I'm Kita, Duran

Original Music Makes

Book.1

Veronica Purcell

Copyright © 2015-2020 Veronica Purcell

Publisher: Katarr Kanticles Press

4th Edition - Revised

All rights reserved.

ISBN: 9798673511831

☆ THANK YOU, READER ☆

Thank you for taking an interest in this novel.
I hope you enjoy Duran Kita's Japanese school adventures.

Original Music Makes - 2015

SYLLABUS

Duran Kita, 2015

♟ ACKNOWLEDGMENTS ✓

Thank you to my family, friends, all the awesome people who encouraged this story during the WeSeWriMo 2015 web fiction challenge at www.epiguide.com and @webfictioneu. This story is possible because of your support.

Hotaka Music Club
Founded by the Original6 of
Hotaka High School, 2015

☆PROLOGUE

Sounds of bass and disco-techno music pounded the air around Duran. The music, pulsing strobe lights, and streams of fluorescent colour sent his senses on a celebratory high.

He took in the scene of the lights bathing the gowns and suits of wedding guests dancing on the dance floor. The atmosphere was surreal to the point of utopia.

Finally, his mother had her one to settle with. A fact Duran was thrilled about. In his mind, he flicked through the number of fathers he had had over the course of his life and, by his mother's standards, were never good enough in the end. But, today was different. He truly was happy for his mother's marriage and for the additional family to enrich his life.

'Hey, my new Nii-san. You're not dancing?'

Duran glanced over his shoulder and greeted his new sister, Himeko Suzuki. He had met her before the wedding at a family introduction. At that time and now, he was relieved she didn't turn out to be a psycho-hose beast and appeared a sensible girl.

'I've two left feet. It's safer for everyone if I didn't.' Duran joked.

He and his sister watched their parents dancing in each other's arms like a pair of love-struck teenagers.

'They look good together eh?' Himeko commented through a warm smile.

'Yeah. I thought I'd be jealous, but I'm glad she has someone else to love. It's only been us for far too long.' Duran reflected on the day he met his new father, Ryuu-chichi. And the instant comfort he felt back then.

'What about you? You're okay being family?' Himeko's words carried a sincerity. Her question made him grin.

'I am if you are,' Duran replied coolly.

'Hmm, well, don't do anything weird. I won't hesitate to smash my guitar on your head if you do strange things.'

'Hah! What a waste of a guitar. In that case, you don't need to worry about this Nii-san being a pervert or such.' Duran laughed.

He couldn't say enough times in his head how happy he was to have a sister and family. He studied his sister's expression from the corner of his eye. She seemed accepting of his words. His goofy grin stretched wider.

'Hey, kids, come dance,' Sakura called out to her son and step-daughter from the other side of the dance floor.

Duran was yanked toward the floor by Himeko before he had a moment to hesitate. Despite her lithe and petite build, she had quite some strength.

'What a she-man.' He chuckled.

He sighed, admitting defeat. It was pointless being aloof now. He moved stupidly to an upbeat pop track, which caused Himeko and his mother into laughing fit.

Duran felt his life was only going to be better from here on in.

♥ THE SHOUJO EFFECT

His breath fell short and dry against his throat as he raced for his first class in his new school. The bell had rung some minutes ago.

'Damn you Himeko,' Duran cursed under his breath.

His sister was supposed to go with him on his first day, but she flaked out last minute with a mad panic attack of having to forget handing in her long overdue spring-break homework. She bolted out the door before he had a chance to say, "Wait up".

He figured out how to get to the school office for his transfer student orientation on his own. Despite the orientation finishing well before the first bell, he was inevitably late to class. It had taken him a good ten minutes to get to the block on the other side of the school grounds with a further ten getting lost.

He, eventually, arrived to his classroom; stopping in front of the door to Class 1-A. He took a moment to compose himself before gingerly opening it and cringed when his homeroom teacher paused his lesson and all eyes were turned his way.

'Please forgive my lateness Sensei. I was attending an orientation at the office,' Duran said as he bowed low.

'Ah the late transfer student. This is Kita-kun all. Close the door Kita-kun and take your seat in the back row next to the window,' Aimi-sensei commented listlessly.

Duran was pleasantly surprised by his teacher's lack of concern but the flourish of whispers from students in the room made him feel uneasy. He glanced at his classmates and almost chortled at the sight before him. Rows of students in starched iron uniforms, neatly preened hair and prescriptive glasses, stared back at him.

'A bunch of *otakus* training to be salary-men.' Duran

deduced in his mind.

He shook off the thought and took his seat next to the window.

Aimi-sensei called everyone back to his attention and the lesson resumed.

Duran's mind wandered to the type of school he had entered. Hotaka High wasn't his first choice, but it was walking distance to his new home and furthest from his last school.

No one questioned his fit since he had top grades to be there. He was somewhat surprised by his principal's instant dismissal of his appearance.

'I feel a slight disappointment now that I've met you in person,' his principal had said upon their meeting during the orientation.

Duran wondered if it was because he wasn't a glasses-wearing otaku.

Well, it's not like he could take an offence from a man wearing last century's tweed suit and fake hair that was way too black and silky-smooth for a man beyond middle-age.

'Can't be helped.' He brushed off the thought and sunk into Aimi-sensei's mathematical drone.

'Aah finally, break time.' He exhaled when the lesson had ended. He stretched away the stiffness he felt in his joints from being seated for too long.

He was crazy for thinking that a boring subject spoken through his teacher's drone was interesting.

'I must be outta my mind. No, it's this school,' he mumbled to himself.

'Dude, your eyes aren't Japanese,' said the guy next to him.

Duran faced the guy gawking straight at him with his chin resting on his desk.

'Man, your face isn't much Japanese either. You from o'seas?'

Duran could take offence since saying such things directly was typically rude. He detected a tone of curiosity behind the guy's words more than anything else, so let his questions slide.

'Nah, born and bred Japanese. My grandfather was French. I inherited a lot of his features so,' he answered politely.

'French mix aye? Cool.'

The guy sat up and extended his hand to Duran.

'Yamaguchi Fumio. Nice to meet you.'

Duran shook his hand and returned the introduction.

He took in Fumio's appearance. He liked his razor-crop hairstyle, where the fringe swept the side of his forehead. It suited the intense black of his hair and framed his manly features well. His eyes wandered over his soft skin, which was almost flawless from imperfections. They lingered on his full, lush lips slightly parted as if they were about to receive a kiss.

He wondered why he hadn't noticed this good-looking guy when he had first entered the room. He certainly was a refreshing change to the other students.

'Sorry for blurting out shit. I have a habit of doing that and getting in trouble for it,' Fumio apologized.

'Not at all Yamaguchi-kun. Being direct can be sometimes refreshing,' Duran replied and wondered if it sounded like a flirt. He decided to be more conscious of his responses.

'You got a cool given name as well. Is that from your grand-dad too?'

Duran chuckled thinking how cute this guy was.

'You really do say what's in your head don't you? Yeah. It was the eyes that made my mother give me his name.'

'Your eyes, they're pretty like sea coloured marbles,' Fumio remarked.

'Yamaguchi-kun if we continue to flirt like this, you'll have me blushing like a love-struck maiden,' Duran teased and laughed at Fumio's awkward response.

'S-Sorry, didn't realize.' Fumio blurted. His cheeks were flushed.

Loud chatter and sounds of shifting seats broke through their conversation. Duran looked around and saw his sister and another girl heading his way.

'Yo, Nii-san, see you got here in one piece,' Himeko said jovially.

'No thanks to you. Did you get your homework handed in on time?'

'On the nick. Sorry, I had to dash like that.'

Himeko took up the seat before his desk and started rummaging through his lunch box on his desk for something to eat.

'Ooh you still have octopi wieners. *Itadakimasu!*' Himeko said and started shoving bits of sausage in her mouth.

'Yeah, help yourself,' Duran said sarcastically with a sigh.

'Geez Hime-chan, just because he's your brother doesn't mean you can steal his food. Where are your manners? And didn't you finish your recess beforehand,' said the girl next to his sister.

Himeko responded with a shrug and continued eating. The girl sighed.

'I'm Okada Mei. Hime-chan's girlfriend by the way,' Mei introduced herself to Duran.

Duran's brows went up at the term "girlfriend" and wondered if alluded toward something other than typical friendship. It was a side of Himeko he did not consider.

'Nice to meet you,' he responded.

He found her eyes scrutinizing him intensely before they went back to Himeko who was still pilfering his wieners.

'*I think I've just been categorized into her database.*' He thought, amused by the idea.

He compared Mei to his sister.

On appearance, they were opposites. Himeko was a bit rough around the edges, although her face was pretty, and she did have nice black hair kept short in a boyish bob with heavy bangs tumbling over her brows.

Mei on the other hand, carried herself with feminine airs of a Japanese princess. Her fine brown hair was kept in a neat pony-tail. She was slender and properly dressed in her navy and white uniform. Her blue bow tie was perfectly positioned in the center of her collar's spread area. Thin trimmed glasses couldn't hide the gorgeousness to her face.

'If she is my sister's lover, holy heck.' He thought.

'You're Hime-chan's new bro aye. Must be annoying living with this Xena,' Fumio said and dodged Himeko's blow to his head.

'I'll cope.' Duran smiled.

'So how are you finding Hotaka so far? Or is it too early to tell,' Mei asked politely.

'It's very different to my last school.'

'How so?'

'I've never seen so many future salary-men and woman in a place that wasn't a train carriage.'

'Salary-men and women?' Mei asked perplexed.

'You know those tax accountant types in boring suits, carrying brief cases,' Duran explained matter-of-factually.

Everyone erupted with laughter surprising Duran.

'Nii-san, you're funny. Scarily it's true,' Himeko said between chuckles.

'Hotaka High is the school that produces top-notch corporate executives, doctors, lawyers and other types of tops.'

'But it's not the school for musos or artists. You go to Emi-Daiki for that.' Fumio added.

Duran tensed at hearing the name of the other school.

'Maths, science, economics, engineering, these type of subjects are staples to Hotaka's academic diet. This is the only school in all of Japan that doesn't have a music and art department,' Mei explained.

No music or art classes? So, what did Hotaka High consider a culture festival if these subjects weren't encouraged? The thought was too weird to even think about. He wondered if there was a club that made up for the shortfall.

'What about a club?' He blurted.

'Club for what?' Himeko asked.

'For music, art and cultures. Is there one?'

'The only cultural club we have is the Otaku Machima Club. That place just talks about nonsense and participate in stupid cosplay games,' Mei replied.

'Shame.' Duran sighed, slumping further in his seat.

'Hey, why don't we start up a music club? I play guitar and you play drums Fumi-chan,' Himeko piped up.

'I play? You mean I kill it 'cause I'm that good. Taylor Hawkins eat your heart out,' Fumio said smugly.

'Mei is good with a cello,' Himeko said for Mei.

'Do you play Kita-kun?' Fumio asked and frowned when Himeko answered for him.

'Of course he does. He's really talented on keyboards. He even sound proofed our rooms, so we could rock out without disturbing the neighbours,' Himeko replied proudly.

'I guess we have a band for a club then,' Mei commented.

'If you could get a club off the ground,' another guy interrupted.

Duran looked around to see where the voice was coming from and came face to face with an honour student.

His neat crop of black hair was slicked back off his stony pretty-boy face, which accentuated a sober expression behind dark almond eyes. He stood tall with a masculine stance; the hint of an athlete showing through his large, sinew hands. The school emblem was still fresh on his navy blazer. His grey pants and loafers emanated a crisp sheen.

If one guy was to carry off the clean cut, salary-man style well it was this guy before him.

'Why couldn't we?' Duran challenged him.

'I believe Okada-chan explained the reasons,' he coolly replied.

Duran's eyes narrowed. Who was this honour student butting into their conversation to shut down their hope for something that could be a good thing?

'Reasons aside, clubs exist to be part of student life not supplementary to a curriculum are they not?'

'Says he who has only started today,' the guy shot back.

'Ugh! Hayashi Kou. You're a pain the butt,' Himeko cried out. She stood, defiant, before the honour student with her hands on her hips. 'It's wrong to eavesdrop you know.'

'You guys were so loud it couldn't be helped.'

'So you're gonna stop us Mr. Student Council.' Fumio interjected.

Duran saw the red armband of a student council representative around Kou's right arm.

'Your club idea is likely to be denied the council's rubber stamp. It's a risk. Should I remind you of the school's purpose in preparing future salary-men as Kita-kun bluntly states.'

The classroom fell silent of chatter. Duran became conscious of his peers interest in their conversation. Hearing Kou repeat his annotation of the school's students made him lower his head with guilt.

'Hayashi-kun, that is true, but we still can't dismiss an application without consideration. That is if they were to submit one.' Another person entered the conversation.

Duran felt a lump form in his throat when he sighted the newcomer who also wore a student council armband to his right arm. He was as handsome and presentable as Kou yet his look was more alluring. His hair was short so it spiked in places and caused a stylish wisp of fringe against his forehead. His athletic build and fine features; flawless china-white skin, natural plump red lips and dark, doll-like, eyes exuded a cool mysteriousness that sent his heart pounding with the *doki-dokis*.

'My god he's gorgeous to be a Calvin Klein model.' Duran blurted in his mind.

He was beginning to think his vision was seriously impaired and his first impression of his classmates was flawed.

'Tsubaki-kun don't encourage them. They're better off being a garage or basement band somewhere else.' Kou brushed off the idea.

Abrupt ringing of the school's bell stopped further conversations on the matter. Duran shuffled out of his seat, packed up his bag and started heading out with Fumio and the others to their next class.

Duran and Fumio strolled down the hallways of Block-B. They were headed toward their science lesson, which was held in the labs of the first floor.

'Hey Yamaguchi-kun, who were those student council guys back there,' Duran asked thinking about the discussion they had at recess.

'Oh, those guys are our first year representatives. Hayashi, Kou is in Hime-chan's class. Tsubaki, Saski is in ours,' Fumio explained.

Duran was surprised to hear that the Tsubaki-kun guy was his classmate and found himself smiling at the thought.

His mind wandered toward the conversation they had had about the music club. He was beginning to doubt the possibility of one existing in a school that didn't practice music.

'Do you really think we have a chance of starting up a music club?'

'Hmm. I thought we might but not sure now,' Fumio said nonchalantly.

His response stirred an itchy restlessness in Duran. He felt he had to do something about it but wasn't sure where to begin.

His attention was momentarily diverted to the heated

argument happening before them; near the stairwell at the end of the floor.

Fumio and Duran paused near the windows, a short-distance away, to eavesdrop on the conversation whilst fend off contact from passing students.

'You can't do this! The Otaku Machima is the only culture club in this school. It'll be sacrilegious to disband the club now,' yelled the guy a short distance ahead.

Duran's impression of the guy was a rock-idol playing student. His hair was cut in razor layers similar to Fumio's with bangs that fell short from the tops of his square framed glasses. Behind his glasses, were fierce brown eyes pitted in a slightly rugged but appealing face. His broad shoulders and solid build could pass him off as an adult. He carried his uniform in the typical fashion of your average student with his top button undone and tie loose.

The rock-idol guy's rant was targeted at an honour student who was an ideal image in a crisp clean uniform and sharp red student council armband to his right arm. Even his navy tie was perfectly set in place.

The honour student stared at the other guy through opaque eyes that refracted light; masking his expression. Duran noticed what set him apart from the others was his dignified stance that meant business.

Next to the student council representative was Saski taking notes in a binder.

'Santo Dai'chi. The club has, once again, caused mass disruption to class time with its noisy cosplay activities. Not to mention the hole in the club room wall that needs to be repaired. You've lost another member during the renewal period bringing it under the minimum count. The club no longer satisfies the conditions to continue,' the Student Council Representative responded coolly with an unyielding expression.

'Please President Saito. If there's no Otaku Machima, what culture is there for this school?' Dai'chi pleaded.

'Once again, you forget Hotaka High's core principles.

Culture you ask? Isn't it obvious that solid grades toward a high-profile career are our culture here? Besides, we do have our many sports clubs. So, we have plenty of enough for this school to manage,' President Saito closed further discussions on the matter.

Duran glanced at Fumio and saw he also had an uneasy expression on his face.

'You've gotta be friggin kidding me!' Dai'chi almost spat out.

'I'm not going to say more on it. As President of the Student Council, I confirm the Otaku Machima Club disbandment effective immediately. Please, your keys Santo-kun,' President Saito ordered.

A silent stand-off between the two students lasted for a few minutes before Dai'chi broke first by throwing a set at the President's chest.

'Screw you!' Dai'chi cursed before he stormed down the hallway past Duran.

'Tsubaki-kun.' President Saito sighed as he pocketed the keys.

'President. I've captured the event and will have a complete report this afternoon.' Saski confirmed his noting of the event for evidence.

'Ah, good then. I'll be going to class. See you in the council chambers later.'

President Saito exited down the stairs.

Duran felt his heart leap to his throat when he saw Saski on his own.

Now was the opportunity he had been hoping for.

'Ah, um, Tsubaki-kun right?' He called out to him.

Saski turned toward Duran's way and clicked his tongue.

'Well, if it isn't the transfer student. What can I do for you?'

'Come on. No need to be like that. I just want to talk with you civil-like,' Duran replied as earnestly as he could.

'Fine. What would you like to talk about?' Saski sighed.

'What'd I need to do to start a club?' Duran asked with a charming smile.

Saski rolled his eyes with a mordant expression. He wasn't surprised Duran had heard the heated discussions about the otaku club disbandment. It had been loud enough for the whole hallway to hear.

'You heard about that club's disbandment didn't you?'

'Yeah. I figured if one club is down another club could open,' Duran stated.

'Wrong.' Saski shot back.

Duran chuckled finding him cute.

Saski's resolve softened at Duran's stupid smile.

'Whatever. Complete this and hand it back within two weeks.' He handed Duran a club application form from his binder.

Duran bowed low with gratitude. 'Thank you Tsubaki-kun. I appreciate it.'

'Ah, yeah well, um, you still need to satisfy application conditions too,' Saski added. 'Let me fill you in.'

Duran and Fumio listened carefully at the absurd lengths they had to go to have an application ready for Student Council approval.

Condition-❶ Source an available teacher and convince them to be their adviser.

Saski made it clear, if the Otaku Machima Club hadn't been disbanded there was no way they would've been able to apply for a club since all other teachers were club advisers. A teacher was only permitted over one club at a time for obvious reasons.

'Sure there's an opening, but it's only one. I have many applications on a wait list from last year to consider,' he stated.

Duran saw it was going to be a dog-eat-dog fight to convince that teacher to sign their form.

Condition-❷ Gather Members. They needed to have five or more members sign on to the club with genuine reasons as to why they wanted to be there, and have a

President, Treasurer and Secretary appointed (by a consensual vote) before the application due date.

Duran figured this should be the easiest one to meet.

Condition-❸ Attach a two thousand-word essay, explaining on reasons why the club should exist and what benefits it would provide the school and its students.

'What's the point?' Fumio scratched his head.

Condition-❹ Complete a fifty question survey on club ethics and etiquette attached to the form.

Duran's eyes bulged at some sensitive questions about boys, girls and where hands were allowed to be at all times.

'The President has to be a third year. All other positions can be from other years. That's about it, really.' Saski finished his club application run-through.

'Woah. That's extreme man!' Fumio complained.

'Seriously?! Gawd, it'd be easier to cut out my spleen and donate it to the student council on silver platter.' Duran remarked wryly.

Saski chuckled and gave Duran and Fumio a patronizing pat on their shoulders.

'Good luck guys. I'll be watching your progress with interest,' he said as he passed them to meet up with a group of classmates further down the hallway.

'Say, Yamaguchi-kun, who was the otaku club's adviser?' Duran asked.

'We're in luck. He's our teacher for our next class,' Fumio replied.

'Aah, so that's what Tsubaki-kun meant by watching.'

Duran felt fired up by the challenge before him. No matter what the outcome, he'd give it his all.

His thoughts constantly changed shape as he walked to class. Always landing on ways he was going to convince his teacher to sign his form.

Before Duran realized it, he was waiting with the rest of his class outside the science lab.

Fumio was talking into his ear on how they were going to approach their teacher after the lesson.

'Sensei Watty is a weird case. We're best to get in quick and hit him hard,' he stated as he slammed his fist, passionately, down on the palm of his hand.

Duran hoped he didn't mean it in a literal sense. He wondered how weird of a man Watanabe-sensei was.

'He can't be that weird. Then again he is a science teacher,' he thought to himself as he pictured his old high school teacher with a hair full of dregs and a scraggly, unshaven appearance. That old teacher had a habit of trying to convince students that eating tree leaves was good for your vitality.

At that moment, Watanabe-sensei walked past him chewing on a green stick, which turned out to be some kind of Pocky.

He was a tall, wiry man in a typical white lab coat. Not middle age but old enough to be past the spring chicken stage of life. His bed hair flopped, unfashionably, just above his eyes.

Duran cringed when his teacher casually unlocked the door with sad sighs. The man's apathetic attitude was going to be a challenge for him?

'Yeah, come in if you can be bothered,' Watanabe-sensei said without caring who walked in.

Duran and Fumio took spots a few benches from the front.

'Have fun,' Saski whispered to Duran as he passed him to the rows at the back.

Duran glanced back and saw him grinning at him with smug attitude. It made his heart race stupidly.

He returned his attention to the front but felt Saski's eyes burning at his back. A moment later, their teacher started the lesson.

'Rawt, awky,' Watanabe-sensei muttered as he chewed and swallowed the last of his Pocky.

'Today's lesson is chemical reactions. I'm going to hand out ingredients for you to mix to your hearts content and see what goes boom.'

The class shuffled about their seats and glanced at each other with concern or interest.

'But!' Watanabe-sensei paused for emphasis before adding on. 'The order of science must be obeyed. I want everyone to write down the order of ingredients then follow them with your experiments.'

Everyone copied his scribbled recipe from the blackboard.

Duran scratched his head at the instructions he had copied, feeling like he had noted a recipe for disasters.

He was asked combine three parts of blue liquid with two parts of red liquid, throw in green pills, hair, powder and some other dubious named ingredients.

'Huh, are we at Hogwarts? What potion stuff is this?' He blurted aloud and caused his nearby classmates into a giggling fit.

'Who said Hogwarts?' Watanabe-sensei demanded, clearly annoyed by the reference.

Fingers were pointed Duran's way to *dob* him in.

'New kid! Come here.' Watanabe-sensei ordered Duran to the front of the class.

Duran gingerly shuffled off his seat and made his approach; feeling apprehensive.

'Potions huh? Well, let's debunk the concept eh Mr. Potter?' The man pulled out a few vials, containers and a burner from a box on one of the front benches.

He had Duran line them up on the teacher's desk for the class to see.

'Mr. Potter and I are going to start mixing stuff to see what happens,' Watanabe-sensei advised the attentive class.

Duran frowned; annoyed by his teacher's reference for him.

The man placed a clean beaker on the tripod above the burner. He set the burner a light with a calm and almost expected attitude. He threw in hair, green pills and shimmering grey powder that Duran hoped wasn't the stuff that went into fire-crackers.

'Okay Potter. Pour the blue stuff into the beaker on my count of three. I'll pour the red stuff simultaneously.'

Duran "tsk'd" as he got ready to pour the contents of the vial.

'One... two... THREE!' Watanabe-sensei counted down excitedly.

They poured to their hearts content. For a moment nothing happened.

Duran noticed a small seed of smoke laze around the base of the beaker.

Unexpectedly, the smoke *poofed* into mushroom clouds of pink smoke, which blanketed the front of the classroom and smothered them.

'What the hell was that?!' Duran coughed as he cursed.

He swiped at the smoke to clear the air but found it going into his eyes and causing it to sting; madly blinking and wiping at his eyes until the stinging cleared. Duran almost fainted at what he saw when he could see.

His whole class was also coughing and wiping their eyes from smoke that had taken over the classroom space. Sensei switched on the pedestal fan in the corner and could clear away the smoke through opened windows.

'Well I guess that concludes today's lesson. Let's make this free time huh,' Watanabe-sensei hastily declared and started shoving the equipment back into the box.

'What'd you mean free time Sensei? What the hell have you done?!' Duran cursed.

He blinked his eyes, hoping his vision would return to normal but it wasn't working. Everyone in the room sparkled in a rose colour and dreamy light like he was seeing them through a shōujo filter.

'Oh my god! Everyone's faces are sparkly roses like a shōujo manga!' He cried out loud and cupped the sides of his face in disbelief and disorientation.

'You too?' Someone else piped up.

'Me too! Oh my god! Everyone looks so hot!' A girl confessed.

'Especially, you Yoshida-kun.' Another added.

'Oh my god. If Yoshida-kun is hot... holy crap, my brain has been fried! *Noooo*!' Another boy panicked.

The whole class lapsed into a mild panic as they saw each other with the shōujo filter.

'CALM DOWN EVERYONE!' Watanabe-sensei shouted.

The room became silent.

'I'm sure we can fix this but I need volunteers,' he asked with his focus on Duran.

Duran released all his tension with a sigh. How could he be mad at a teacher who stared at him with imploring, sparkling eyes? They were adorable.

'I'll do it. I need your signature anyway,' he blurted.

'I'm in too!' Fumio called out.

'Me-me as well!' Chimed a boy eagerly.

'Me too! I can't say no to Sensei's cute, adorable face.' Another boy yelled out from the back then let out a dreamy sigh.

'Isao! Snap out of it. It's the shōujo effect.' The boy next to him said with a violent shake to his shoulders.

A few others called out to offer their help but Watanabe-sensei waved them off. He wondered if he should bother to remove the effect, but thought that if the condition were to go fatal attraction that probably wouldn't be ideal for the school's image.

'Okay, okay, I have plenty enough volunteers now. You four boys who offered first, see me after school,' he said dreamily and shook his head violently to shake off the shōujo effect the best he could.

The room fell into chaos again when everyone realized they had to spend the rest of the day viewing others through the shōujo effect and suffering the consequences. Chaos gave way to dreamy sighs, *oohs* and *aahs*.

↗

The news of Watanabe-sensei's shoujo effect, impacting the salary boys and girls of Class 1-A, had spread fast and wide across the school by the time the lunch bell rang out.

Other students seized the moment to have the affected return their unrequited feelings. Or payout on the unfortunate souls in embarrassing ways.

The problem was escalating at an unpredictable rate as infection spread.

Duran trailed after Fumio and Saski, who were attempting an escape from girls across the open courtyard between buildings.

'Yamaguchi-kun, what you think of me?' One girl persisted as she followed at their pace.

'Do you think I'm pretty.' Another desperately chimed. Knocking the other girl to the ground when she overtook her run.

'Fumi-chan! Say you like me too!' A girl cried out to him with a flirtatious, sing-song, voice.

'Tsubaki-kun, go out with me! I beg you!' A girl begged as she tried to hinder Saski's run with her leaping hug. And found herself flat on the ground.

So many girls pushed their way in and fought among each other to be by the boys side.

Although, they practically kicked Duran out of the way.

Duran squealed at the unexpected push and deviated off his path. He bolted back to the Block-B classrooms to find his sister.

He entered the upper hallway and found himself cornered.

'What now?' He groaned as he slowly backed away from the older boys advancing towards him. The air was thick with the same rivalry Fumio had faced with the girls.

'Dude. You're cute.' A burly senior leapt for Duran.

Duran was pushed and yanked back and forth into each of the boys. Their whole psycho-manic routine wasn't doing wonders for his mood. He managed to duck and dodge grabs, and flee up the stairs. Not hanging about to hear his "hot guy" ranking from his male peers.

He escaped up to the roof-top as fast as his legs could carry him.

'And stay out!' He yelled with frustration when he slammed the fire stair door behind him.

He was relieved when no one had followed him. And ecstatic when he found Himeko and Mei eating their lunch, peacefully, near a bird's-eye view of the interesting activity happening in the courtyard beneath them.

'Himeko!' He cried out and rushed to her.

'I was groped by maniacs,' he said as she hugged him.

Himeko gingerly patted his back.

'There. There. I can see it's been hard on you.' She cooed into his ears.

'It's awful.' Duran cried into her chest.

Himeko gave a sideward look to Mei.

'So it's true you were doused with Sensei's love drug,' Mei commented.

'Not doused, smoked.' Duran corrected her as he calmly pulled away from Himeko's hug.

For some reason, he couldn't look Himeko and Mei in the eye. They were too damn sparkly.

'Really? Come on Nii-san. Tell me how gorgeous I am.' Himeko joked.

'Shut up. This is embarrassing. *Gênant soeur.*' Duran grumbled.

He turned his back on her and stared at the carnage happening in the courtyard below.

'Don't tease Kita-kun. Looks like he and his class are going through an awful time.' Mei berated Himeko and faced Duran kindly.

'Awful? So looking at someone through a lover's eyes is awful,' Himeko answered back.

'Yes if it's forced upon you!' Duran snapped in response.

He saw members of his class chasing or being chased

by others. Fumio was still running for his life to escape from the mob of desperate admirers.

'Suppose I should go back there and save him.' He mumbled, feeling instantly calmer. And felt like a coward for having ditched him and Saski.

'Don't mind her.' Mei calmly said.

She beamed with a sparkly smile too bright in Duran's eyes. They were tearing-up.

'Oh no. Did I make you cry?' She asked, concerned.

'No, it's not that. The effect has ramped up to a scale of fifty, causing my eyes to ache,' Duran explained.

He wondered if his other classmates were experiencing similar changes in symptoms, and felt bad for ditching Fumio.

'Damn.' He sighed.

Feeling a boost of courage, he turned to head back down the stairs.

'Where're you doing?' Himeko asked with concern.

'To save Yamaguchi-kun,' he said as he raced out of the roof-top and back the courtyard to save his friend.

He saw Fumio cornered by girls from another class and raced up to them.

'Hey Yamaguchi-kun. Teacher wants you!' Duran shouted at him.

He yanked Fumio away from the complaining mob. They sprinted so hard that everything sailed past them like a big blur. They made their way to Himeko and Mei.

'Wow. You're both fast runners,' Himeko commented.

Both boys crouched over before her. They were panting for breath.

'Geeze. You abandoned me dude!' Fumio puffed. He slapped Duran's back.

'Sorry! I panicked. I'm really sorry! You can hit me again if makes you feel better.' Duran yelped.

He bowed low, and repeatedly, almost kissing Fumio's feet.

'Aw. Nah. How can I when you look cute as.' Fumio

sighed.

He helped Duran straighten up. They both stared into each other's eyes with longing. And leaned in for a kiss.

'Woah!' Duran cried out as he came to his senses and pulled away. He realized the Shoujo Effect had evolved to Shounen Ai.

'This bad. Bad. Bad. Bad!' Duran muttered.

'Dude. I can't last the day like this,' Fumio said as he slumped down next to Himeko.

'It's that bad?' Himeko said with concern.

It had been a long time since she had seen her childhood friend so rattled.

High-pitched squealing and desperate screaming caught Duran's attention. He peered over the railing and saw Saski being chased by a mob of girls.

On instinct, Duran fled the roof-top, down the stairs and corridor. Keeping track of Saski's plight.

He waited inconspicuously under the eaves of the doorway ahead of the mob. When he saw Saski racing toward him, he stepped out and yanked him toward himself.

Duran led their escape to the roof-top where they collapsed next to Mei and Fumio.

He saw two other boys had joined the group. He recalled that Dai'chi Santo guy from that conversation he had eavesdropped on before his science class. He had never met the other boy before. The other person was skinny, smaller, and adorable for a boy wearing thin-framed glasses.

'Geez Nii-san. How much more running you gonna do?'

Duran laid himself down on the ground. He stared up to a clear spring sky.

'Just let me die will yah.' He exhaled. Exhausted.

He closed his eyes for the moment. When he opened them, he saw the cute glasses' boy staring down on him with a wide grin. Saski's face was next to his.

'Wah!' Duran abruptly sat up and almost knocking his head on Saski's jaw.

'Don't freak me out like that!'

'Sorry. Just seeing if you were okay,' the cute glasses' boy politely replied.

Duran felt his heart leap up to his throat. He was certain that it was the shoujo effect causing the unbearable stiffness in his groin, and hot flushes to his cheeks, at the sight of the boy's soft pink lips and gorgeous almond eyes. A sensation of lust overcame him.

'You're a beauty. I wanna kiss you.' Duran blurted.

He slapped his hands over his mouth to shut himself up. Stopping himself from jumping the boy.

'Woah! Whadya saying?' The cute glasses' boy stammered. He awkwardly backed away from Duran.

'Sorry!' Duran shook his head clear.

'Me too. Fujita-kun, you're way too cute.' Saski chewed his lip to stop himself from saying more.

He faced Duran with intentions to thank him for saving him from those girls. Instead, he pounced on him when their eyes met. Unable to resist his uncontrollable urges to ravish him.

Duran struggled against Saski's insistent kisses and groping. He screamed for him to get off.

'This is serious shit.' Dai'chi sniggered as he and Fumio pried Saski off Duran.

'Don't snicker Senpai.' Saski whimpered.

He went to cower in a corner away from Duran.

'This is horrible. I was chased by packs of girls. No vixens! No matter how many turn offs I think of when I look at people, nothing works! Now with Kita-kun. THIS SUCKS!'

He wrapped his arms around himself to hold back the chills he felt to his bones.

'Wow, you make me feel so special Tsubaki-kun,' Duran said sarcastically.

Saski ignored him.

'Dude. Those girls were gonna eat me alive.' Fumio shuddered. His face paled at the horrid thought.

'Gawd. Look at you guys complaining about something that'd never happen to your average high school boy in any lifetime.' Fujita-kun chuckled.

'Fujita, Aki. This is no laughing matter! It's the shoujo effect that has caused all of this.' Mei scolded the cute glasses' boy.

'Yeah. I guess you're right. I can't imagine girls wanting to chase them for any other reason,' Aki replied.

'Hey!' Fumio yelled out.

Aki's eyes met Duran's again.

Suddenly, he felt his heart pounding against his chest. His palms became clammy. Thoughts in his head were begging him to "do" that handsome, green-eyed and chiselled face prince before him.

He leaped for Duran and pinned him to the ground with his hands feeling up his body.

'Ugh. Get off me! Guys! Help please!' Duran screeched.

He saw Saski and Fumio yank Aki off him.

'Whada hell you're doing!'

'Sorry. Sorry. I dunno know what came over me just then,' Aki said with a perplexed expression.

Duran realized he was affected.

'Ugh! It's gone all Yaoi!' He gasped.

'YOU THINK?!' All the boys shouted in unison.

'Hang on. Aki-kun's not in 1-A. So, how can he be affected?' Dai'chi asked.

'The condition is viral. Others outside 1-A can be contaminated on contact?' Duran gulped.

Dead silence fell upon the group as the penny dropped.

'That's it! I'm going to see Sensei and demand he fixes this right now.' Saski declared.

He stormed off towards the door.

'Hey. Hey. Wait up!' Duran yelled after Saski.

He hurried after him.

'Hey. Yamaguchi-kun. You come too,' Duran called out

to Fumio over his shoulder.

Fumio sighed and followed.

The others gave each other pensive glances that said, "I'm not going to miss this".

Everyone packed up their bags and hurried after the boys.

They weren't the only ones seeking out Watanabe-sensei. The staffroom hallway was packed with Class 1-A students screaming out demands.

'If you don't get to your next class you'll all get detention for a week!' Harada-sensei threatened with a coarse voice.

His students' insistent demands and shouting were going over his cauliflower like ears.

Duran flicked his friends an uneasy look over his shoulder and noticed Watanabe-sensei cowering behind a door at the other side of the hallway. They crept away from the fuss and approached their science teacher who failed to slam the door on his face.

'Sensei! Don't you dare! You and I need to chat.' Duran hissed through gritted teeth.

'I'm busy. Go to class,' Watanabe-sensei whispered to shoo him off.

'Sure. I'll go but I'm going to scream out to everyone you're here first,' Duran said in a threatening tone of voice.

'You wouldn't!'

Watanabe-sensei glanced down the hallway and the mob of first years bailing up poor Harada-sensei. He knew it was pointless to attempt discipline on a bunch of students in a near psychotic state.

Duran took a step back and opened his mouth to scream out Watanabe-sensei's location. His science teacher pulled him into the room and slammed the door behind them before his voice was let out.

'It wasn't meant to work.' Watanabe-sensei fretted.

Duran felt his teacher was more excited than panicky.

'Why are you excited?! You have to fix this!'

'Fix? Well, you could have a cold shower.' Watanabe-sensei mused.

'And that would return me to normal?'

'No, but it'll calm you down.'

'Calm down?! I want my friggin science teacher to fix the wrong he caused me and all the others!' Duran screamed.

'Now, now, Kita-kun. Your pheromones are absolutely sparkling with hotness right now. You're a lady killer. Isn't that every teenage boy's dream?' Watanabe-sensei attempted flattery.

'Only I'm not attracting the ladies.' Duran grumbled to himself. 'Hang on! Whadya mean pheromones?'

'Oh the ingredients we mixed were an attempt to recreate Androsterone, but it somehow ended up as a cloud machine,' Watanabe-sensei recounted.

He wasn't fazed by Duran's obvious distressed expression on the matter.

'Andro-what?' Duran nervously gulped. Praying it wasn't some new kind of virus they needed WHO intervention.

'Androsterone. Boosts the sex pheromone to a mating call.' Watanabe-sensei chuckled when he found it amusing that such experiment had actually worked.

He wondered at the actual emotional intelligence of his students.

'To be honest. I thought the most that would happen is a small bang and fizz.'

'It banged alright.' Duran thought to himself. He clenched his fists as he felt his testosterone escalating.

'So you're saying that some stupid teacher wanted to make a love potion in his class?!'

'Stupid? Tsk. Students never appreciate science. But, yes, I would conclude that.'

'Tell me why I shouldn't punch you right now.' Duran gritted his teeth, suppressing the urge to slam his fists into something.

'Why? Because it's science!' Watanabe-sensei answered childishly.

Duran detected a tone of wonderment to the man's voice. He realized his teacher was really, unexpectedly, both proud and surprised of his discovery. Perhaps he had no intention to harm in the first place. He knew he had to calm down or face an unsightly experience and consequence. Despite the anger he felt at that man, he was still his teacher.

'Okay, why are people outside my class affected?' Duran slowly exhaled to calm down.

'Well they have pheromones too and you're reeking of a mating call right now. So, they are naturally responding with the same intensity. Should anyone affected lock eyes for more than three seconds, it'll activate a mating call for those sharing the right amount of, ahem, chemistry. Once the mating call is sated, one way or another, pheromones will return to a normal level as well.'

'Whaaat?! Have sex with people?' Duran said aghast at the idea.

'Dreadful boy. This is a school not a swingers club. You keep your filthy ideas in your head!' Watanabe-sensei scolded him.

'Then what's the alternative?' Duran felt his tensions rising again.

'Make an elixir that will negate the effects of a mating call and return the levels to normal for both parties. The ingredients needed are mostly from plant extracts so should be harmless to humans.'

'Okay, let's do that!'

Finally! A solution that didn't sound like a sexual harassment lawsuit.

'But, well, it's not going to be easy finding the ingredients at this school,' Watanabe-sensei said as he mulled over the recipe in his head.

Banging on the door paused their conversation. Watanabe-sensei goaded Duran to say something.

'Yeah?' Duran called out.

'Duran open up, please!' Fumio called out in desperation.

He opened the door and jumped back as Fumio and Saski rushed into the room and slammed the door hard.

'Good, we've escaped.' Saski huffed with his back against the door.

Fumio was panting next to him.

'Sensei dude?! Dude, you have to save us, but Harada-sensei more. He's getting eaten alive,' said Fumio.

'Sexual harassment cases are piling up. The whole school's going love crazy!' Saski reported.

'Hmm, so it's even the staff now,' Watanabe-sensei muttered.

He found himself sizing up Saski with high interest. He shook his head clear from his impure thoughts and returned to the problem at hand.

'We'll obtain the ingredients you need to make the antidote. Give us a list and places to go,' Duran volunteered.

'Okay, I suppose it's only fitting. Give me a moment,' Watanabe-sensei said.

He quickly wrote down a shopping list for Duran and the others to procure and provided them names of places where they could find the items.

'Here are special permissions slips. Keep them on you, should someone ask questions.' Watanabe-sensei handed them signed slips that excused their absence from school as official errands.

'Right, got it,' Duran said as he pocketed the list and slip.

'But, in doing this I want something else from you.'

'What do you mean? This is to save the students so why would you bargain?' Watanabe-sensei eye's narrowed.

'Yes, save the students from your experiment. I'm surprised you won't be summoned to a board hearing very soon,' Duran said formally.

Fumio and Saski were surprised at Duran's switch to proper speech. They watched in silence at the business assumed between Sensei and their classmate.

Saski wondered who Duran was for him to be calling shots with a teacher on his first day. His mind went back to the moment when he walked into their classroom with that air of confidence and slight arrogance. The scene before him confirmed his thinking.

'You're threatening me now?' Watanabe-sensei said levelly.

'No, stating a fact that I think you're already aware of anyway. What I offer is a soft blow,' Duran replied.

'And that is?" Watanabe-sensei asked not sure if it was a good thing to entertain a student's extortion.

Yet, from Duran's controlled composure, he felt his student's shift in attitude was an effect of a higher purpose calling upon him at that very moment. It piqued his curiosity.

'I'll return the ingredients and help apply the antidote either way. I ask you to sign my club application form and become the music club's adviser,' Duran requested of him.

Watanabe-sensei laughed at the absurdity of Duran's request. How was that a soft blow?

Duran felt like an awkward kid at his teacher's reaction of his demand. His efforts were shot down in that one moment of Watanabe-sensei's hearty laughter.

'Geez Sensei, you don't have to shoot me down like that,' he said with a defeated voice.

'So yah just talking big time there then.' Fumio worked out.

'Well, it was worth a shot.' Duran sighed. 'I did say I'll get what is needed regardless.'

'Aah, but I do admire your tenacity Kita-kun. Okay, I'll be your club adviser only if you set some respectable conditions. You may be right about it being a saving grace if your case is compelling before the student council and school board,' Sensei said once he had calmed down.

He couldn't resist Duran's drooping shoulders and the dejected look on his face. Charming.

'Oh, okay, let's do this!' Duran piped up with a burst of enthusiasm and yelped when he felt his butt being massaged.

He turned and saw Fumio's hands becoming friendly around his body.

'That's enough! It's bad enough you called out to me by my given name earlier,' Duran scolded him with a deep frown and flushed face.

'I can't help it Kita-kun. *So* cute,' Fumio apologized with a look of a sad puppy.

'Oh my god. I can't take it!' Saski cried out and pulled Fumio into a lustful kiss.

He was pulled off by Duran.

'Calm down Tsubaki-kun! This is not how a student council representative should behave. You have to fight the effect harder!'

Both boys stared back at him with strong blushes mixed in with an aroused expression.

'I think you need to be chaperoned by someone unaffected,' Sensei suggested.

Duran signed up his sister, her girlfriend and Kou for the job.

'Okay, here are three extra passes. I'll send word to their teachers.'

Sensei gave them a time for the return and sent them on their way. The three boys hurried out of the room to gather their other friends to the cause.

ひ MATSU RAMEN HOUSE

Duran met the others outside the north gate, which was a smaller and more discreet exit out of the school grounds. His clammy hands twitched by his side.

'Keep calm - keep calm,' he chanted to still his fast racing heart pumped with adrenaline.

He forced pages and pages of boring maths in his mind to keep his desires and reactions in-check.

'Gawd, you guys look like nervous wrecks,' Himeko blurted out when she caught sight of her brother, Fumio and Saski waiting at the gates.

She frowned at Duran's twitching, clammy hands, Fumio's sweaty brow, dark rimmed eyes and Saski's shivers, sweaty face and the sleeves of his shirt plastered to his arms.

'This is beyond a joke. How could Sensei be so irresponsible?' Mei said with concern as she came up behind Himeko with Kou by her side.

'And not just these guys. I've never seen the infirmary so busy with people waiting in the wings.'

'So we're to be your helpers and moral conscience for this task?' Kou said bluntly.

'Thank you, any of your help is fine,' Duran said with a low bow.

Kou faced him with an awkward expression.

'Eh, er, um, it was by a teacher's request, so I couldn't refuse,' he replied and checked on how his childhood friend was holding up.

'Your pheromones aren't going to cause embarrassment out on the streets?'

'Tsk. You don't have to be blunt Kou-kun.' Saski grumbled and wrapped his arms around himself in an effort to stop his shivers. 'I'm doing my best.'

'Tsubaki-kun, you look feverish. You should go home,' said Mei; worried he was going to collapse on them.

'I wanna come. I'll be worse off if I stop now,' Saski answered.

'Okay. So, what's first to get? By the looks of Tsubaki-kun, we're on a time limit.' Himeko gathered everyone around Duran who held Watanabe-sensei's ingredient list before them.

'We need five ingredients.' Duran ran through the list.

The first two were something they could easily buy at a shop. The tricky part was the expense. Mei and Saski agreed to hit-up Sensei for cash then go to the stores near the station.

The other ingredients involved a bit of a run around the streets. They had to find two plant extracts; rose and lavender. Hunt for a young male cat, pat off and bag some of its fur. Why on earth it was needed was beyond Duran's understanding. In his state and itching for a cure, he'd scrap the scales off a snake if he had to.

'Hey isn't Aki-kun's dad manager of that nursery place?' Fumio added.

'Yeah, yeah, he is. Fumi-chan let's grab Aki and get the plants,' Himeko confirmed.

'That leaves Hayashi-kun and Kita-kun to hunt for cat fur,' Mei ticked off.

'Okay. Before we take off, we should all exchange numbers in case of an emergency,' Himeko ordered.

Duran felt awkward when he swapped numbers with Saski. Especially, when his heart raced at a million miles an hour.

'Let's go!' He cried out and turned to flee.

Everyone else hurried off to secure their part of the cure.

The mellow chirping of crickets in the warm spring afternoon lulled Duran in and out of a sleepy state as he trailed behind Kou who was power-walking ahead of him.

'Hey Kita-kun, I saw a stray near the station when I was coming to school this morning,' Kou called out.

'Huh, yeah,' Duran said absent-mindedly.

The shōujo effect had pushed his body to a limit. However, Kou's presence could keep him grounded and aware of his surroundings.

They came upon an alleyway, which was nestled between a bustling café and ramen house. Both places were full of patrons enjoying each other's company over bowls of steaming food, cake or cups of beverages. Sure enough, they found a young male cat lounging on top of a dumpster mid-way in the alley.

'Stay behind me. I'm going to try to chase it toward you. Catch it when it runs to you,' Kou whispered his strategy to Duran.

They gingerly approached it. Duran took a few steps back from Kou for the catch.

He peered at the cat's fur, which seemed too sleek for a stray. It was all black save for a tuft of white streaking the top of its head like a Mohawk. It regarded them cautiously.

'Good kitty, nice kitty,' Kou said with soft tones and a maniacal glint in his eye. He crept slowly toward it; extending his hand.

The cat's orb like green eyes kept its vigilance on Kou's approaching hand. Its body tensed when his hand was almost on its back. Quickly, it leapt off the dumpster and went head on for Kou's face. Kou stumbled backward onto Duran.

The cat slipped past their legs and fled toward the eateries and crossroad at the end of the alleyway.

'*Chikushō!*' Kou cursed under his breath as they chased the cat inadvertently into the al fresco area of the ramen house.

'You kids! Get back here!' A surly waiter yelled at them as they turned tail to flee back up the alleyway.

'*Sumimasen!*' Duran cried out as he followed Kou's hunt.

They chased the cat to the other side of the street; barely dodging an oncoming courier worker on a push-bike.

Duran cringed when the worker screeched to a halt in

their path and went flying, unceremoniously, over his bike.

He landed flat on his face-butt in the air to the footpath. Envelops littered his body and the surrounding ground.

'Really, very sorry.' Duran frantically apologized and bowed as he helped the courier worker to his feet.

'Where you're rushing too?!' The courier worker snapped at Duran.

Duran bowed his head apologetically and gathered the courier's letters from the ground. He heard Kou yelling at him from a distance.

'Here. Very sorry again!' Duran rushed out as he shoved the pile of letters into the courier worker's hands and raced off down the street to Kou.

'I GOT YOU!' Kou screamed as he leapt for the cat as if his life depended on it.

He gripped the cat's small, wriggling, body and yelped in pain from its desperate scratches to his skin.

'Hurry Kita-kun!'

Duran cursed, feeling the scratches to his arms as they gathered the fur they needed from it. He patted the cat the best he could, stirring up fur balls into the air and onto his hands.

He transferred the fur to a tissue, crumpling it to contain it and shoved it in his pocket.

'Got it!' Duran confirmed.

Kou released the cat. It escaped down the street and around the corner at lightning speed.

'Phew!' Kou panted. He tensed with guilt, realizing the mess they had left back at the ramen house.

They sprinted their way back to school, skirting the ramen house.

Fortunately, all the other kids were in class. Kou and Duran could rush down the hallway of Block-B's first floor science labs without distraction.

They ran up to Watanabe-sensei, who was opening the door of the far end laboratory.

'Watanabe-sensei. We have the cat fur.' Kou puffed.

'Not bad,' Sensei said as he invited them inside.

Duran and Kou took a moment to recapture their breath.

They entered the room and were reunited with Himeko, Mei, Fumio, Aki and Saski.

Duran carefully placed the crumpled tissue next to the other ingredients that were lined up on the teacher's bench.

'Déjà vu.' Duran thought as his mind wandered back to the start of the snafu. He felt he had been running a yearlong marathon and ached that way too.

They gathered their teacher and attentively watched him mix the ingredients in a vial over blue flames of a Bunsen burner.

Watanabe-sensei covered the top of the vial with a funnel, where the thin hole was an entrance to space of a white paper bag. The bag expanded as purplish smoke filled it. He quickly disconnected and tied off the bag when it was at bursting level then swapped it with an empty one.

'Fujita-Kun. Can you and Okada-kun release the contents into the air conditioner unit down in the maintenance room? Tanaka-sensei is expecting you,' he asked the boy and handed Mei the responsibility of holding the bag.

'How are we supposed to put this stuff in the aircon?'

'Open the bag before the main vents. Ask Sensei who will tell you what ones,' Watanabe-sensei answered.

Aki and Mei raced out of the room to complete their mission.

'Okay my affected lab-ra, er, students. Breathe this in and go back to being the shy, awkward students that you are.' Watanabe-sensei chuckled as he unhooked the bag from the vial and passed the purplish smoke under everyone' noses.

Duran felt the same sensation he experienced the first time around. This time there were no twinkling stars or roses. Everyone and everything had returned to being dull and boring. Even his heart lacked the pace and flutters it once held in his chest.

'I dunna wanna be in love for a long time.' Fumio sighed deeply.

'I never thought I'd be so happy to feel dull and boring.' Saski sighed with relief. He still looked worse for wear.

'I thought all student council guys were happy being boring.' Himeko joked.

'Humph. Joke all you like but now that we're back to normal. I'll be expecting a full report from everyone affected. Especially, from yourself Sensei.' Saski demanded.

'A report on what?'

'On how everyone suffered under a botched experiment from their science teacher. The school board would want to be advised of this issue ASAP.' Saski stated.

'Tsubaki-kun. You are way too serious minded for a student of your age.' Watanabe-sensei retorted.

'I'll consider your comment a compliment. My report to the student council and the school board will be swift. You won't be able to wheedle out of this one Watanabe-sensei.' Saski spoke his piece, turned and stormed out of the room, letting the door slam behind him.

'Can't blame him for being pissed.' Fumio commented.

'Me neither. His response was reasonable. Was it not Sensei?' Duran commented levelly.

'I suppose so. Well, I imagine my review for employment is on the line. So, your music club will need another sponsor eh?'

Duran sighed when he realized it was like that. He left the science room feeling dejected and drained.

He was glad the remainder of the day passed like any other school afternoon, although the atmosphere was so thick with embarrassment a knife couldn't even slice through it. When the end-of-the-day bell rang out, all of Duran's classmates scrambled for their escape and didn't look back.

'Phew. What a first day aye Nii-san?' Himeko said as she meet up with him before the lockers near his class.

'Tell me about it. I'm so embarrassed I don't know if I should come back,' Duran replied and dodged eye contact with the other students.

The incident left a bitter aftertaste to the day.

'Kita-kun,' a small voice came up behind him.

Duran turned around. He saw a tall and slender pale-face boy, behind thick rimmed glasses, standing before him. The boy bowed so low the fringe of his neat black hair flung forward over the top of his glasses. He wondered where he had seen the guy before.

'I'm really sorry about today. I don't know why I did what I did, and to a freshman on his first day. Please forgive me,' the boy apologized.

'Aah, yes, today in the hallway,' Duran said as he remembered seeing the boy among the group that had tried to seduce him when he was making his way to the rooftop.

'It's okay. It wasn't you but the effects from a botched experiment in our science class. So, there's nothing to forgive,' he said kindly.

The boy sighed with relief and flashed a warm smile.

'Thank you. I'm Izuki, Isao, a second year. If you ever need a hand in getting around school, with your studies or anything, I'm happy to help. It's the least I can do.' Isao introduced himself.

'Nice to meet you Izuki-senpai. Actually, do you play a musical instrument by any chance?'

'Y-you called me Senpai. Thank you! Music? Um, well, er, yes. I sort of play the flute. Why do you ask?'

'My sister and I are thinking of starting up a music club,' Duran answered.

'Oh really! Then I'd love to join if you need members.'

'Excellent! Should the club be approved, I would like you to join.'

'I'll also let my friends know too.' Isao bowed.

'Thank you Senpai,' Duran said with a courteous bow. He felt his phone vibrating in his pant pocket concurrently.

'Senpai. Please excuse me.'

Isao cordially left them and met up with his friends at the end of the hallway.

Duran read the text he had received from Kou with Himeko.

'Why does Hayashi-kun want you to meet him outside a ramen house?' Himeko questioned, highly curious.

She wondered what had happened between the student council representative and her brother for them to start exchanging that sort of email.

'Because we stirred up some unpleasantness at that place,' Duran winced.

He explained the event to his sister as they made their way out of the hallway and for the main gate.

Himeko couldn't stop her laughter. They were half-way down the street toward the train station when she finally calmed down.

'Oh man Nii-san, you're entertaining.' She smirked and wrapped an arm around Duran's head to brace him into a head-lock. Her other hand ruffled up his hair.

'Himeko! Cut it out!' He yelped as he struggled free from her Tarzan grip. She was more of a guy than he was.

'That aside. What're you gonna do about the ramen house mess? You know they'll ask for compensation,' she said soberly.

'I'll cross that bridge when I get to it.'

He wasn't sure what to do about the issue, but he couldn't run away from the trouble he caused either. Whatever compensation they demanded, he would have to pay it somehow.

His mind wandered to the issue facing Watanabe-sensei and the formation of the music club. He continued walking lost in thought and following Himeko's lead down the busy streets.

The sun's spring-like glory had waned into early evening by the time they reached the ramen house.

Kou and Saski were standing beside an outdoor dining table, near a fiery red awning displaying the name Matsu Ramen House in free flowing calligraphy.

Duran couldn't see any obvious damage. He hoped the trouble he and Kou had caused ended up trivial.

'Tsubaki-kun you're here.' He squealed with surprise. He blushed and averted his eyes from the others.

Himeko chuckled.

'I guess we need to make good on our reputation.' Kou sighed.

He felt tense by the situation.

'Especially for the school's reputation.' Saski added to the reason's for Kou's nervous tension.

The restaurant's door swung aside to reveal a burly worker whose head was covered with a labourer's handkerchief. His body donned in a white t-shirt, jeans and waiter's apron tied around his waist. Although, his features were predominately manly, his face held a softness to the edges. It was almost as if someone decided to mix the body of a construction worker to the face of a part-time rock star. Garnish his chin with a goatee patch and set a stern expression in his eyes.

'You kids that caused trouble earlier eh?!'

'J-ju-just me and him,' Duran stammered and pointed to Kou.

The worker towered over Duran and Kou. He peered at them with a stern expression.

'Yeah. I recognize the uniform and both of you. So, where's that cat?' he asked them.

'Es-escaped,' Duran timidly answered.

He bowed low before the worker and politely asked to speak with the manager, so he could apologize to him.

'Well you can talk to me. I co-own this place.'

Duran frowned when he noticed Kou still standing upright next to him. He prodded him into a low bow.

He explained on their reasons for chasing the cat and causing the ruckus.

'Huh? Good grief. Come in. Better to retell with my bro.' The worker sighed.

They stepped into a set-up that was far from fancy. The mould stained plasterboard walls were softened with a few faded pictures of the country side, which was probably somewhere in the Kansai area. The tables themselves were lacklustre with their butcher paper table cloths and condiments centrepiece. Duran counted three dining sets (able to seat four people per set). And a long front counter with a row of stools where people could watch meals being made in the kitchen area beyond.

The place had enough space to be cosy. He envisioned the place cramp on busy days.

'Jiro-san. I've finished setting the tables. Do you need me to stack the shelves?' A young worker said as he entered the restaurant through the staff's entrance behind the counter.

'Yeah. That'll be good.' Jiro-san confirmed.

The worker was about to leave when he spotted Duran and Himeko standing near a table.

'Kita-kun!' The worker called out excitedly.

'Izuki-senpai. You work here?' Duran said when he recognized the quiet boy he had met earlier.

'Yes. Just started my shift. You've come to eat?'

'Er, well, not really,' Duran mumbled. 'I and Hayashi sort of caused problems today.'

'Bwahaha! You're the culprits with the cat. Jiro-san was complaining to me when I got here and started drilling me on the school's complaint person,' Isao laughed.

'It sounded funny.' He added but changed his tone upon noticing Jiro-san's curt glare. 'But terrible at the same time.'

'Yeah. We copped many complaints from our regulars as well. Had to kiss butt to keep their patronage.' Another person entered the conversation through the staff entrance and stood before Duran and the others.

Duran's eyes sized up another worker with an uncanny resemblance to the man Isao called Jiro-san.

Unlike Jiro-san, his face was goatee free and much manlier.

'So you came to kiss butt and beg forgiveness.'

No beating around the bush with this guy.

On cue, Kou and Duran bowed low and profusely asked for forgiveness.

'Hmm well how about this. You and jade-eye kawaii-kun here work for us for a month to pay off the damages. You'll work Wednesday and Friday afternoons, Saturday mornings. Do this and forgiveness be yours.'

'Huh? What damages? There was only mes-' Isao blurted and was cut short by Jiro-san's death stare.

'Er, um, yeah. I-I've gotta load stuff in the back,' he muttered and disappeared through the staff exit.

'You'd like our labour as compensation?' Duran rephrased.

'Yeah. Give me your body. Let me make you sweat for a month.' The man chuckled at Duran's flushed cheeks and nervous expression.

'I g-guess th-that is reasonable compensation.'

'Like we have a choice.' Kou groaned.

'You dare complain!' Jiro-san hissed through gritted teeth.

Everyone took a step back.

'Hayashi-kun. See this as an opportunity huh? I mean, it's as Kita-kun has said. A reasonable compensation,' Saski said to soothe the atmosphere.

'Hah! Sensible boy. It's settled,' the other man said as he drew his hands together in one loud clap.

'You kids call me Shiro-san. You two fools who'll be my slaves can call me Shiro-sama,' Shiro-san beamed with a cocky grin.

Duran felt he had been played at some level. He sighed away the feeling. As Saski had alluded, maybe it was a disguised blessing. Especially, since he would get to work with Senpai. Either way, he was going to have to suck it up and do the time.

'Geez Nii-san. You fall right into it,' Himeko joked as she slapped his back.

Duran grimaced at the sting he felt.

'No fear. Don't think dad will be mad. Mum might go Judge Judy on them though.'

He pictured his mother's slight frame confronting the almighty Shiro-sama. Her feminine voice yelling out terms for rights violation and other legal references coupled with adult ways of saying idiot.

'Like a David slinging legal stones at Goliath.' He shivered at the thought and decide it was better for everyone that he did his compensation without complaints.

If his mother saw his humility by the experience, maybe she would receive it positively.

'Thank you Jiro-sama, Shiro-sama. Yes, compensation is fair and I'll work as you have said.' Duran agreed with a formal bow.

'You too?' Shiro-san said to Kou.

Kou bowed in response.

'Okay. Both of you. After school this Wednesday.'

The group left the shop shortly afterwards. Tired and aching for home.

The first thing Duran did, when he had arrived home, was collapse to his bed.

He had survived a weird and wacky first day of his new school. Moreover, he found himself locked into a work agreement that saw him working three days a week at Matsu Ramen House. His penance starting the coming Wednesday.

'What else could go wrong?' He thought wearily.

His mother flung his bedroom door wide open with a curt wham! Her green eyes burned fierce with anger and her usually composed face was twisted in an ugly expression.

'Kita, Duran Akihiko. Tell me you didn't!' Her irate voice pounded against his ears.

Yep. The shit had hit the fan.

The only time she ever called him by his full name was when she was highly pissed off with him.

He buried his head underneath his pillow hoping she would get the hint and leave him alone. It only made matters worse.

'Get your head out of that pillow and face me!'

Duran gulped back his fear and slowly faced his mother's unnerving presence and scowling face staring down on him.

'I receive a call from a ramen house telling me you'll be working for them for a month. Himeko tells me you're doing it for free because you damaged their shop. Are you that much of a *baka*?!' She bellowed.

Duran cringed. He knew it was a terrible idea to Shiro-san his mother's number before he had left the shop. Shiro-san had insisted on informing her as some sort of duty of care. So, he hoped they had told her he got a job with them and left it at that.

Himeko's explanation of his circumstances would have definitely screwed it up for him.

'What the hell Himeko?!' He cursed in his mind when he saw his sister cowering near his door from the corner of his eye. An apologetic expression was written on her face.

'Don't you give me that look young man! You're damn lucky they didn't press charges nor made any complaints to the school.' His mother continued to scold him.

'B-But it was an accident. I was doing errands for my teacher,' Duran explained with a timid voice.

'Errands? Well. I'll check with the school either way,' she declared, adding her warning for emphasis.

'Don't do any more stupid things or I'll ground you from hanging out with friends for a month!'

She stormed out of his room and sight.

He let out a sigh of relief. His mother was usually an

approachable and fair person, but her personality took on a scary change when she was angry. Akin to a Jekyll and Hyde complex.

'I'm really sorry Bro. She cornered me with that scary look on her face.' Himeko apologized as she tip-toed into this room.

'You're quick to change,' Duran said to change the subject when he noticed his sister in a blue t-shirt and ripped jeans.

He couldn't be mad at her. It wasn't her fault for his predicament nor did she do anything wrong for telling his mother. His mother would have found out eventually.

'Always. I get more wear of my uniform if I get out of it straight away,' she said lightly with a big grin.

He sat up and noticed his room felt cosier. Almost as if the white wallpaper had taken on a soft creamy tone to ease the sterile brown of his flat-pack furniture. He gestured for his sister to join him for chit-chat. She plopped herself onto his bed and patted his shoulder.

'Don't worry D-man. I'm sure tomorrow will be a better day. At least you made friends today,' she consoled him.

Her eyes landed on the fire-brown burnished guitar propped up on a stand at the foot of his bed next to his keyboard.

'Hey is that a Loar?'

'Yeah. Did some part-time work at my music sensei's store for a few months to get that. It's one of their archtop cutaway's,' Duran said smugly. 'Wanna give it a try?'

Himeko didn't hesitate as she held the guitar's curvaceous frame against her front and started to pick out a tune. Her heart trilled with delight at the vibrant rich timbre the guitar strings allowed her fingers to play.

'Now this is a guitar!' she said excitedly and kept picking out the tune of a Bleach theme song.

Duran moved to his customized keyboard next to her and chimed in with her playing. Moments later they were jamming away the entire song in a sweet-melodic unison.

In his heart, he felt light and at peace. A kind warmth embraced his body and soothed away his troubles for that moment, so his mind was floating in a state of euphoria.

His mind was so enrapt that he didn't realize Himeko had stopped playing and was staring at him with a wonder-stricken expression on her face.

'Nii-san!'

Her voice let out a slight choked up sound that reeled his mind back to his small-sized room.

'Did you stop playing?'

'Friggin hell dude! You're like a freak of nature on the keyboards.' She praised him.

'Really?'

'Hell yeah! A season prodigy.' She went on. 'We so have to get that club started.'

Their conversation moved to Duran's suggested plan of attack for getting a club up and running. They talked and played throughout the nigh. Until their parents interrupted their fun with orders to eat, do their homework and go to bed.

Duran went to bed that night feeling a mix bag of emotions as he recapped his day. It all led to a conclusion that, despite the weirdness, he kind of had fun. He was looking forward to waking up to a new day and see what else would come into his life.

'Maybe the music club will be a good dream come true,' he said to himself before he closed his eyes and succumbed to sleep.

♪ I'M KITA, DURAN

The action to start up a music club kicked off at the start of his second week of school. First arduous task towards the cause was a visit to the principal's office on a Wednesday.

The summons came to Duran when he was passing through the school gates.

'You're wanted at the principal's office ASAP. I hope you haven't been a naughty boy.' The handsome teacher at the gates had chuckled when he had given him the order.

This did nothing to allay Duran's worries as he tentatively made his way to the office. He was practically shitting himself with all the things he could've done wrong before the principal's door. Disrupting the peace at Matsu Ramen House was definitely one of those wrong doings.

'Enter,' he heard a stern voice grumble from the other side.

Duran closed the door and stood upright before his Principal's wide desk, which was some sort of polished cedar.

Its pristine condition was a bit over-the-top. The pens were too upright and even in the sleek black pen cup perched on the right corner and the papers, Principal Kimura was busying himself with, were kept in crisp neat piles toward his left.

He glanced around the rest of the room and took in two bland chairs, which sat as audience before the desk. Toward his right was a tall bookshelf with rows of books stacked neatly and evenly so not an edge was improper. Impersonal white walls closed off a small sized space.

It was a stifling room to stand in. Duran was certain his discomfort was due to anticipation for the worst. Of course, he wasn't brave to take a seat.

'I heard you submitted an application for a music club.'

The unsparing tone from his principal's voice made

Duran flinch with unease.

Principal Kimura sat back from the piles of papers and fixed his stern eyes on him. Duran cringed under the man's glare.

'This is your second week is it not? Already you demand the impossible.'

'Sir. Why do you think it's not possible?' Duran lowered his eyes.

'I'll tell you something Kita-kun. Hotaka has a long standing tradition of grooming top corporate executives, honorary doctors, lawyers and national sports champions.' His principal stated proudly.

'Sir, You're saying to host a music club would cheapen the school's reputation.' Duran clenched his fist at the words that rolled out of his mouth.

'Yes.' Blunt was Principal Kimura's response.

Duran felt he wasn't in the position to negotiate for another answer. He realized then that his efforts for a music club was as pointless as Kou had advised him. If it was going to cause trouble for the school's reputation and his classmates by pushing for one then it was probably best he resigned from the idea. He was sure his friends would understand.

He opened his mouth to start off a string of apologize and agreement toward his principal's view but his moment was interrupted by a polite knock on the door.

Upon Principal Kimura's order, Aimi-sensei stepped into the room.

'Sir. You asked for me.'

'Yes. Close the door Aimi-sensei.' Principal Kimura ordered the teacher.

Aimi-sensei did as he was told and stood next to Duran.

'Did you know that your student has submitted an application for a music club?'

'Er, yes. The student council are reviewing its acceptance.'

'So what are your thoughts Sensei?'

Duran stared at his homeroom teacher from the corner of his eye and saw the man's throat twitch nervously.

'Eh, um. I think i-it's not a problem.'

'You're young and foolish. It's a huge problem from what I can see.'

Duran went through his submitted application in his mind. He could write out the essays, fill in the survey and even secure Watanabe-sensei's endorsement. His teacher had only received a warning and a small cut in pay as compensation for unintentionally setting the entire school on an orgy rampage. There were rumours that Watanabe-sensei's father was the school's chairman and had pulled some strings to ensure he was still employed as a science teacher.

'This boy is serious about the club's purpose and wishing to represent this school at music events.' His principal went on.

'Sir. Why is that a problem? The events he suggests are reputable school and community exhibitions.'

Principle Kimura waffled on about the school's exclusive image and a music club wasn't going to happen in his lifetime.

He was about to dismiss Duran and Aimi-sensei with his ultimate decision of declining the club's existence when Watanabe-sensei barged into the room.

'Pardon the intrusion, but I figured you're talking about canning the club before it begins.'

'I've just told Kita-kun here that the club is a no.' Principal Kimura affirmed not hiding his displeasure at Watanabe-sensei's untimely intrusion.

'Are you sure about that?'

'It's a music club Watanabe-kun! It goes against the exclusiveness of this school.'

Watanabe-sensei made himself comfortable in one of the chairs without invitation.

'You know, my old man played in the Tokyo University

Orchestra when he was a student. When I mentioned there was a group of kids who wanted a music club to break the boredom of study - oddly he was all for it.'

'I don't believe Our Chairman would defy the rules of this school. Even he is bound to principles.' Principal Kimura scoffed.

Watanabe-sensei's eyes narrowed with a defying expression behind them. Surprising both Aimi-sensei and Duran.

'Who said it was a rule to disallow music?'

Duran watched a silent stand-off between the men. He was surprised when his principal broke first with a fumbled come back.

'Either way. At least allow Kita-kun to go through the same acceptance process as any other club application.' Watanabe-sensei recommended.

'Why would I endorse such a request Watanabe-sensei?'

'Why not? Even if Kita-kun is good enough, the club would probably be a flash in the pan like that otaku cosplay one anyway,' Watanabe-sensei said lightly.

'No. No. I'm still against this,' said Principal Kimura, stubbornly.

'Why not set a challenge?' Aimi-sensei suggested. Everyone stared at him like he had said the devil word.

'I mean, if he's good enough to play, he'd be good enough to motivate a club right?'

Principal Kimura paused with his mind ticking on an answer.

'Okay. I present a challenge..."

Everyone listened as their good principal issued his challenge.

Duran was to play before the entire school body at their Thursday morning assembly. He's to the end of the same day to earn his own year's vote; on whether his playing was good to lead a music club or not. If he were to receive more than half of the votes being negative, the club would never see the light of day.

'The number of freshman attended is 263. So, your goal to achieve is well over half of this number,' he said with a haughty chuckle.

'So if he gets at least 135 positive votes, the club will get the rubber stamp of approval?' Watanabe-sensei concluded.

Principal Kimura nodded his head.

'A ballot vote tallied at the end of the week's assembly will determine the results.'

'Well then. Better state this on the application form as a precursor for acceptance.' Watanabe-sensei grinned.

He removed a folded up application form from his pocket and smoothed it out on the principal's pristine desk.

They waited and watched with anticipation as their Principal gingerly pushed the form toward himself with a pinkie. He scribbled a condition at the bottom with little contact to the paper as possible. His face contorted with disgust as he finished his sign-off.

'There you go!' Watanabe-sensei said to Duran as he whisked the form away from the Principal's view and folded it back into his pocket.

He stood to leave the room.

'Sensei, Principal Kimura, thank you.' Duran bowed his respects to his teachers.

His Principal huffed and gave Duran the gesture of being dismissed.

Duran hurried out of the room at the same time his teachers did. The three of them blew out a sigh of relief.

'Well looks like you need to impress your peers,' Watanabe-sensei said with a wry smile.

'I guess so,' Duran gulped down a nervous knot he felt to his throat.

He was queasy thinking the number of students his music would have to impress. Playing music was one thing but playing before a massive judging audience was a different experience. He would have to push aside his nervousness and do it. It would be rude to waste the opportunity that his teachers had fought for.

He yelped at the sting he felt to his back from Watanabe-sensei's manly "cheer-up" slap.

'It's almost the first period. Better get to class music-man,' he said and chuckled at Duran's face contorted with worry.

Duran was relieved he had made it to class before the first lesson had begun. He saw Fumio talking casually with Aki and a couple of other classmates near his desk.

From the corner of his eye, he spied Saski leaning against his own toward the middle row; surrounded by a bunch of glasses wearing boys and girls who seemed to hang off his every word.

'Here's trouble,' Saski said when he saw Duran strut past him.

'Aim to please my friend.' Duran flashed him a cocky grin and chuckled at the incredulous *pffts, tsks* and eye-rolls from the Saski's posse.

'Sup. You're Mr. Popular this morning.' Fumio lightly joked.

'Haha. Well, I'd hate to steal Tsubaki-kun's thunder, but can't help the admiration his posse gives me when I say those things.'

'Infamous dude. Speaking of, heard you got called into an early meet with the Princ. How'd it go?'

If it was one thing Duran had learned about his new friend Fumio. The guy seemed well informed with people and topics. At least those that seemed to be of interest to him. He was slowly discovering the sharp mind beneath his friend's aloof exterior.

'It was scary.'

'Yeah. I guess having to face up to the popo can be like that.' Aki joined their conversation.

'Have you had to deal with him before Fujita-kun?' Duran asked him politely.

'Geez. Call me Aki. I feel like my old *aniki* when you

call me that,' Aki said and chuckled at Duran's flushed-red cheeks.

'Heehee. It's not like I'm asking you out on a date. Just call me Aki as a friend would aye?'

'Um, er, okay. Aki-kun.' Duran complied with a mousy voice and yelped at Aki's "mate's" slap to his back. For a small guy, he had a heavy hand.

'Geez man. Just Aki okay? Even the honorifics makes me feel old. We're the same age after all.'

'Dude you call me Fumio too. I can call you Duran? Been saying I'd like to call you by your given name. It's too cool not to be used.' Fumio jumped in.

'Um, yeah. I'm cool with that.'

'So. Yeah, we were called into his office when he found out the Otaku Machima Club was gonna happen. He was real pissed about it.' Aki continued with his story on his visit to the principal's office.

'Oh yeah. Didn't he tell you to prove the worth of the club or something like that?' Another classmate said.

'Something like that Isao-kun, but he predicted the club wouldn't last more than six months. So let it go. Turns out he was right. No fault to anyone but our members too. Man Dai'chi was pissed to the high heavens about it all,' Aki explained.

'But to start a music club. Now things are getting interesting huh?'

'It's interesting to see what Kita-kun has to satisfy to get one.' Saski called out, having eavesdropped on the conversation.

'Hey Tsubaki-kun. Whadya mean by that?' Aki's eyes narrowed at Saski's comment.

Saski made his way to them. He took over Fumio's seat. Ignoring Fumio's complaints and scowls.

'Just. For that type of club request to be approved. Something has to give right?'

Duran's heart pounded madly at his chest. He knew Saski's sole intention was to rile him up about the music club, but his composed mannerisms, cool eyes and the smirk on those luscious lips aroused him.

He slunk low in his chair, squeezed his knees together and started chanting the first few paragraphs of Pillars of the Earth in his head to shrink his twitching member. Everyone else saw his reaction as one of intimidation.

Saski continued his taunt, which made things worse for Duran. He dipped his head to hide his beetroot blushes. Adding to the misinterpretation.

'Stop it Tsubaki! Can't you see you've made him nervous!' Aki snapped at Saski.

Saski bowed his head low with apology.

'I'm sorry Kita-kun. I sometimes get carried away and didn't consider how nervous you must be about the club. I should also add how brave I think you are too for trying for one.'

'Did something just hit your head Tsubaki?!' Fumio retorted.

'Huh? No sarcastic comeback this time? Well done Kita,' said the boy Aki had referred to as Isao-kun.

Duran slowly raised his head when he felt the Pillars of the Earth had done its job. He was composed enough to face Saski.

'It's, um, okay Tsubaki-kun. I guess you have the school's best interest in mind. So, I've no hard feelings. You're right. I'm nervous as hell and can't stop thinking I've signed myself up for a lost cause.'

'Well don't force yourself. Do your best and thing's will work out as they're meant to I guess.'

Saski's gentler response both surprised and warmed Duran's heart. From the gaping mouths and gawking eyes of everyone else, it was a shock for them too.

'Saski-kun. Did you smile at Kita?' A girl squealed.

'Oh-my-god! So cute!' Another girl chimed in.

Duran felt a weight of eyes checking him out. His face blushed with embarrassment that caused more girls to swoon his way.

'Hey. You seem alright to me after all. Tsubaki's was harping on about how over confident you were, since that time you saved him from being chased by girls,' said one of the guys from Saski's desk. He walked over to introduce himself.

'Hey! I did not.' Saski cursed at the lanky boy standing before Duran.

'Mikumo, Osamu. I've known this guy since grade school.' Osamu introduced himself.

Duran returned the greeting.

'Don't mind Tsubaki. He talks brash sometimes. But he's just your average boy like us,' Osamu whispered and laughed at Saski's tsundere reaction.

At first glance Osamu was your typical glasses boy and future salary-man type of student. His uniform clung to his tall build nicely. His hair was cropped in a safe clean cut. Dark orb like eyes glistened with a sparkle behind thin square frames. Duran felt they carried an expression beyond a boy of their age. He wondered if he was experienced in a few aspects of life that were still beyond the comprehension of his peers. He also wondered how much of that life experience was lived with Saski.

'That's reassuring.' Duran smiled.

'Alright everyone back to your seats!' Aimi-sensei called out as he entered the room, drawing everyone either out of the room or to their seats and his attention.

The bell rang. The first lesson began.

Throughout the day, Duran's name was whispered everywhere. Someone had leaked about his performance for a music club during morning recess, which had spread through the grounds as wild fire.

What kind of transfer student would try to shake tradition on his first week of school? This question and many others circulated around his ears as he navigated through halls of gossip to his last class for the day. He was glad for his friends comfort.

'Nii-san you're a novelty right now. Next week

someone else will be a victim.' Himeko reassured him with heavy slap on his back.

Duran wasn't convinced. He had already spent a good part of the day dodging accusations about his intentions and abilities. He was baffled by the fuss it caused. It's not as if he was going around shaving his head and declaring his love for Minami Minegishi.

He was concerned of the effect the gossip could cause his sister and friend's reputation by being associated with him. The last thing he wanted was to be trouble for them.

'Yahooo Kita-kun!'

Duran glanced up from the hallway lino he had been staring at and saw an image of an AKB48, girly-girl, making a beeline for him.

She had a buxom figure of woman already; lithe waist, slender legs, big boobs and a seductive look in her large brown eyes. Yet she carried the image of a middle-schooler with her hair up in pig tails, skirt riding way to high up her smooth thighs, her bag jangling with Hello Kitty and other mementos of innocence. Probably other guys saw her as the ideal fantasy girl wrapped up with a navy bow tie. A prowling bear was a more accurate image in his mind.

He shrieked and took a few steps back to hide behind his sister and Fumio.

'Oh Kita-kun. I hear you're performing tomorrow. You're so brave!' She squealed as she dodged his sister's shove and wrapped her arms around his waist.

'Um, er, ah, yeah.' Duran answered, flustered with bright red cheeks and a nervous twitch to his lips.

'Watanabe Chiasa. Call me Chiasa, please. I sit behind Tsubaki.'

'Um okay.'

It was the first time he had seen her. He really needed to take note of his class surroundings more earnestly.

'Hey Watanabe if you hug Kita like that you're gonna break him.' Himeko frowned.

'Says the Warrior Princess. Though, I'd thought it

would've been you to break him first.' Chiasa teased her and chuckled at the obvious embarrassment on Duran's face.

'Geez Watanabe. Give the dude breathing space. He's goin' delirious?' Fumio teased.

'Oh Kita you're so sweet. Breathe in my oxygen.' She teased further and forcefully kissed his cheek.

'What the hell?!' Duran was startled by her brashness. He managed to wiggle free from her hold.

The school bell twanged through the halls.

'Let's go,' she ordered and grabbed his arm. She ignored Himeko and Fumio's protests as she pulled him into brisk walk.

'Hey Kita-kun. I need to talk with you for a bit,' Saski called out from behind them.

Duran struggled out of her grasp. He fumbled out apologies as he hurried towards Saski and pushed him into sprint around the corner.

'Geez that's the second time you've done that Kita!' Saski huffed.

'S-sorry. It's just that, um, well.' He couldn't bring himself to say that he was scared.

'Yeah. Guess Chia-chan can be scary when she's obsessed.' Saski laughed at Duran's obvious reaction.

'I can't blame her.'

Duran's heart pounded so hard that he felt the throbbing at the back of his ears. He couldn't move when Saski pinned him against the wall and whispered into his ear.

'Makes someone like me want to bully you too.'

His words were scary, but his voice flowed through his ears like honey. Electricity tingled the places of his arm that were held against the wall. Their lips were a hair's breadth away from a kiss, so Saski's breath burned his cheeks. Duran felt he would surely melt if they did kiss.

He closed his eyes and waited, but it never came. His cheeks went cold.

'Huh?'

'Jokes aside, I wanted to talk to you before we got to class. Shall we walk?' Saski released his arms and stepped away.

Duran sighed. Of course Saski was crudely teasing him as a way of showing his superiority as a Student Council Representative. His mind went over the near kiss as they made their way to class.

Saski talked about his music club application.

'I don't think it's fair you perform tomorrow not knowing what's at stake.'

'Um, I already know I'm fighting for a music club,' Duran responded nonchalantly.

'It doesn't sound like you do. Otherwise, you wouldn't be causal about it.'

'I'm casual?'

'Yeah. Listen.'

Saski elaborated on the risk of failure. Should he fail to convince his peers for a music club would ensure no music club would ever exist in all of Hotaka High School's future lifetimes. Duran couldn't believe the fate of all music clubs rested on his performance tomorrow. He started stressing about the consequence.

'You suck Kita!'

'Go to hell Kita!'

'Weirdo Kita, creepy Kita. Die. Kita die…'

Harsh words circled his mind. Ghosts from his past surfaced. His mind flashed to the face of a young teacher. His teacher's voice echoed acutely in his ears, shouting out his name with desperation.

Intense pressure and pain surged through the back of his head. He felt the weight of his body pull him down. His thoughts lost all form and became black.

'Sensei, I'm sorry I caused you trouble, please forgive me. I'm sorry Sensei…'

Duran woke with a start. His mind eased out of a memory as the present environment appeared before him.

He soon realized he wasn't where he should be. The last moment he remembered was talking to Saski in the hallway near their classrooms.

'Nurse be here shortly. I was told to wait 'til she comes back.'

Duran glanced around the sterile white-washed walls and ward bed he was lying on. A curtain provided privacy between bed spaces. Fumio was perched on the edge of his bed. He was still in uniform.

'Fumio-kun. Um, where am I?' He asked, still hazy.

'The infirmary. Man, you passed out in the hallway K-Pop style.' Fumio's voice was apologetic. 'I shouldn't have let you go off with Tsubaki.'

'It's okay, not as if I was led astray to be trampled upon by screaming Justin Bieber die-hard fans desperate to touch their god.' He reassured Fumio and felt a chill down his spine thinking of it.

Fumio chuckled.

'Still, how'd I get here?' Duran asked perplexed.

Fumio explained how everyone in their class saw Saski racing down the hallway with him in his arms. Fumio bolted out of class and caught up to them outside the Infirmary. Saski left Duran in his care.

Duran blushed at the image of himself being carried like a princess in Saski's arms. Surely, it would've taxed a lot of that guy's strength to ensure his arrival in the infirmary.

The place was a distance from his classroom block. He would've had to carry him across the courtyard and down the hallway of the Administration floor.

'How strong is that guy?' Duran spoke this thought out loud.

'He's our kendo prince, so guess the dude's gotta have some guns. Then again. You look light enough to be carried like a princess.' Fumio lightly joked.

Duran looked over his scrawny body and hid further under the thin blankets. His height was a mere average 165 centimetres and his figure was light and skinny as Fumio said.

He felt guilty by troubling Saski and his friend. Would a simple thank you be enough to show his gratitude?

'Dude. What's with your red face? You ain't got a fever have you?'

'Oh, um, no. Don't think so. Thank you for being here and all. I'm sorry I caused you trouble.' Duran fumbled his thanks.

'It's all good. You gave me a valid reason to skip history.' Fumio reassured him as he ruffled up his hair

Duran felt relieved his friend was being normal around him, but he wondered what his other classmates thought of him.

'Don't worry what people think. Passing out is what people do sometimes. If anyone said bad things about it, I'll smack their brains in,' Fumio said out of the blue. Sharp guy.

'Yeah, thanks mate.'

The school nurse shortly arrived to take his temperature. He was released when she saw it was at a normal level, and he looked well enough.

The end of the day bell rung when Duran and Fumio approached their footlockers in the front foyer of the classroom block. Himeko, Aki and Mei were waiting for them.

'Nii-san!' Himeko called out. She raced for him and yanked him into a bear hug.

'Get off me, it's embarrassing,' Duran said, but found himself holding on to Himeko's warm hug.

'Nah! When Aki-chan told me what happened, I wanted to skip class to see you, but well.'

'She's already skipped too much English. Sensei told her she'd have detention the next time she wasn't there,' Mei said to finish off Himeko's explanation.

'English's boring and too complex. Who wants to speak like a *yankee* anyway? Besides, my brother's more important!' Himeko pouted then stopped and released Duran when she remembered he was fluent.

'Glad to see you haven't lost a body part,' she brushed off with an awkward grin and pat to his shoulder.

'Yeah. Your *yankee* speaking brother is okay, although I felt my pride go down the chute. It's embarrassing,' he sighed.

'Sounds like a normal teenager to me.' Aki added with a cheeky smile. He swung his arm around Duran's shoulder.

'You feel well now Duran?'

'Er, yeah.'

'Excellent. Then how 'bout we go for ramen and see you work!' He suggested.

'Yeah. Nii-san I wanna see you work it too. I am hungry for good ramen.' Himeko piped in.

'Um, yeah, guess so. Don't cause trouble for me, 'kay?' Duran said as he pulled away from Aki and started swapping to his outdoor shoes.

He felt his friends concerned eyes on his back, but no one said anything else about his mishap.

'It's settled. We go for ramen!' Fumio said, motivated. He kicked Duran into a walk and chuckled at his reaction.

'That's mean!'

'Got you moving, though. Everyone, lets go-go!'

'Ramen! Ramen!' Duran and his friends chanted cheerfully as they made their way out of school.

The five of them weaved their way through people as they strolled along suburban streets that were surrounded by a mismatch of weathered apartment blocks, modest family eateries and small shops with windows overflowing with all kinds of loud and colourful advertising.

Duran's mind wandered toward Saski and their near kiss. What was that guy thinking back then? Was he really going to kiss? His questions led a fact that a couple of times Saski had come to his rescue about the music club when others were against the idea. Why was that?

His friends' talk turned to the style of music and bands

they liked. Duran brushed his questions aside and focused on his friends' conversation.

'Man when it comes to pop, western bands are cool,' Aki declared and was met with contention from Mei who wasn't shy in confessing her like for home-grown bands.

'Of course chicks would be into packaged groups with good-looking guys.'

'Hah! Like to see if you can sing, dance and look cool at the same time.'

'Yeah I can do that,' Aki said and busted some moves that caused him to stumble on his feet comically.

'*Pfft*, very cool. NOT!' Himeko laughed.

'Just you wait! I'll be all cool like a pop idol and make all the girls go gaah,' Aki declared with great conviction, which only caused more hearty laughter from his friends.

'Dude, stick to playing guitar and studying maths,' Fumio said with a slap to Aki's back.

Thoughts of the music club stirred up in Duran's mind again. If he got an actual club off the ground, would they really be willing to play as a band?

'Hey. We all really play an instrument?' He asked.

'Not sure about the rest of yah, but I'm a legend on guitar.' Aki cocked his head to one side.

'Pfft! You keep on dreaming and reaching for the stars Megane-chan.' Himeko chuckled.

'Shut up Xena! Jealously get you nowhere.'

'Yeah, yeah.' Himeko brushed off his words with a light kicked to his backside.

'Wow, what cool fate for all of us to be musos.' Duran thought aloud.

'True. I mean you know how good I am at guitar. Aki ain't bad either, although I'm better,' Himeko said matter-of-factually.

'I like to see you run a riff at the speed of light like I can.'

'Says he who's never won against me.' Himeko argued.

'I could get the music club of the ground. We could all

be a band!' Duran said enthusiastically with a clenched fist. 'How awesome that would be!'

'You're really hell-bent on setting up a club aren't you?' Aki said, dropping his argument with Himeko.

'The principal challenged me, so too late to turn back now.' Duran let out an awkward laugh.

He couldn't shake the feeling he was being set up to be a disciplinary example for everyone to see either way.

'Hey guys, do you hear that?'

'Aki-kun?'

'It's Granrodeo!' Aki answered.

They all stopped and fell silent with their ears perked toward melodic guitar riffs sounding from some nearby building.

Duran closed his eyes and pictured the crisp twang and pluck of each note, which danced in the air effortlessly. The troubles he felt in his heart and mind eased the more he soaked in every run. Whoever was playing was a skilful master.

'*Sugureta.*' He let out a breath full of awesome wonder.

'I wonder where that's coming from,' Himeko said enthusiastically as she searched the buildings hoping to zone in on the playing.

The five of them found themselves called to the music and abandoning their thought of ramen as they chased the riffs through the streets.

'It's close!' Mei panted.

Duran was surprised to see the same feverish look in her eyes.

They raced through an alleyway and stopped before the back of an eatery that was next to other over-lived-in apartment buildings.

Everyone's jaws dropped when they saw Jiro-san fingering out a Grandrodeo tune on a Fender. What was this? Was this fate?

'Jiro-san!' Duran breathed out.

'Awesome!' Himeko acknowledged.

Jiro-san stopped playing and looked up to the faces of five awestruck students.

'Kita-kun? Oh, you're early.'

'Early?' Duran was still in a semi-trance from Jiro-san's playing.

'Yeah. You're here for your shift right?'

Duran took in food crates and the sign for Jiro and Shiro-san's shop. The music led him to work.

'Jiro-san you play in a band?'

'Ah, yeah, but just for kicks. Doesn't earn the money though.'

'Sensei, dude! Please teach me those cool riffs!' Aki pleaded with a low bow. 'I beg you!'

'Huh?' Jiro-san rubbed his chin as he sized up Aki. 'Depends on if you can play some already.'

He handed Aki the guitar.

Aki stood transfixed. His hands shook as he carefully positioned the Fender to his chest and portable amp to his belt.

Everyone waited with anticipation.

Duran's eyes widen with delight and surprise as Aki started playing a Fo'x Tails song almost as good as the original. He was disappointed when his playing stopped.

'Come with Kita every Friday,' Jiro-san said when he claimed the Fender back.

'Thank you!' Aki beamed with a grateful bow.

'You, kawaii-kun, get to work!'

'Hai!' Duran replied.

'What about me?' Himeko cried out.

'You're a legend already right?' Aki replied with a cheeky smile.

'Shut it Megane-man.'

Duran frowned. He wasn't keen to see Jiro-san's generosity pushed further.

'Himeko, you're already good with riffs.'

'Not like that.'

Jiro-san sighed. 'Okay both of you come on Fridays.'

Himeko squealed with delight, clapping her hands.

Duran escorted everyone into the front of the shop then made his way to back room to get ready for his shift.

The afternoon flew as Duran worked hard beyond his friends' eat and go time.

Kou had changed to different days to balance the rosters.

So, he performed a lot of the work on his own, alternating tasks with Isao. He didn't mind his duties of chopping and peeling vegetable, sorting packages on shelves, serving patrons and constantly cleaning up the dining area to closing time. It felt no different to what he would do at home.

Before he realized, it was nine o'clock when his bosses called it a night.

'You'll be alright getting home?' Shiro-san asked Duran who was wiping the last dirty table clean.

'Yeah. My Step-father's coming to pick me up soon.'

'Okay. Let me know when you're about to take off. Good work today Kita-kun. A lot of our regulars were impressed with your service. You're a quick learner.'

Duran blushed as Shiro-san's large hand fondly ruffled the top of his head.

'Um, ah, thank you. Good work today as well.'

He watched his boss exit to the back room as he waited in the dining area for his step-father.

The place assumed a calm silence, which was a complete contrast from the din of bustling conversations, chinks of chopsticks and cutlery on plates, and the sounds of a working kitchen an hour earlier.

Duran sunk into one of the seats and breathed out a sigh of relief that his shift was over.

'Hey Kita-kun. Nice work today. You really made a big difference to this place,' Isao said as he entered the dining area ready to take off for the night.

'Oh Izuki-senpai. Good work today too. I'm glad I was useful.'

'Definitely useful. We could serve food faster because of you. The patrons seemed to like the look of you.'

'Like the look of me?' Duran frowned at the thought, not sure exactly what his senpai was indicating. Judging by the amiable expression on his face, he took it as a compliment and left it at that.

'Make sure you get enough sleep when you get home,' Isao said as he made his exit.

Duran didn't think that was going to be a problem. He'd most likely crash as soon as he reached his room. He relaxed back into the chair and allowed himself to doze off.

A commotion from outside jolted his body awake. A pang of worry struck his heart as he heard yelling and screaming not too far from where he was.

'Otōsan,' he muttered as he bolted for the exit and stepped outside.

He ran up the street and saw three surly delinquents cornering another guy beneath a street light and entrance of an apartment block. One of them rammed a fist into the guy's stomach. The guy keeled over with clear agony on his face from the punch.

Duran's eyes widen with a mixture of concern and anger when he saw Isao was the victim of the attack.

'Hey!' He yelled out at the top of his voice, which drew the attention of the delinquents his way.

'What yah think you're doing?!'

The delinquents started making their way to him with their full display of toughness.

Instinctively, Duran flipped out his phone and started dialling the cops.

'Hello. I'm seeing a bunch of delinquents attacking a man in the streets. Please hurry.'

'Yah think we be 'fraid of pigs!' A delinquent snickered.

'You should be afraid of me.' Duran heard a man say behind him. He turned around and saw the towering frame of Ryuu-chichi.

'What yah gonna do old man? Yell at us,' said the tallest of the delinquents.

He had a formidable build, bleach blond hair and piercings all the way up his left ear. His baggy sweat pants and athletes jacket reminded Duran of one of those American rappers.

'I'll give you a chance to beat it on your own. Or make you forcefully,' Ryuu-chichi answered coolly.

'Ha-ha. Old man, this gonna be fun.'

The three delinquents rushed at Duran and Ryuu-chichi for the kill. Both were quick to evade the attacks. Ryuu-chichi could disarm the group on his own and send them running off down the street with their tail between their legs.

'Izuki-senpai!' Duran rushed to check on Isao's condition.

'Ki-ta, th-thank you.' Isao breathed and coughed up some blood.

Duran wrapped his arm around his shoulders as he helped him stand up.

'We need to get you to the hospital.'

'Duran, what did dispatch say?' Ryuu-chichi said as he supported the other side of Isao.

'The number didn't connect. Let's go back to work. The bosses will be still around,' Duran replied.

They helped Isao back into the ramen house.

'Shiro-san, Jiro-san!' Duran called out as they entered the dining area.

'Baka! I told you to tell me when you were leaving didn't I!' Shiro-san yelled when he saw Duran enter the shop. His anger left him when he saw Isao struggling to walk and had to be assisted into a chair.

'What happened?'

Jiro-san entered the dining area. Duran recounted the incident to both of them.

'Those damn punks!' Jiro-san hissed through clenched teeth.

'No use getting riled up when he needs to get to a hospital,' Ryuu-chichi said.

'I've called in a report to my boss.'

'Boss?'

'Um, yeah, Otōsan's a police officer,' Duran answered.

He saw his bosses size-up his step-father carefully and wondered of their first impression of him.

Ryuu-chichi resembled a stoic salary-man more than a detective. He was a head taller than Shiro-san, broad at the shoulders with a leaner and more toner build. It was rare for Duran to see his step-father wear anything but a business suit outside the house. His thoughts went back to the day he first met him, and those piercing black eyes that seemed to be able to see through minds and absorb everything.

'Okay. I'll take Izuki to the hospital and call his parents,' Shiro-san said, having calmed down at the mention of a law enforcement officer in his presence.

'Good, we'll leave him in your care,' said Ryuu-chichi. 'Izuki-kun it'll be safer if you had someone pick you up on late nights. A student shouldn't be exposed to this type of risk.'

'As bosses, ensuring the safety of your staff when leaving work is just as important,' he directed to Duran's bosses.

'Hai, thank you.'

Jiro-san and Shiro-san gave him a humble bow.

Ryuu-chichi and Duran left the restaurant.

'You'll be alright working there during the week?' Ryuu-chichi said as they stepped into his car.

'I'll be fine. It's only for a month anyway and as long as you or mom can pick me up at nights, I should be okay.'

'I'm more concerned with your studies.'

'My grades are okay and school work isn't too much anyway. I think I'll be fine.'

'Well okay. I trust your sense of judgment Duran. You're your mother's son after all. Let us know if it becomes too much.'

Nothing more was said between them on their ride home. As Duran had predicted earlier, he fell asleep as soon as he had reached his bed.

A few days later, the moment of truth arrived. Duran felt he wasn't prepared enough as he packed his Loar for the fight. Winning the challenge would come down to his musical experience. If he wasn't good enough, he would fail without mercy with the entire school as witness.

It didn't help that his thoughts were also filled with Isao's attack. He hoped his senior was recovering well and made a mental note to check on him later in the day.

'Ready Nii-san?'

Himeko stepped into his room and made herself comfortable on his bed. At first glance, she seemed relaxed and carefree as always.

'I guess.'

He was unable to calm the nervous twitch in his hands, which were further aggravated by his dark thoughts. Was it arrogant of him to believe he could make music happen in an institution that denied and discouraged it?

If he had won a club what else would he have to fight against? He was certain just having a club wasn't going to be enough to ensure its continual existence. The Otaku Machima Club's disbandment was proof of this. He would have to follow through with a serious purpose for the club's survival.

'Nii-san. Nothing ventured, nothing gained. You can do this.' Himeko reassured him with a seriousness unlike her.

He stared at his sister, accepting her reassurance. Of course, it wasn't just for himself he was fighting for. He had to believe he could pull off the best performance of his life and win his peers over. No point in thinking otherwise.

'Hai!'

He grabbed his bag and armed his guitar to his back. They both left his room for school.

They filed through the school gates as all the other students. Obvious chatter and glances were fired Duran's way as they made their way to their classroom block. He was relieved that no one had approached him.

'Duran! Hime-chan!' Aki called out to them from the top of Block-B's entrance. He came bounding down the steps to them.

'You look ready to rumble eh?' His eyes sized up Duran's guitar.

They made their way to the footlockers and exchanged their shoes. Duran made light chit-chat with his friends in attempt to distract his roulette of nervous thoughts. It worked for a short-lived moment.

He soon found his mind wandering back to those dark places as they made their way to their classrooms. His body moved through his whole morning routine

'Duran! Hime-chan!' Aki called out to them from the top of Block-B's entrance. He came bounding down the steps to them.

'You look ready to rumble eh?' His eyes sized up Duran's guitar.

They made their way to the footlockers and exchanged their shoes. Duran made light chit-chat with his friends in attempt to distract his roulette of nervous thoughts. It worked for a short-lived moment.

He soon found his mind wandering back to those dark places as they made their way to their classrooms. His whole morning routine automatically with his mind and mood occupied elsewhere. He didn't notice his friends' concern nor the teasing from other classmates. He was completely oblivious of the Student Councils' watchful eyes on him.

He was standing in the school hall with his classmates for morning assembly before he realized it. His guitar on his back ready and waiting to go.

'Students. Stand attention!' A teacher called everyone to order as Principal Kimura made his way to the center podium on the stage.

The podium mic cracked and hissed for a split moment as he pulled it closer toward himself. It drew Duran out of his thoughts and toward the stage.

His mind fell into a trance by his principal's run-of-the-mill announcements and weekly accolades. He heard Saski's name mentioned with favour on one of the announcements, but everything else escaped him.

'Kita Duran, approach the stage!' There was no warmth to his principal's words.

The school hall ignited with a buzz of whispers.

'Silence! Kita here, now!'

Duran stepped out of his line and gingerly made his way up the stage; trying to block out the burning stares and glares from the students. His heart pounded feverishly as he approached his principal.

'No, calm down, calm down. You can do this,' Duran muttered in his mind, struggling to keep his nerves and racing heart at bay.

He felt dwarfed by the man's authoritative presence. A flurry of dark and horrid thoughts raced through his mind to stir up more nerves.

'You could fail. You could lose. Give up now and go home. You could be forgiven...' Could he be forgiven for failing or for giving up?

He closed his eyes and took a deep breath.

'You can do this Kita-kun! I know you can,' a boy called out from the crowd.

It made the silence thicker than before, but his heart's racing eased a little.

'Silence! I will not tolerant deviant behaviour. This deviant boy dares to suggest that he can lead a music club in this school! To challenge his cockiness, he will play for you now. All freshman has to submit a ballot vote to your homeroom teacher by the end of the day. Yes, for a music club. No, not for one. Kita-kun's performance being your motivation.'

Duran swallowed a nervous gulp at the curt glint in his principal's eyes and nasty smirk to his lips.

'The floor is yours Kita. Don't go beyond three minutes or you will fail.'

Duran unpacked his Loar and portable amp, suited up and prepared himself for his performance.

This was it, there was no going back now. All he could do was play what he knew best to the best of his abilities.

'This is Miyavi,' he exhaled to the anticipating audience.

The first pluck of the G-string pulled his racing heart together. He soon found his nervous fingers working for him as they raced over the guitar strings; plucking, pulling and banging percussion against the Loar's face. His stance became stronger and powerful as the song took over. He was calling to his army and leading them into a battle with fierce conviction. No one was left behind or left out. His fingers keep playing out his defiance until the message was clear.

'I'm Kita Duran. I am not afraid to fight for our music!'

His battle came to rest after a couple of minutes.

The assembly erupted into warm whistles, cheers and feverish clapping not even the principal could calm down.

Duran stood still, soaking in the energy.

'Kita back to your place,' Principal Kimura sneered.

It took him a moment to register the command. When he did, he returned to his place as quickly as he could.

He was grateful it was over and prayed he was a success.

263 first year, 186 second year and 198 third year students. Equalling 647 heads in total. 198 valid votes were received favouring a music club after Duran's performance.

However, they received a total of 605 votes across the school with the total of 485 of those affirming acceptance of his music. Neither the principal nor the student council could deny the right of the club when many student votes were in favour for it.

Principal Kimura included his endorsement, but he was far from gracious about it. He ranted and raged the whole time Duran and Watanabe-sensei were in the student council chambers receiving the keys and budget for the club.

Duran's mind wasn't occupied with the music club at that moment. He was concerned for Isao who wasn't coming to school since around the time of the attack. His concern deepened when Ryuu-chichi told him that his senior had dropped all charges and apologized for causing trouble. He wondered what was going on in his senior's mind.

'Sensei, I'm sorry I caused you trouble.' His mind wandered back to this past conversation.

Was his senior going through something similar?

'Sorry, please excuse me.' He bowed and raced out of the council chambers, unable to ignore the urge to find Isao.

'What was that all about?' Kou blurted out, not hiding his annoyance at Duran's spacing out and abrupt exit. They were still doing their handover too.

'It seems Kita-kun has a lot on his mind,' Watanabe-sensei answered.

'I thought he would've been thrilled at having achieved the impossible,' Saski said both concerned and annoyed.

'I'm not surprised of his arrogance. I am annoyed at his attitude of ingratitude,' said President Saito.

'Ingratitude? Arrogance? I think you've completely misunderstood this boy,' Watanabe-sensei said in Duran's defence.

'Misunderstood? His actions speak for themselves.' President Saito retorted.

'Are you any different, President Saito?'

Watanabe-sensei chuckled at the boy's stern expression.

'I think he's very grateful, but right now there is something troubling him.'

'A boy like that is trouble, so I'm not surprised. This matter of a music club is shameful in my eyes. I can't understand why an honour student would want to defy this school so much.' Principal Kimura went back to the music club argument.

'Honour student?!' Kou and Saski blurted in unison.

'Why are you surprised? He's in your class Tsubaki-kun.'

'I thought he was filling a gap like Yamaguchi,' Saski answered. He blushed, feeling embarrassed by his words.

'Kita, Duran scored in the Top Ten of your year. He scored in the Top Five of his former school's Entrance Exam. Tell me if he's filling a gap now?' Watanabe-sensei asked Duran's Student Council peers.

He wasn't sure why he was defending Duran so much, but it made him feel good in his heart for doing so.

'He may not appear it, but he's a very dedicated and intelligent student. He received some glowing recommendations from his previous teachers too. Since you all didn't see this, in this respect, I see him anything but arrogant.'

Saski sighed. His science teacher had a point and maybe his perception of Duran was misconstrued.

'You may be right Watanabe-sensei, but it still doesn't excuse his behaviour just now. I'll be watching him cautiously as I expect of you and Aimi-sensei as well,' said

Principal Kimura.

'Of course, I'll be keeping a watchful eye on him as the club's adviser and his teacher. I think you should be more open-minded. Not everything is as it seems. Now if you excuse me, I have a class to teach.' Watanabe-sensei ended his discussions and made his exit.

'Keep an eye on him.' Principal Kimura ordered the council members.

He left the council chambers.

'I leave that task in your care Hayashi-kun, Tsubaki-kun,' President Saito said as he picked up his books and left the room.

'Actually, that task is for you Saski-kun since you're in his class.' Kou teased Saski with a firm pat to his shoulder.

Saski groaned at the realization that he would have to keep tabs of Duran's coming and going from this point on.

He found himself observing him in class from his desk, which had a safe line of sight to Duran's side profile.

Duran was indeed a dutiful student. His slender fingers took notes when they should, soft green eyes paid attention to their teachers' lectures and delicate full lips rested pensively as he quietly worked at his notebooks.

Saski's further observation took note of the way he sat with proper posture. He appreciated the way his silky gold-blond hair reflected the daylight around his high cheekbones and the delicate curve line of his jaw.

'If I didn't know him better, I'd mistake him for being gentle.' He wryly mused and swallowed the rest of his absurd thought.

Towards the middle of the day, he mulled over Duran's behaviour when he handed over the club keys at the end of their class.

'Thank you Tsubaki-kun. I'm sorry for leaving the meeting early.' Duran had respectfully thanked and apologized to him with proper manners.

Saski concluded that his western good looks gave him the impression of arrogance. The truth of his personality was something else.

He sighed with relief when the lunch-bell rang, and he could ditch his observation duties on Duran, satisfied he knew enough of his classmate.

His heart began to race at the sight of Duran's form receding from him up the hallway.

'What the hell?' He thumped at his chest and shook off the weird feeling he felt. He made his way out of school.

'Tsu-ba-ki!' He heard Osamu call out his name with his usual flirtatious manner and braced himself for a bear hug.

'Why you look so moody?' Osamu whispered into Saski's ear as he wrapped his arms around his waist.

'I'm not moody Miki-chan. Let go of me, you're sucking the life out of me.' Saski gasped and gulped in air when he was released.

'You're a tease.' Osamu joked.

Saski caught curious glances from other students passing them by in the school hallway.

'Miki-chan let's go to the roof.' He led the way up to the rooftop of their building.

The day was crisp and sunny and the air felt refreshing. Other students also decided to eat their lunch up at the rooftop. In the distance, he spied Duran sitting with his other classmates and a few other circles.

'His popularity has soared since his guitar solo,' Osamu commented as they made themselves comfortable in a shady spot conveniently in eye line view of Duran's group.

'Sickening isn't it?' Kou said as he sat down next to them. His hair was wet like he had come out of a shower.

'I thought you didn't have any basketball practice today?'

'I didn't that's why I can have lunch with you monkeys,' Kou joked. 'Actually, it was meant to be a meeting, but when you enter a gym full of guys all fired up it ends up as quick practice. Five minutes was enough for me to win over Kudo-senpai.'

Kou's attention wandered over to Duran and his ever

growing circle of friends. Something bothered him about the guy, but he couldn't put his finger on what it was.

'Looks like Watanabe's attached herself to him,' Osamu said casually as they saw the AKB48-like girl pounce on an unsuspecting Duran.

They laughed at Duran's comical response to her advances, which was an awkward attempt to fend her off whilst not tripping over.

'He's definitely going to get eaten alive.' Saski chuckled. He felt both lucky and guilty that he was off her radar.

His chuckles subsided when he saw Mayuzumi Chihiro initiate a conversation with Duran. Why was that second year talking causally with him?

'I'd say I'm surprised, but I'm not,' Kou said through mouthfuls of seaweed rice.

Saski was. Associating with that despicable guy didn't match with his observations of Duran behaviour.

'I figured Kita-kun's many things, but associating with Mayuzumi is something he's not.' He frowned at the interaction between the two. Something felt off, which was highlighted by the reactions from Duran's friends who also seemed surprised by the encounter.

He wondered if Duran's brash from the Student Council Office was related to Mayuzumi. He pulled out his phone and fingered through his contact list for Duran's details, glancing back to the group to see Mayuzumi walking away. The expression on Duran's face made him feel uneasy. It was as Watanabe-sensei said. Everything wasn't as it seemed. Something was up.

'Maybe he made a deal with the devil. Could explain why he received so many votes,' Osamu said.

'You could be right. If that's, so I'd need to look into this further,' Saski said.

'Hey Miki-chan, I'll meet you back at class.'

Saski packed up his lunch and trailed after Mayuzumi.

He checked the time on his phone, there was still fifteen minutes before the end-of-lunch bell was scheduled to ring.

He hurried through the hallways searching for Mayuzumi and found him at a set of lockers leering over a couple of scrawny first year boys with his Yankee gang by his side. It was clear they were performing extortion. Saski clenched his fists and gritted his teeth.

'Mayuzumi!' He spat out.

Mayuzumi left the fate of the first year boys to his thugs and approached Saski. He was a head taller with his muscly body detectable underneath his loose fitted shirt with sleeves rolled up and pants snug around his backside.

Saski had heard of girls gushing over the look of his manly face and ash-blonde hair. He couldn't find anything to admire in his senior. The guy was repulsive with scheming grey eyes and slimy thin lips always twisted in a sly smirk.

'Mr. Student Council what do you want?' Mayuzumi snickered.

'Extortion is a crime. I will not allow it at this school.' Saski straight out accused his senior.

Mayuzumi stopped a hand-space away from his face.

'What are you talking about? Who's doing any extorting? We're just having a friendly chat with our juniors.'

Saski skirted around Mayuzumi and skilfully pushed his thugs away from the trembling first years. They swung punches at him, but ended up hitting locker faces instead. He pushed them further away, so they stumbled to the ground, defeated.

'Now you could say that I went for an attack. There're no marks on my body, but a lot on your friends here. Or you can shrug this off as a play fight, tell your goons to let these first year's go and move on.'

'Well done Tsubaki-kun. You're a true hero.' Mayuzumi sarcastically clapped and gestured for his Yankees to beat it.

Everyone left the hallway to leave Saski and Mayuzumi

alone to sort out their business.

'You look like you have something you want to say to me. It wasn't by chance you're here is it?'

'Kita. Why were you talking to him?'

'Pfft! Is that why you sort me out? Jealous I'm hitting on your boyfriend?'

'You're not even close. I'll ask again why?'

'Why should you be interested in who I talk to?'

'Because the Student Council is always left to deal with crap from your scandals.'

'Ah, I get it, so you think this good son of our prominent politician pulled strings for him huh?'

'Did you?'

Mayuzumi resumed his stance before Saski who wasn't backing down. He chuckled.

'Sheesh you're too pent-up. Once again, you go deciding things for yourself. I do find that side of you very sexy Tsubaki Saski.'

'Again Mayuzumi. What did you talk about with Kita-kun?'

'Trivial matters. Nothing to concern your pretty-boy face with.'

'Fine. If I find out you were up to more scandalous behaviour, I'll ensure you're kicked out of this school.'

'Even if it involves Kita-kun in the process?'

'Even that.'

'Have fun with your interrogations then.' Mayuzumi stepped away and turned to leave.

'Don't you think a vulnerable Kita is sexy?' He threw over his shoulder and smirked at Saski's glare.

'I'll find out what you're up to and stop you.' Saski soberly declared.

'Try if you can.'

Mayuzumi made his way down the hall, leaving Saski behind.

Saski made sure Duran was always in his line of sight.

He watched his peer move from room to room with an

effete mannerism. Not even the cheerful jokes and efforts from Duran's friends did much to improve upon his mood.

'What's going on with you?' Saski muttered to himself.

A fat lot of good he could squeeze out from Mayuzumi. Looks like he had to go to the source for some idea. What would he do if Duran had been cheating the system with that delinquent's help?

'Did you?'

'What are you mumbling about my sweet honey?' Osamu said as he assumed his usual seat at the bench next to Saski. They readied themselves for their home economics lesson.

'Nothing.' Saski brushed off and refocused on the lesson.

Both the lesson and the rest of the school-day was quick to end. Or maybe his mind was so full of thoughts of Duran, and whether he had fudged the votes for a club, that it appeared that way. He decided to go with his instincts, believing that Duran was a vulnerable creature as Mayuzumi had suggested.

Maybe he got it wrong and that time with Mayuzumi was by chance. It didn't explain their casualness nor the uneasiness on Duran's face.

He thought back to the delinquent's words about Duran being vulnerable and sexy.

'Sexy? Pfft, as if!' Saski argued with himself as he stepped up to his footlocker.

He paused, remembering that time he teased Duran with a near kiss. Ugh! What was he thinking? The guy had even fainted, so he had to carry him all the way to the infirmary. He was running on instinct at that time.

No, he was only teasing Duran to see how far he would go with his concept for a club. Then he also jumped him when he was affected by the Shōujo Effect. What did that say about his like for him?

'It's not like that. I don't like him!' Saski yelled out to no one in particular and felt embarrassed by the thought of it. A few guys from his class chuckled as they strolled past him. He cringed and quickly swapped his shoes, so he could get the hell out of there.

'Hey, Saski-kun!' Kou called out to him as he made his approach from the other end of the lockers.

'Kou-kun, you're working today?'

'Yeah. Doing my penance. Luckily, the contract ends before we have to start thinking about exams.'

Exams, of course. Many clubs were whittling away their activities in readiness for the hold period all clubs had to endure during mid-term examinations. The Music Club had just been approved and was still in its grace period. So, Duran wouldn't be able to complete his setup of the club nor gather more members until mid-terms were well and truly over. It would be a couple of months before the club would be able to open its doors. It was an apparent fact that clubs that formed before mid-terms had died a sudden death because the interest would have waned.

'I'll come with you and have some ramen. Dad's working late shift again and I don't have kendo,' he said feeling less troubled.

'Yeah, okay. But don't cause trouble for me 'kay?'

'Since when do I ever cause trouble for you?' Saski said as he ruffled his friend's hair.

'Yahoo Saskicchi!'

Saski shuddered at his name being called out by Chiasa Watanabe.

'Pyscho-hose beast alert,' Kou whispered.

They both went stiff at the sight of three AKB48-like girls bounding their way to them with breasts jigging up and down like Jell-O cups.

'Saskicchi!' Chiasa squealed as she slammed into him and wrapped her arms around his waist.

Kou wasn't safe from attention either as her two best friends plastered themselves to his sides.

They were both well and truly trapped in the thralls of

the booby-babes.

'Hayashi, Tsubaki, die a thousand deaths!' A guy yelled out to them.

There was a clear misunderstanding with guys who ached to have those girls wrap their arms around their waists. To those type of guys, Saski and Kou were lady-killers who had dated a score full of girls like Chiasa. Of course, it was furthest from the truth.

'Don't mind them Saskicchi. They're just jealous,' Chiasa coyly said into Saski's ear as she toyed with the buttons on his blazer.

'Maybe if you didn't pounce on me all the time. They wouldn't come to those conclusions,' Saski said as he struggled free from her hold.

Why was he still on her radar? Wasn't Duran her target now? The light bulb in his mind went ding.

'Hey, Chia-chan. You were with Kita at lunchtime weren't you? What did he and Mayuzumi talk about?'

'Eh? What's your interest with Duracchi?'

'It doesn't look good for you to mix with someone who's up to no good. With Mayuzumi on top.'

Chiasa surprised him when she assumed a defiant stance before him, hands on hips and a strong a glare in her eyes. She was firing daggers his way.

'Duracchi is good guy. He was cruelly teased by Mayu-san who called him a pansy!'

'A what?'

'I didn't think you could be so judgmental. You're the worst Saskicchi!'

'I'm what?'

'Come on girls were going.' Chiasa huffed and pulled her girls away from Kou. They stormed off down the hallway.

'That was what?' Kou was surprised and relieved.

'I think I received my answer. I don't know what to think any more.' Saski sighed.

They left the school grounds talking about other things.

Saski's mind was still mulling over the troubles with Duran, which left him feeling confused. He was usually good at reaching to the core of a problem by now.

He couldn't shake off the feeling that Mayuzumi was up to no good and somehow Duran was connected even if indirectly.

'You've been brooding ever since we left school,' Kou commented as they made their way down the street to the ramen house.

'I can't get this whole Kita and Mayuzumi thing out of my head.'

'Huh? What's Kita got to do with Mayuzumi?'

'It's something Miki-chan said,' Saski mumbled then shook his head to brush the explanation away. 'Never mind.'

Kou peered at his friend, weighing up the troubled expression on his face. It wasn't like him to be this invested in the troubles of others without some sound reason.

'Look. I've known you since elementary. So, I know you wouldn't be worked up about something unless you had grounds for it.'

'That's the thing Kou-kun. This time I don't really know.'

They were about to enter the alley that led to the back of the ramen house when they saw Duran and Mayuzumi in conversation toward the middle near the dumpster.

'You can't be serious!' Duran cried out. 'Why would you do that?'

'I didn't do anything. I only ascertained my position,' Mayuzumi replied smugly.

'You have no conscience?'

'What has this got to do with you eh? In love with him too hmm?'

Saski couldn't see the expression on Duran's face, but from his clenched fists and the tension in his stance, it was clear he was pissed-off.

'I only claimed insurance for the trouble your senpai caused.'

'Bastard! Go to hell.'

'Pleasure. Maybe I'll see you there someday.' Mayuzumi breathed smugly into Duran's face.

He stepped back to make his exit, seeming somewhat satisfied by his reaction.

'See yah Kita. Hope you sleep well at night.'

'Screw you!' Duran yelled, huffing and puffing with rage.

Kou and Saski ducked back into the street when they saw Mayuzumi stroll in their direction. They waited until they were sure he was out of their sight before heading back into the alley. Duran was gone by then.

Saski felt confident of Duran's innocence. Maybe his name was used for some dishonest dealings, and he found out. The concerns he felt earlier had shifted to a curiosity.

'Didn't think he had the side to him.' Kou's voice was sober. 'Kita comes across as mellow, although he did challenge me.'

'Mayuzumi must've caused some trouble for him,' Saski replied somewhat absent-minded as his thoughts recalculated possible causes.

They entered the front of the ramen house and saw Duran in a white T-shirt and blue-jeans with an apron around his waist. He was scrubbing tables clean with a dark expression. His eyes were slightly bloodshot.

'Kita-kun you're here today?' Kou said.

Duran's expression relaxed when he saw them standing at the counter.

'Oh Hayashi-kun, Tsubaki-kun. Yeah, I'm covering for Sasaki-san.'

'Eh? Okay.'

There were many things Saski wanted to ask, but the situation was delicate. He took a seat at the table near the window whilst Kou made his way to the workers' area.

'You're eating today?'

'Do you recommend anything?' Saski asked and flashed Duran a reassuring smile.

Saski allowed Duran to order for him and watched him go about his work. His mind was constantly ticking with a million questions and pieces of the conversation he had spied upon in the alleyway.

Patrons coming and going provided some distraction from his thoughts. He kept his watchful eye on Duran, for a different reason this time.

The restaurant was a lot quieter about an hour after Saski had arrived. Unable to hold back his curiosity and the whirlwind of thoughts in his head. He approached Duran about the incident in the alleyway.

'Hey Kita, I saw you arguing with Mayuzumi before I came here.' He threw out with no other way to put it.

Duran paused his cleaning and faced Saski. His lips were twitching with words.

'Don't say anything yet. I'll speak first. Let me know if I'm wrong.'

Saski told Duran about his suspicions of the votes, how some council members thought he wasn't grateful and a few other perceptions. He was blunt, honest and factual. It was only fair and respectful of him to be. It was Duran's reaction that gave him a pleasant surprise.

'I bet you feel relieved getting that off your chest.' Duran smiled, his eyes welling with tears. 'I understand Tsubaki-kun why'd you'd see things that way. I can't deny, I am involved in something troublesome.'

'Kita-kun what's going on?' Saski gently asked.

Duran occupied the seat before him with a heavy sigh.

'About three weeks ago I caught a group of thugs attacking Izuki-senpai. My step-father and I had intervened, but Senpai was hospitalized.'

Saski listened attentively, praying no one would walk through the door as Duran poured his heart out in a calm and controlled manner.

As Saski heard more he realized how far from the truth

and dangerously close he was from stirring further trouble. He wanted to kick himself hard for seeking out Mayuzumi before talking to Duran. The situation was sensitive.

'So, Mayuzumi's thugs were behind Izuki-senpai's attack?'

'Yeah, but I don't have any proof. I happened to overhear Senpai and Mayuzumi arguing at school when I went to check on him. Senpai told me he was being threatened because he and his friend happened upon Mayuzumi about to do horrid things to a middle-schooler.'

'I see, so they were threatened to keep quiet,' Saski responded.

Duran nodded his head and continued his story.

Whilst Isao was recovering in hospital, his house was broken into and the only things stolen were pictures of him and his childhood friend, Shouta Meiko. When Isao had returned to school, a few days later, he saw the pictures of them all over pin boards in the hallways to class, carrying accusations that they were gay lovers being exposed. Some photos were suggestive too, half naked shots and group photos that showed the closeness between Isao and Shouta. Nasty rumours were spread around about them.

Saski cringed remembering the rumours, but didn't realize how much of an effect it had caused.

'Their parents also received the same thing in their emails. It was cleverly woven together that no one was going to give Izuki-senpai and Meiko-senpai a benefit of a doubt. The rumours lead to bullying and isolation. Meiko-senpai was taken out of school, possibly for a transfer. Izuki-senpai ran that day and hasn't been back,' Duran said with his face scrunched into a serious frown.

'I've been visiting Senpai after school, trying to get him back. Senpai's become a shut-in. Rumours continue to spread about him and stir trouble. The frustrating thing is, Izuki-senpai is the only one that can turn it all around. He needs to for his scholarship,' he sighed.

Saski's doubts about Duran's integrity and underhandedness were washed away. However, he couldn't understand why Duran would involve himself with other people's problems.

'Why get involved?'

Duran stared him hard in the eye before answering.

'Because he's my senpai. He is a good guy. I don't care if he's gay. I do care that his rights to an education are being robbed from him because of all this. He doesn't have anyone in his corner. For me, this is the right thing to do.'

Duran's words struck Saski's heart with resolve.

'What you're gonna do about it?'

'Focus on getting Senpai back to school. I might need the Student Council's help.'

At that moment a group of patrons entered. Duran stood to attend to them.

'Kita-kun whatever you need I'll help you.'

'Thank you.' Duran bowed low before going back to work.

Saski left the ramen house with his thoughts more unsettled. He gripped his heart and closed his eyes thinking about Duran's words and what he had said before leaving. A warm and fuzzy feeling washed over him. His thoughts cleared to the only truth remaining, to help their seniors recover their status and school life.

☠ BULLIED

Duran ended an exhausting work shift, but it was mostly from feeling emotionally drained. He was glad he had talked this troubles with Saski and set matters straight before the man had reached the wrong conclusion.

He and his mother walked through the door of their home to see his step-father and Himeko watching TV in the lounge room, which barely had enough space for the family two-seat sofa. Neither asked about his work or school nor about the mood clearly written on his face. He wasn't in the mood to talk about anything either.

The situation with his senior troubled him into a despair with a desire to help him out of the problem and back onto his feet. He felt lost on how he could help without being too intrusive.

Mayuzumi boxed him into a corner, making any form of retaliation a sensitive situation. Duran could meet aggression with aggression. What good would that do? It would only make the matter more troublesome and not bring his senior back to school.

'Think!' He grumbled to himself as he worked around the kitchenette, making his bento.

'Hey Nii-san, you can't keep doing this,' said Himeko carefully.

'You haven't been sleeping well. Izuki-san has shut everyone out. Maybe you should let this one go.'

'No!' Duran slammed his lunch box to the bench.

'Izuki-senpai has been isolated. He needs someone to fight for him. I will never give up on him.'

'Nii-san.' Himeko's voice quivered, her eyes welled with tears. She pulled her brother in a sisterly hug with all the care and pride she felt for him.

'You're the strongest person I know.' Her voice was coarse with emotion. 'What can we do? We're only students. The most fight we can bring is music.'

The noise in Duran's head went silent. His heart pounded feverishly as his mind gathered on an idea that could bring his senior back to school. It would only work if he had the support of the student body, his family and friends.

'Himeko, I know what I need to do.'

For the first time, he felt very sure of a plan. He smiled at his sister as he realized part of the answer was right before his eyes.

'Sis lend me your voice. There's a song I want you to sing.'

'Huh?'

Duran shared his plan, which fired up Himeko's support for the cause. When the plan was laid out, they sent a round of emails to their friends to rally them to the cause.

Hi Guys, You're my best friends, I love you deeply. That's why I beg you for your talent this Saturday, so we can get our seniors back to school. Our seniors who've been bullied out of school because of Mayuzumi-san and his thugs. Please tell me you can come.

The last email Duran sent for the night was a request to his other step-father, Akira-san.

'Please Akira-san, I beg you, say yes to this one,' he pleaded to his phone before he powered it off and called it a night.

Akira-san's answer arrived to the phone's inbox at the middle of the night. It flashed as a guiding light whilst Duran was lost in his dreams.

Duran went about his plan the next day, cautiously

manoeuvring things into place without alerting attention from Mayuzumi and his people. Plan talk was discussed carefully during a lunchtime meeting with his friends in his homeroom class.

'This is what you meant by your weird email,' Fumio said with a secretive tone. 'Mistook for spam at first.'

Duran had his friends huddled around his desk to talk over the details that had all of them nodding and looking invested in the plan.

'It's a big task. It will work if Prick doesn't get wind of what's up. I beg you to keep a tight lip,' Duran hushed.

He had given Mayuzumi the code name of Prick.

'Why'd we need the Student Council's help?' Aki hissed in protest to the idea.

'I know your love for the SC runs deep Aki. Whether we like it or not they hold the weight of the student body.'

'Can we trust them?' Aki kept up his argument.

'Do we have a choice?'

Aki sighed, realizing Duran was right. To get their message across in the shortest amount of time. The Student Council's help was a necessary evil.

'Okay, so we enlist the SC's help for supporters, what about the soundtrack?'

'My step-father is willing to help us.'

Fumio and Aki gave confused stares at Himeko and Duran.

'I don't mean Himeko's dad,' Duran chuckled. 'My father's partner.'

'You've got a confusing family dude.' Fumio dropped trying to understand the many fathers his friend had.

'What does your father's partner do?' Mei asked, bringing the subject back to the matter at hand.

'He owns a music studio and runs an independent record label.'

'Woah! Dude you're holding out!' Fumio perked up.

'Man, you're my best friend for life!' Aki said through a cheesy grin.

'It's not like that guys. This is the first time Akira-san has agreed to one of my requests for some studio time.'

'Really? No family freebies or discounts?' Fumio asked innocently.

Duran laughed, and even harder at Fumio's frown.

'Oh, man, um that'll be a no,' he said after he had calmed down.

'He was all for the cause, but we only have two hours this Saturday to make it count.'

At that moment Dai'chi Santo entered the room.

'Hey Duran!' He called out when he saw him at his desk.

Duran waved him inside. Dai'chi grabbed a seat into their pow-wow.

'Thanks for coming Santo-senpai. We're going over the plan.'

'Geez how many times do I tell you to call me Dai'chi?'

'You're our senior and the club president,' Duran said with a horrified expression.

'Hey it's friends before status. Being a third year doesn't make me any extra special.' Dai'chi smiled.

'I second that.' Aki joked and yelped at the clip to his ear from his senior.

'Don't be a smart-arse. I'm Santo-senpai to you Aki-man.'

'Shut-up Santo Claus.'

'Okay, okay. Let's get back to it before the bell rings.' Duran called them all to attention.

Every one brought Dai'chi up to speed.

'We can cut a track at your Akira's studio? Wow! That's big.'

'Are you going to let them know?' Mei asked.

Duran nodded his head.

'We need to practice a track first.'

He pulled out copies of a song he composed with parts for each of them to learn and practice.

'Learn this 'till your fingers bleed.'

'What about bass?' Aki looked over everyone and screwed up his face at their clueless expressions.

Duran turned to Mei, 'Do you think you could use your cello skills to play bass?'

'Um, not sure. I've never touched one before.'

'I can help you.' Himeko piped up. 'It's not much different. We can use my dad's bass guitar.'

'Why can't you play it Hime-chan?'

'Because I'm needed for guitar solos,' she answered smugly, ignoring Aki's pouting.

'Actually, Aki will do lead guitars as you're the singer,' Duran stated.

'Huh? I can do both you know?'

'Well we might need you as a bass backup. Besides, not much guitar solo anyway,' Duran said considerately and flashed a wink to Aki when she wasn't looking.

Himeko sighed and shrugged her shoulders with her reluctant agreement.

At that moment the end bell rang out. Duran was satisfied he got across what he wanted everyone to do.

'Remember, keep this a secret guys. Prick must never find out the plan. If people ask about the music, say it's for the club welcome after mid-terms.' Duran reminded everyone before they dispersed.

The next task of finding a moment to speak with the Student Council played on Duran's mind. He found his moment to speak to them at during a free period in the afternoon. He had approached Saski during class, who was true to his word of wanting to help.

'Come. I'll take you there now.' He had nonchalantly said over his shoulder to send Duran's heart racing.

Duran reigned in his feelings to focus on the matter at hand when they reached the Student Council room.

Saski opened the door to let him in.

'Oh you're here.' Kou greeted him with his usual aloofness.

'I can come in?'

Kou stood on the threshold, pondering on the question.

'Or I can cut my losses,' Duran answered for him with a strong hint of sarcasm.

Kou rolled his eyes and stepped aside to allow him further entry.

'Thank you, Jeeves,' Duran said through a cheesy grin and received eye rolls from the man.

He raised his brows. The important room of power, for the student body's elite council members, was a cheap, weathered ex-teacher's office with a few crusty desks, chairs, a rusted filing cabinet and a weathered old principal's desk that now acted as the president's seat of power.

Sure it was in Block-C, which was the oldest block of the school, and housed the third year classrooms. At least the school board could've replaced the crappy, grey, coffee-stained carpet.

Duran hoped the dark splotches near his shoes were coffee stains.

He flicked aside the sinister thought that flashed through his mind. And faced the Student Council members who were gathered around the president's desk in an impromptu meeting.

Was it wrong of him to think they resembled the Third Reich? Maybe that was too strong an image. He hoped they were open-minded like Saski.

'Kita-kun.' President Saito acknowledged him.

'Sorry for intruding.' The formality rolled off Duran's tongue.

'Tsubaki-kun tells me you need our help, for something important.'

Duran stood a few meters from the group. He decided to be direct.

'I need the Student Council's help to bring Izuki-senpai and Meiko-san back to school.' He gulped at the blank stares from the council members.

'Um, well, you see, many bad rumours and stuff were spread about them. They won't come back to school because of it. I have a plan to help them. I would like, no, need the Student Council's support.' He rambled and bowed low, hoping it would appease their decision.

He felt President Saito's eyes checking him for lies.

'Why would we help you or them? Considering the rumours were true, they left on their own. I've not heard of any physical harm happening to students.'

Duran rose and faced the man with a frown.

'Left on their own? No physical harm? Let me give you a scenario, you might understand. If you were made out to be some sleazy gay when you weren't, people constantly harassed you by spreading lies behind your back, isolating you and calling you horrible names. Your belongs are trashed. Constantly your name and face are being verbally put down, every single day you live and breathe at this good school.'

He braved a few steps closer to the president.

'Not just school, but your family, neighbours, anyone associated to you now has a thought in their heads that you are some sleazy gay predator. Tell me you won't be suffering the injustice. Tell me that your good status is strong enough to face persecution from the masses.'

'You sound like you speak from experience,' President Saito coolly answered.

'I've seen good people hurt in this way. President, are you a good man?' Duran calmly addressed his answer.

A heavy silence hung about the room. President Saito observed Duran's expression, until he felt satisfied he saw a truth to the matter.

'What are you expecting us to do? We deal with school business.' President Saito's question broke the silence.

'This is school business. Hotaka High School has had a hand in the damaged reputation of its two students,' Duran soberly answered.

'Rumours sprout from a seed of truth. Nobody is a

good person,' President Saito replied levelly.

'I disagree. People choose to be good. My seniors are people who live for honest hard work and a good life.' Duran stood firm before the Student Council.

His voice carried his bold statement around the room.

'I cannot forgive that this school has allowed them to be used in a witch hunt.'

The atmosphere felt heavy under his defence for his seniors. Duran knew he was risking a lot with his daring statement, which could lead to further problems than good. He was banking on the Student Council's integrity.

'You may have a point. Maybe the rumours were spread too fast or too much, but if they were innocent, then rumours shouldn't stop them from coming to school.'

'They don't even have that chance any more. It was taken from them.' Duran sighed.

'I can see you haven't been listening. I'm wasting my time.' He turned to leave.

'Wait, Kita!' Saski called out and turned to his President.

'I believe in what he's saying. Those two upper classmen need our help. There's another thing. Mayuzumi is likely the cause behind it all.'

'Mayuzumi?' President Saito said, revealing an expression of shock for a split-second.

Saski nodded his head.

'From my investigations, Mayuzumi started the rumours because Izuki-senpai and Meiko-senpai saved a middle school kid from being violated by him. It was his way of getting payback,' Kou stated.

'Your investigations?' Duran asked Kou, but his question was ignored.

He frowned when the mention of Prick's name stirred a reaction from the other council representatives. He wasn't convinced they saw his seniors as victims, but whatever other reason motivated them towards their cause was something he'd have to accept.

'Mayuzumi caused this.' President Saito acknowledged.

His face was expressionless, but his body became tense. He met Duran's eyes.

'Okay. I acknowledge what you say Kita-kun. If you're right, the students of this school need to be held accountable for the inconvenience caused to those two second years. Especially if they aren't guilty of a crime.'

Duran sighed. 'The Student Council will help me?'

'Yes, but there are conditions—'

'You will follow my orders.' Duran interrupted. 'Otherwise, you'll screw up everything I've planned.'

It was the first time Duran saw a clear expression on the President's face. Albeit one of tight-lip annoyance.

'Kita, Duran, do you not need our help?'

'Yes, but if you're not going to go by my plan I'd rather not bother.'

President Saito sighed, appearing worn down all of a sudden.

'Okay, we'll follow your lead,' he responded and pinched his nose like he felt an onset migraine.

'Thank you.' Duran bowed low with sincere gratitude.

'I'll share my plans with you, but you must keep it in this room. Everything must be organized in secret. If Mayuzumi were to find out, the plan is an instant failure. Oh, from this point on, Mayuzumi's code name is Prick. Remember that.'

The heaviness lifted with laughter at Mayuzumi's code name. Even the President had relaxed.

Duran smiled at the Student Council group for the first time.

He heaved a sigh of relief when he stepped outside. The energy he had needed to sell his case to the council president was expected, but he wasn't prepared for all the convincing arguments he had had to throw at the man.

In the end, the support was achieved through Mayuzumi's name. Saski had mentioned before the meeting that the Student Council were united in stopping that man's corruption. If Duran's plea wasn't going to work, he'd use that angle as their trump card. Regardless, he had their support.

His next part of the plan was gaining the support of Isao and Shouta's homeroom teachers.

'Kita-kun.' He heard as the door opened and closed behind him; turned and saw one of the council members approach him.

Like all the other council representatives, he was an image of a model student. About the same height as himself and appeared younger with round cheeks, gentle brown eyes and cherub lips. Duran saw a troubled expression in his eyes.

'What you said and your plan is very brave of you. I don't think I'd have such resolve to carry through what you're doing. I'm Kiyoshi, Teppei, a second year.' Teppei extended his hand.

'Nice to meet you Kiyoshi-san.' Duran accepted his handshake.

'Can I walk with you for a bit? I'd like to have a chat with you.'

'Sure.'

Duran controlled the pace and direction of their walk as they recapped on what he spoke about. They were cautious with their terms and names of people to deter eavesdropping.

'I'm in your M-senpai's class. I saw him slowly fall to pieces. He's not a guy to crack under-pressure easily. So, I believe you. For me, I don't think I'd be able to handle it. The plan you have is good Kita-kun. You have my full support,' Teppei said with a cordial smile.

'Thank you.' Duran bowed.

'Kita-kun, be careful. Prick attacks his targets mercilessly. If you're on his radar, he won't stop until you and everyone dear to you is hurt.'

Something bothered Duran that he needed to get off his chest.

'Kiyoshi-san. Why is that guy still attending this school if he causes so much trouble?'

'Good question. His father is a prominent councillor for Inage ward and has some financial weight in this school. So, you can imagine what would happen if his son was expelled. Prick is not stupid. He covers his tracks extremely well, making it difficult to pin anything on him. We've been fighting him for a while now.'

Duran was relieved he had taken the path away from seeking direct vengeance on Mayuzumi.

'We have to be extra cautious.'

'Exactly Kita-kun.'

'Um, Kiyoshi-san, when do you see your homeroom teacher next?'

'After lunch. He'll most likely be in class now if you need to speak with him.'

Duran smiled and nodded his head.

He followed Teppei to his classroom, which was on the second floor above his. He felt awkward being surrounded by so many upper classmen, but brushed aside his nervousness. It wouldn't be long before he was in one of those rooms.

'Come on in.' Teppei invited him inside.

Duran felt a few eyes size him up and down as he entered.

'Hey aren't you that guitar dude?' A guy mocking called out. They were ready to fire off some taunts.

'Leave him be Nakamura or I'll burn your Maeda poster book.' Teppei sternly ordered the boys that surprised Duran. Even more so when the guys obeyed him and went back to their chatter.

'Sorry about that. As you can see my class has a few smart-alecs,' he whispered.

'Too much for one homeroom teacher to manage. I swear the smarter the student the harder they are to keep in line,' said Teppei's teacher who approached them from behind.

Duran recognized the handsome teacher who had given him the message for the principal's office.

He wasn't as tall as Watanabe-sensei and a lot younger; a bit on the skinnier side with likeable features, welcoming amber eyes, thin lips where one side was curled up in a grin, high cheekbones and stylish bangs that touched the tops of his shaped brows like a K-Pop idol.

The young teacher was presentable in a navy suit, tie and shiny loafers. More the image of a promising salary-man than school teacher.

Duran wondered if this was his first teaching post since graduating from college.

'Kato-sensei, this is Kita Duran.' Teppei introduced them.

'I know. The talented guitarist who had this whole class talking,' Kato-sensei said politely as he vigorously shook Duran's hand to make the boy's head nod in time.

'Are you friends with Kiyoshi-kun?'

'We just met a while ago. There's something he needs to speak to you about. In a private area,' Teppei explained.

'Really?' Sensei raised his eyebrows. 'Okay, let's go to the backroom to talk.'

Duran followed Teppei and his teacher to the small utility room behind the class, and closed the door behind them. When he was sure no one was nearby, he gave his spiel.

Kato-sensei's eyes didn't leave him the whole time he spoke nor did he interrupt. He only nodded his head in places.

'So, that's it.' Duran ended his explanation.

'An ambitious plan, but if you're really doing this for Meiko-kun and Izuki-kun I'll support you. I've been visiting Meiko-kun's home numerous times, but his parents constantly push me away,' Kato-sensei said wearily.

'Izuki-senpai's a good guy.'

'Meiko-kun is too. Kiyoshi-kun is correct in saying that he's not a person to crack under pressures.'

He looked earnestly at Duran with many questions.

'Sensei, I care for my seniors well-being. Izuki-senpai's on a scholarship, so he needs to be back at school. To waste a future because of all of this is criminal.'

'Kita, Kita, if only all my students could be considerate, sensible and brave. I'll speak with Izuki-kun's homeroom teacher in private after school.'

'Thank you Kato-sensei.' Duran bowed low.

They end-of-lunch bell rang.

'I better return to class.' Duran opened the door. He paused on the threshold when Teppei called out to him.

'Kita-kun remember to be careful, okay?'

He nodded and left the room, ignoring questioning glances from other students as he made his way back down the stairs to his floor. He didn't see Mayuzumi watching his exit from the other end of the hallway.

Duran happened upon Isao's homeroom teacher before the end of the school-day, and could gain his support. Everything was falling into place, which made him feel more uneasy.

He passed through the main school gates and into the streets, headed for the ramen house. All of his friends and council members had after school activities. So, he made plans earlier to meet them at his workplace and go over what was needed for the coming Saturday.

He was lost too in his thoughts that he didn't notice the group of students tailing him until he entered the narrow alleyway to the ramen house.

'Kita, Duran.'

He heard his named called out from behind; stopped in his tracks with an expectant sigh.

'Mayuzumi,' he said without turning around.

'Well, you've been busy haven't you?'

Duran swallowed his nerves and was doing his best to calm his unsteady heartbeats.

Did Prick find out? He braced himself for the worst as he turned to face the second year. His eyes widen when he also came face to face with his Hose-Beast Squad.

'I don't know what you mean.'

'Oh come on my sexy, cute kouhai. I'm not stupid and I'm definitely not blind. You have a plan going on involving your senpai.'

'You brought your lackeys along for, what, tea and scones to talk about a Tupperware party?'

'Ha-ha, that's what I like about you Kita. You're a funny guy.' Mayuzumi feigned a laugh.

His expression sobered.

'I know you plan on getting your seniors back to school.'

Duran stilled the screaming in his head and his racing heart, putting on the best acting of his life.

'Wow, you're a true genius. Well done, you caught me out.' He clapped sarcastically and saw Mayuzumi's face twitch with anger. His eyes narrowed. 'What you're gonna do now?'

'Not me. I'm just here for tea and scones. But, my boys are keen for blood. Who am I to deny their wants?' Mayuzumi answered coolly.

He gave a signal for his boys to attack.

Duran gripped the strap of his satchel. If he learned anything from his former school life, it was how to survive a closed in fight. He scanned the positions of his attackers, counting seven thugs circling him from what he called star-point angles. He scanned the area's advantage points close to where he was positioned. Then exhale the last bit of his nerves to still his mind.

They came at him fast, but he was faster. He avoided their swinging fists and low kicks, kept his back near the wall, so they had no choice but come at him face to face.

He swung his bag at thighs and vulnerable parts of the body with all his might, estimating the weight of three half kilo textbooks among the rest of his school junk would cause impact when swung at a certain speed. His analysis was correct as well as his landings, which caused the thugs to stumble into each other.

They were taller and stauncher in build than him, so his next best shot at taking them out were their knees.

One of the thugs managed to land a swing to his side, which caused him to stumble to the ground. Instinctively, he grabbed a handful of dirt from the gutter and chucked it into his assailants' eyes.

They reeled backward. This gave him a chance to bring them down. He tightened his grip on his bag and whacked at knees, knocking them to all fours.

From the corner of his eye, he saw the rest of the thugs advancing on both his sides with baseball bats.

He took a step forward, so they were in-line with each other. He dodged their swings before they met his head. The thugs yelped and fell to the ground when their bats' blow landed on themselves.

The attack was over within ten minutes. Only Duran and Mayuzumi were left standing.

'Now you. Whadya gonna to do.' He coolly threw the challenge back to the senior.

Mayuzumi gritted his teeth and clenched his fists, but didn't move.

'I thought so,' Duran said.

He took steps away from the fight scene, keeping his eye on the thugs who were still squirming on the ground. When he was sure they weren't going to recover for a second round, he turned and resumed his way down the alleyway.

'KITA! THIS ISN'T OVER! I'LL GET YOU! YOU'LL PAY. ALL OF YOU WILL PAY!' Mayuzumi shouted.

Duran stopped.

'Give it up.' He ordered over his shoulder then resumed his way to his workplace.

When he was out of their sight, he pulled out his phone and sent a broadcast email warning people away from the alleyway.

'Crap,' he cursed as he pocketed his phone.

The last thing he had expected was a run-in with that guy. Mayuzumi was going to be nastier than ever now. He had to ramp up the plan.

He raced for the ramen house and felt woozy as he entered the back of the shop. His thoughts blurred and became muddled.

The world spun about his head as fuzzy blobs. He wobbled up to the door, stretched out his arm to turn the handle and lost his footing.

He stumbled into the boxes stacked up to one side, gripping his nauseated stomach to hold back the sharp pain he felt to his spine. The pain overwhelmed him that he collapsed to unconsciousness.

'Kita-kun!' Saski cried out when he and Kou found him unconscious at the ramen house's back door.

He carefully turned Duran over onto his back and checked for breath. His breaths were faint and heart beats were dangerously slow.

His mind went back to Duran's strange text sent earlier and suspected there had been a fight. He unbuttoned Duran's shirt and checked for physical damage, he noticed a deep-purplish swelling on the side of his abdomen. His suspicions for ecchymosis deepened.

'Kou-kun, give me that crate over there,' Saski ordered him.

Kou handed Saski a medium-sized crate and watched him carefully balance Duran's legs on it, so they were alleviated.

Saski pulled out his phone and dialled Emergency. He calmly told the emergency operator of the suspected injuries and other details.

'An ambulance will be here shortly,' he said when he ended the call.

He checked again for Duran's breathing and began to panic when he couldn't feel his breath nor a heartbeat. He had watched his father perform CPR to patients many times that it was ingrained in his memories.

On instinct, he began to force air into Duran's mouth, and push down on the appropriate space beneath his heart to get it beating again. Counting and timing each breath and pump.

Duran's sister and his friends arrived at that moment.

'Hayashi-kun, what's going on?' Himeko asked Kou.

She cried out when she saw her brother lifeless on the ground and Saski doing his hardest to revive him.

'Don't!' Kou said firmly and held her back from interrupting. He turned her around to face him and forced her to calm down.

'Go to the front. Tell Shiro-san and Jiro-san what's going on,' he calmly ordered.

Duran's friends lead Himeko away from the scene to do as Kou had asked.

'Come on Kita!' Saski cried out between pumps and breaths.

His mind became flustered from Duran's lack of response. His hands were aching from the pumping and his breath was falling short. He wasn't going to give up. Duran was not meant to die like this!

Is this the feeling Duran had when he thought up a plan to save his senior from grief?

It was the first time Saski felt the urge to save someone's life. His heart was beating feverishly. He had to keep his mind clear to keep going. His mind was filled with relief when he felt Duran's heart beating again, but he still wasn't breathing. He continued forcing air into his lungs with up his timing.

'Hayashi-kun!' Saski heard from behind him and saw Shiro-san next to Kou from the corner of his eye.

'No focus!' Saski thought and willed his mind to calm down.

He sighed when he felt Duran's breath faint on his cheek.

Two paramedics arrived to take over. Saski sat back to reclaim his breath.

'You did well kid,' one of the Paramedic's said to him.

Saski provided a report before they took Duran away on a stretcher with Himeko by his side.

Everyone else Duran had invited to the meeting arrived at that point. Shiro-san invited them all into the restaurant.

★ THE PLAN

'You're the strongest person I know.' Himeko's voice soothed his troubled mind.

'There are people who will try to destroy a beautiful person because they see their own ugliness reflected back at them when they look at such a person.' Isagi-chichi, his paternal father, reassured the demons of his nightmares.

Many other snippets of thoughts, past conversations and events swam in and out of his sub consciousness.

What was he doing again? There was something important he had to do. Something he had to finish no matter what.

He felt an icy coldness run up his arm and a dull pain to his stomach.

His eyes fluttered open and blinked in the sight of heat lamps blaring against a white-washed ceiling. He stared downward and saw his arm connected to a drip. The smell of ammonia and chlorine overpowered his senses. He felt certain he wasn't in the school infirmary.

'You never fail to make me worry,' said a familiar voice next to him.

Duran squirmed at the ache he felt as he tried to get up.

'Here,' said the voice soothingly.

He felt familiar hands assist him, so he could sit up, and saw he was wearing his pyjamas.

'Thank you.' He panted and faced the man next to him.

'Dad.'

His father who appeared his usual calm and collected self.

The man he fondly called Isagi-chichi was rarely an emotional person on the surface. A cool, confident and extremely stylish man with warm dark almond eyes.

His father stared at him with neither anger nor

disappointment. Instead, there was a sense of relief that he had recovered consciousness. Duran noticed the fine red spidery veins in his father's eyes.

'Where am I?'

'Hospital.'

'How long have you been sitting here?'

'A while. You've been lying here for two days now.'

What? How could that be? His memories flooded back to him. He was meant to meet with his friends and members of the student council at the ramen house to talk over the plans for Isao and Shouta's comeback.

'Wait. Two days? No, where's my phone, I was meant to meet up with some people.' He panicked.

'Calm down, Son. Don't worry about your friends or your plan, they have that in control.'

'Whatya mean have it in control? I have to call them. Dad, it's Saturday!'

'Don't make me discipline you! Drop it!' Isagi-chichi furrowed his brows as she scolded Duran.

'Dad?' Duran's voice quivered.

He sighed and lowered his head, feeling drained.

Isagi-chichi dropped his scold with a weary sigh.

'Son. Sakura and I, we were scared.' His voice quivered.

'You know what your mother is like. She was going off about filing a lawsuit, giving her usual tough lawyer talk, but inside she was scared out of her mind. This time, you might not come around.'

Duran saw his father's weariness in his eyes. He gripped his hand tight.

'I can't thank that boy enough for what he did for you.'

'Boy?' Duran frowned, perplexed.

'You stopped breathing, your heart gave out. He revived you with CPR.' Isagi-chichi's voice trembled with tears, which welled up in his eyes. 'If I had lost you, I don't know what I'd do.'

'Who revived me Dad?' Duran gently insisted.

'I feel ashamed I don't know his name. He was like

your guardian angel. They told me he never stopped until you were breathing. By that time the paramedics had arrived. He saved your life.'

Their conversation was interrupted by an attending nurse who wheeled in a blood pressure monitor.

She routinely checked his heart rate, temperature and the amount of saline solution left in the drip's sack.

'Good to see you conscious. You've worried your family to no end,' the nurse scolded Duran as she wrote down his readings to a clipboard.

'Very sorry,' Duran apologized.

'Recover well and be healthy. Don't make your parents fret again,' the nurse added as she wheeled out the monitor and left them alone in the room again.

'She's right. The last time you were in hospital, you were a scary sight, but you were conscious then. I don't know if my heart could handle it if this was to happen again.'

'I'm sorry dad for causing you worry.' Duran bowed his head with shame.

'Son, everything you do causes me to worry. That comes with being a parent. But you also make me smile with pride.' His father smiled through his tears and squeezed his hand tighter.

'Dad.' Duran sobbed.

'I'm sorry I wasn't there that time for you,' his father whispered and gently pulled him into a hug. 'I love you too Son. Don't ever forget that.'

His mother and Himeko walked into the room.

'Nii-san!' Himeko cried out. She jumped on him and Isagi-chichi with her hug.

'Ow, Ow, careful.' Duran winced.

Himeko pulled away and stood next to his mother who also looked like she hadn't been sleeping for days.

'Tell me why I shouldn't slap you right now!' Sakura cursed and let out all the tears she had been storing when she was keeping a brave face.

'Sakura, he'll be alright now.' Isagi-chichi reassured her and released Duran.

'Dad's been hell-bent on trying to find out what happened to you,' Himeko said with a sober voice. 'What happened?'

Duran sighed and told them about the attack in the alleyway.

He closed his eyes and waited for his mother's cursing and shouting. Instead, she surprised him by pulling him into a hug.

'When you were here because of that time, I was worried and angry. This time, you scared me. I don't want to find you in a hospital because of another attack on you every again.' Her voice sounded tired.

'No more of this.'

'I'm so angry right now. I want to kill them.' Himeko cursed and clenched her fists.

'Himeko-chan. Helping Duran recover his strength is more important right now,' Isagi-chichi said to calm her down. 'But I thank you for thinking so well of him.'

Himeko sighed and shook away her anger. He was right. Her brother was alive and would recover. That was more important than retaliation.

'That aside, what are we going to tell Ryuu-san.' Sakura sighed.

'I guess the truth,' Duran answered and leaned back into his pillow.

His mind was heavy with explanations, weighing up his step-father's possible reactions.

Duran was released from hospital a few days later. He had a couple of small wounds near his right rib cage from where he had been sutured. The doctors had recommended that he stay home and recover for a few more days to allow for the wounds to heal.

They had discovered one of his ribs had cracked upon an impact that caused some internal bleeding, and him to collapse to unconsciousness. If he hadn't been revived by

CPR, at that time, it was likely he would've internally bled to death. His father was right when he said a boy had saved his life.

Fortunately, his rib could be patched, so he could walk away with a few war scars at the end of it all.

He realized how extremely lucky he was that day, but also sad that he wasn't able to see his plan through to ensure Isao could go back to school.

He shuffled out of his bed and glanced about his room, which had an unusual silence to it.

Of course, it was a Wednesday so Himeko would be in school. His step-father had taken time off work to care for him since his mother had no choice but to be in Kyoto for a case.

'Duran-kun, you are hungry?' Ryuu-chichi called out to him and poked his head into his room.

His step-father was dressed in casual clothes and still wearing bed-hair. He looked exhausted and unlike his usual stoic self.

'Yes, thank you.' Duran smiled and followed him into the dining area.

A drama show was playing on the lounge-room TV, but neither were interested to watch it.

Duran sat at the low round table, near the lounge, before a bowl of steaming miso soup. He watched his step-father coolly move about the modest sized kitchenette; gathering other bits and pieces of the meal they would share together. He waited for him to be seated before getting into his meal.

'Itadakimasu,' they said and started eating.

For a while, the only chatter was coming from the TV show. Duran and Ryuu-chichi were lost in their thoughts.

It was Ryuu-chichi who broke the silence between them first.

'Your wound is still dry,' he asked.

Duran nodded and checked the bandages underneath his t-shirt. They were clean. He didn't feel the pain as much as before, but it was still a struggle for him to bend.

'I think I'll be okay to go back to school tomorrow,' said Duran softly.

'Give it another day to be sure. Last thing we'd want to hear is your stitches re-opened at school. Your mother's been through enough worries.'

Duran bowed his head toward his miso soup and poured all his guilty thoughts into its cloudy mixture.

This wasn't the first time he had this type of conversation with one of his fathers. He honestly wasn't looking for trouble, but somehow trouble found him. It made him realize he had to focus harder on doing well in school. His idea of a music club wasn't as meaningful to him any more.

'I'm sorry I caused you trouble. It's my fault I made you worry,' he said into his bowl of miso.

His step-father released a long sigh. 'Himeko was seven when one of her friends was being bullied by a group of boys. Back then, she stood up to those bullies and defended her friend. Boy, did she give them a licking.'

'She won the fight, but broke her leg in the process. Her mother was alive at that time. She was furious at Himeko, yelling at her, telling her she had to be like all the other girls. Little girls didn't fight boys and break their legs.'

Ryuu-chichi smiled.

'Himeko's answer to her mother was "I'm not like other girls". All daddies are proud of their daughters, but I felt very proud of her that day. She was strong to stand up for her friends and for herself. That's why I understand why you were in that fight. Why you're determined to see that kid back at school. It's something she would do too.'

'When did her mother—' Duran couldn't finish the rest of his sentence.

'Two years after that incident. It broke Himeko's heart and for a short while, she kept herself away from people. Most kids came to see her as this angry girl. She had a few who were willing to be with her. When you and your mother came into our lives, I think you helped her to move on.'

They resumed their silence as they finished eating but the atmosphere was a lot of lighter. Duran helped his step-father clean up the dishes and was glad when their chatter turned to trivial topics.

He excused himself and went back to his room to complete his catch-up school work. His thoughts chopped and changed between his studies, friends and family.

Everyone and everything had a meaning in his life. He felt his meaning to everyone else eventuated in a failure.

He dropped his pencil and studies, and moved to his keyboard.

His fingers started playing a song, but his heart wasn't in it. The sounds came out flat and awkward. He hung his head with shame at feeling useless.

Who was he to believe he could make a difference to someone else's life when he couldn't even change his own? He was still getting into trouble, causing his mother grief and worry, and now Ryuu-chichi, his sister and a few other people were involved.

'Damn it!' He cursed.

His phone started ringing, breaking through the cycle of his depressive thoughts. He picked it up and saw the caller was Isagi-chichi.

'Dad,' he answered.

'Just checking if you're healing okay. Are you eating well?' His father's voice flowed into his ear.

'Yeah, Ryuu-chichi's home with me today. I had miso soup.'

'That's good to hear. You're okay to go back to school?'

'Seems Friday is a good day for me to go, the wound's healing really well and I'm getting rest.' He tried to sound chirpy.

It was the least he could do to ease his father's worry.

'Great. I'll come to see you then.'

Duran could hear some background chatter and voices calling his father to them.

'Son, listen to your mother and Suzuki-san. He's a good guy.'

The background chatter was becoming more prominent. As well as the people calling out for Isagi-chichi.

'Dad, I, um.' Duran couldn't find the nerve to finish off what he wanted to tell his father. The thoughts he wanted to get out of his head that only his dad could soothe away.

'I'll talk to you tomorrow. Bye, I love you son.'

The conversation ended with a click.

'I love you too dad,' Duran replied and placed his phone back on his desk.

His phone's ringing woke him up from an afternoon nap he didn't realize he had been having. He shuffled upright and answered the call still groggy from being half-asleep.

'Hello?'

'Sorry. I hope I didn't wake you,' said a timid voice.

Duran checked the Caller ID. His mind was awake.

'Izuki-senpai. No, it's okay. I haven't heard from you for a while. How are you?'

'I'm doing okay. I heard you were in a fight. Are you okay?' Isao's voice sounded strained.

Duran wanted to tell him so many things, but he was concerned about adding to his seniors worries, so he said he was doing fine.

He brought Isao up to speed about what was going on in school and the ramen house. Their talk moved to sports, shared interests and other trivial topics.

'My teacher came to my house today to give me school work. He didn't say much. I wonder why he still bothers.' Isao's voice trembled into Duran's ear.

Duran closed his eyes, taking in his senior's pain.

No matter how much he doubted himself, he couldn't give up on the reason behind why he was at home recovering from a wound.

'Senpai. I'm going to go back to school tomorrow. I'm going to go to your house afterwards. When I do, I'm going to make you come back to school kicking and screaming because you belong there. You belong with us. I'll kick your door down to get you back to us!'

There was a long pause on the other side of his phone. Duran could sense his senior was choking back his tears.

'K-Kita-kun. Why would you do this for me? I don't understand.'

Duran remembered the conversation he had with Saski who asked him a similar question. His answer was simple.

'Because you're my senpai.'

His senior's tears were more audible on the phone this time. Duran sat there with his phone to his ear, allowing him to pour out his emotion. It was the closest thing to having a shoulder to cry on.

'I can't imagine what you went through, but I understand what it feels like to be seen as different. That's not a bad thing, not at all. Senpai, you sometimes didn't get my stupid jokes, you were hard on me when you taught me how to wait tables, you even made me feel like a sex object at one point.' Duran chuckled, recalling the first time they met each other during the shōujo effect fiasco.

'Never once did I think you were less than a good person.'

'Kita-kun. I've never met anyone like you.'

'Doubt you'd find anyone as dashingly charming as me.' Duran joked.

'Senpai. I meant what I said about dragging you back to school. Believe it or not, there are people who miss you, people who want you back. I'll make you see that.'

The conversation ended with light talk.

It left Duran's heart pounding like crazy. How could his step-father expect him to stay another day away from school after a call like that? He felt he was ready to resume his plan.

He couldn't go back to sleep after Isao's call, so he went back to his homework.

Checking the time, he realized Himeko should be out of school. Thank god! He never thought he would miss her noise around the house so much. It was way too quiet with just him and his step-father.

He refocused on the maths sheet before him, which he figured he'd be able to finish by the end of the night. His mind was swarming with algebra patterns that he didn't notice his mobile phone vibrating with a call until it brushed against his hand.

His body went stiff when he checked who was calling him.

'Hello?' His voice came across slight flustered.

'Kita-kun?'

'Yes?'

'Sorry to call you out of the blue. Um, how are you?'

'I'm fine. Looks like I can go back to school tomorrow.'

'Really?'

'Yeah.' Duran's heart thumped so loud that he was worried it could be heard on the other end of the line.

'That's good. Your sister looked a bit worried. It made me wonder how you were.'

Was he dreaming? Could this call be real? Why was Saski calling him and asking how he was? He didn't care if he was put up to it. The sound of his voice coming across the receiver made him feel special.

'She was strange.' Saski continued.

'What do you mean?'

'She was really nice to me and kept giving me all these sweets. I thought she was going to pounce on me like Chia-chan does.' He chuckled.

'Hey! Don't mistake my sister with that AKB48 clone. She's got more going for her than that girl,' Duran said a bit fired up.

'I thought that would get a rise out of you.'

Duran smiled, feeling he was on cloud nine. He was on

the phone with Saski! They were talking causal-like!

If he had a megaphone he'd scream from the rooftops about how happy he was right now. He prayed in his heart that Saski was the boy who had saved him.

'Come on Tsubaki-kun. You called because you can't get enough of me.' He flirted.

'Maybe I wanted to see if we had succeeded in scaring you away.' Saski joked.

'Never.'

'Hey Kita-kun are you dressed?'

Woah! This was getting intimate way too fast.

Duran was highly flustered at this point that the phone fumbled in his hands. His face flushed red as if the heat in his room had cranked up to 45 degrees.

'Kita-kun?'

'Hai, hai. Still, here,' Duran piped up. 'Um sort of. Gotta get a shirt on. Maybe take a shower.'

Take a shower?! What was he saying?

He smacked his forehead realizing how weird that sounded.

'Ah, um, okay. Just get dressed and meet me at school. There's something I need to show you. But take your time, don't want you falling down again.'

Meet him at school? Was this a date? Wasn't this guy going too fast?

'Now who's being cheeky. I'll have my step-father drop me off.'

'In that case, be in here in twenty minutes.'

'Should I come wearing my Sunday best?' Duran said teasingly and waited for Saski's reaction.

There was a long pause. He was worried Saski had ended the call. No, he would've heard a dial tone.

'Decent. Dress decent.'

The conversation ended.

'Dress decent.' Duran repeated with the biggest smile on his face.

He forgot about his wound as he started pulling out

clothes from his wardrobe to go out.

Twenty minutes later, he had arrived to a ghost town for a school. It was too quiet and completely void of people. He'd hear a pin drop if one fell.

'Tsubaki did say meet here?' He questioned himself, feeling panicky that he had heard the details wrong.

He cautiously made his way to his classroom block to be sure.

'There they are.' He sighed when he saw his sister, friends, Kou and Saski waiting on the entrance steps for him.

'Duran! Looking good man.' Aki greeted him.

'Dude, you're okay?' Fumio expressed his concern with solemness.

'I'm fine.' Duran reassured him.

'You took your time for being fine.' Kou grumpily called out.

'Hey, show the injured some courtesies, please. Your instructions are shonky. I could've ended up at a different block.' Duran pouted in his defence.

'You found us. I say we failed.' Kou huffed.

Duran gave the guy a wry smile. Yet he was happy his friends were there. Although slightly disappointed it wasn't going to be only Saski and himself meeting up. Of course, why would it be a date?

'What's going on here?'

'Your plan,' Kou answered and opened the doors to let everyone into the building.

Duran didn't question further as he followed everyone through the hallways and corridors.

'Nii-san. We're not going too fast for you?' Himeko checked on him.

'Sis, I'm okay.' He reassured her with a smile.

They entered the second-year floors and stopped before Isao's homeroom class.

Duran's eyes went wide. Was it possible they were actioning stage two of the plan? But he didn't even get them to stage one!

'Duran.'

His eyes lit up when he saw his father and step-father waiting outside the room.

'Dad. Akira-san! What are you doing here?'

'We're here for you and your cause. Look,' Isagi-chichi said

He drew Duran's attention to the inside of the room, which had all of Isao's classmates chatting with one another near their desks. There were various spotlights and a couple of video cameras propped around the main area of the room with a professional crew checking each one. A heightened buzz was among all the students who were trying to keep their cool about being part of a video shoot.

'Is this for real?'

'I called in a favour from one of my film production buddies. When I told him your plan and your reason behind it, he jumped on-board since his only son faced a similar situation. We're doing stage two of your plan today.'

Akira-san grinned proudly as he said this, which made him appear younger than thirty years old.

Duran recalled the first time he had met him almost three years ago and how he innocently mistook him for a high school student. Even now, dressed in a mature navy jacket, T-shirt, blue jeans and boots he still looked as old as a third year high school student.

'I told you Son that your friends had this all under control didn't I?' Isagi-chichi confirmed.

'I'm offended you didn't trust us to deliver,' President Saito said as he walked up to Duran.

'Sorry, no, it's not that, I'm a bit baffled,' Duran said scratching at his head.

'It seems Mayuzumi and his friends came down with a mysterious case of food poisoning, so wasn't at school today.'

'You sound very sure that would happen.' Duran gulped, feeling a shiver run down his spine.

'I swear it was a lucky break. Hyuga-san had a free slot for the day, so we could do stage two for your seniors,' President Saito said through a smug smile.

'This is the last shoot for the day,' said a burly man in jeans and a dark t-shirt sporting a company logo.

'Thank you Hyuga-san,' said Akira-san

'Wait last one?' Duran looked to Akira-san for answers and received them from Himeko.

'Yeah Nii-san, we've been filming in and out of clubs and rooms all day. The principal was pissed about it, but the Student Council made sure to schedule shooting times so it didn't affect classes,' Himeko answered proudly with the goofiest smile she had ever given him.

'Come watch Nii-san,' she said as she prompted him into the room where Hyuga-san was calling everyone to attention.

Duran sat on one of the large lighting cases that were stacked in the corner away from the shooting area.

All the desks had a white card on them that were large enough to cover the desk's face.

On cue from Hyuga-san, all the students took their positions in their seats, sat up straight and went quiet. Their hands were ready to raise the cards.

'I need to learn that trick from Hyuga-san,' Kato-sensei whispered into Duran's ear.

Duran acknowledge his presence then resumed his watch of the show being made before him.

'Cue the music,' said Hyuga-san to Akira-san who was behind a DJ setup connected to two free-standing speakers.

Duran's eyes glistened with tears when he heard Himeko's voice among an arrangement of strings, keyboard accompaniments and gentle percussion coming out of the speakers. It was the song he had his friends learn for the cause.

She sang in English with a voice so powerful and beautiful. He couldn't believe she could sing the words so well. The song flowed through the classroom carrying a strong message of hope and love.

On a silent cue, one by one the students raised the cards that carried one word on each. No voices from their lips. The cards said it all. The flow of words touched Duran's heart. It was as he had envisioned; the hope that his seniors needed to see to believe they belonged in this school and society again.

'We're - Sorry - Izuki - Meiko - Come - Back - We - Miss - You.' Duran mouthed the words.

He cupped his mouth to hold back his voice from cracking and ruining the moment.

The filming ran through the entire class until it was a sea of white cards carrying a message for Isao and Shouta to come back to school.

Hyuga-san called it a wrap after fifteen minutes of shooting. There was whooping, cheering, clapping and show of support among the student's afterwards.

Duran sat in the background; overwhelmed with emotion. All the heaviness in his heart he had been carrying for his senpai was being shared across his senpai's class and the entire school.

'Are you okay Nii-san,' Himeko gently asked.

'I'm fine sis. This is exactly what they need.' He shuffled off the case.

'Akira-san, Hyuga-san, thank you very much. I can't say enough how appreciative I am for all this.' Duran bowed to them.

'Kita-kun, look at me. Your generous heart is what makes us want to help you.'

'If my son had you as a friend, he might still be in my life. Your seniors are very lucky they have you,' Hyuga-san said with a slight quiver to this voice.

'Hyuga-san, I'm very sorry to hear.'

'Well this project gave me hope there a good kids out there,' Hyuga-san said as if in thought.

Duran offered him a reassuring smile.

'Is it okay to ask when the message will be ready?' He asked politely.

'We'll try for tomorrow. I'll give it to you so you can deliver it to your senpai,' Akira-san answered.

'Akira-kun couldn't stop raving about you when he asked me. You're the son he always wanted,' Hyuga-san said to lighten the mood.

'I feel like a proud mother right now.' Akira-san beamed and ruffled Duran's hair.

'Akira-kun, I'll be working on the edits as soon as I return to the studio. Good work Kita-kun.' Hyuga-san ended the conversation and wheeled equipment out of the room.

Duran sat at one of the front desks and watched the rest of the equipment being wheeled away, students packing up the cards, tidying up the room and filing out of the doors.

'Good work Kita-kun,' said one of the students with a pat to his back.

'You're a good guy. Izuki's lucky,' a girl said to him with a bow before leaving with her friends.

A few other of Isao's classmates smiled and bowed his way before leaving. Eventually, the only people left were his friends, father, Akira-san and the Student Council.

'I'll work with Hyuga-san on the edits. You spend a bit more time with our boy,' Akira-san said to Isagi-chichi.

He patted Duran's shoulder before leaving the room.

'Satisfied. We helped you,' Kou grumbled.

'Correction, you helped our seniors. I'll be satisfied when I hand deliver the message to them and drag them back to school.' Duran reconfirmed the thought.

'You're persistent,' Teppei said through a warm smile.

'Among my many other charms.' Duran relaxed into a cheeky smile.

'Oh my god, I'm gonna hurl. You're so cheesy Kita.' Kou grimaced.

'Hey, you chuck, you mop up buddy. No one here's

your janitor.' Duran joked.

The room erupted with laughter.

'Man, I miss you. When you come back dude?' Fumio rested a hand on his shoulder.

'Himeko's dad says Friday. I say tomorrow.' Duran confirmed.

'Are you sure?' Fumio frowned.

'I second that question.' Isagi-chichi jumped in.

'Dad, I'm close to fighting fit. As long as I don't lift weights, I'll be fine.'

'Okay, let's talk later about it.'

'A stubborn devil too.' Teppei added.

'We need to wrap things up. It's getting late.' Saski interrupted the conversations.

'Thank you Tsubaki-kun. Back to the plan, you'll take the message to your seniors tomorrow or when it's ready. I expect a report of when those two will be back to school.' President Saito summed up with final orders.

'Yes sir!' Duran saluted and grinned at the President's long sigh. 'Seriously, I will let you know when they're coming back.'

'You're sure they will?' Saski voiced a doubt.

'They will.'

Duran shuffled out of his seat. He stood and bowed low to everyone.

'Thank you very much for your support. The plan was achievable because of all of you.'

'Okay this is a wrap. Nii-san straighten up. You're still recovering you idiot.' Himeko scolded him and went to stand next to him.

All of Duran's friends gathered around him and wrapped him in a group hug.

'Alright, alright, enough with the embarrassing hugs.' He tried to sound tough.

'Good work today.' Dai'chi congratulated everyone.

He pulled away from the hug first.

Everyone else followed suit, patting each other the

back and telling each other they did good.

President Saito turned off the lights and locked.

'I told your father Himeko-chan I'll take you both home,' Isagi-chichi said to Himeko and Duran.

'How is everyone else getting home?' Duran asked the others.

'We have our means,' Saski reassured him with a smile. 'Kita-kun get well and come back to school.'

'Thanks for calling me earlier Tsubaki-kun.' Duran responded to his smile.

He felt butterflies in his stomach and a fuzziness in his heart as he watched Saski go ahead of him with the rest of the student council guys. His heart went for a marathon when Saski glanced back at him with another weak smile before returning his attention to his group.

He wasn't imagining it, was he?

'I have to pinch myself later,' he muttered to himself.

'Eh? Aah, I see.' Isagi-chichi chuckled next to him.

'Dad?'

'It's nothing.' Isagi-chichi brushed off with a knowing smile on his face.

The ride home was quick. Ryuu-chichi was waiting up for them when he and Himeko walked through the door on a high.

The three of them gathered around the dining table and talked well into the night about the video shoot. Himeko talked excitedly about making the track and Akira-san being awesome with them. Duran felt disappointed he wasn't there. They were making his song, so figured he was with them in that sense.

His thoughts went back to the fight and his time in the hospital.

'Hey, Himeko. Do you know who revived me?'

She began biting her lip with worry.

'Sis, I'm here talking to you, it's alright.' He reassured her with a few pats to her back.

'Nii-san, it was as mom and dad said, scary. You were

just lying there.'

'We don't have to go back there. I only want to know who I need to thank for saving my life.'

Himeko heaved a sigh and released her lip. She gave him an answer.

'Tsubaki. It was Tsubaki,' she whispered as she shuffled out of her seat to call it a night.

'You better get to sleep too,' Ryuu-chichi said.

Duran nodded his head and went back to his room.

Saski had saved him, as he had hoped. What was he going to do next? What did Saski think of him now?

He fell asleep with a load of questions circling in his mind. At least, he wasn't aching with pain as much as before.

The next day was being back at school, defying his step-father's protests with repeated reassurances that he was fine. Although step-father remained unconvinced. Regardless he dropped him and Himeko outside the main school gates.

NYAA! Duran yelped at the angry cry near his feet.

He saw a black and white mohawk cat staring back at him with a cranky scowl on its face.

And the cat was really scowling at him with a deep frown.

'Oh. Where'd this cute cat came from?' Himeko knelt to give a friendly pat and rub to its head. The cat didn't seem to mind.

'You call that cute?' Duran gulped as he tried to do the same and yelped when the cat's left paw did a fierce swipe attack for his hand.

'Cranky beast.'

Himeko laughed as she rose and bid the cat farewell.

The mohawk cat gave Duran the stink-eye before it fled down the path and around the corner.

A few of their peers passed them, giving them warm greetings. They returned welcome smiles, gestures and greetings as they crossed the courtyard to their classroom block.

'If only Meiko-san and Izuki-senpai received the same thing.' Duran thought sadly.

His mind cycled with thoughts about his seniors and stopped on one fact that he didn't really know much of Shouta before the incident.

He checked the time on his mobile phone and saw he had some minutes before the homeroom bell rang.

'Hey Himeko, you can go to class ahead of me, there's something I need to do before the bell rings,' Duran said and ran off before she could get in a word.

He entered the second years' floor and breathed out a sigh of relief when he saw Kato-sensei headed in his direction.

'Sensei, can I ask a question?'

'Of course, anything.'

'Who was Meiko-san's friends aside from Senpai? Was he in any clubs?'

'Clubs? Sure, he was in the Soccer Club. A striker and good one too,' Kato-sensei answered.

'I realized I don't really know Meiko-san before the incident,' Duran explained.

'Well if you want a better insight, you're best to speak with Miyagi, Rintarou. You'll find him at Block-C and Class 3-C. He's the club's captain.'

'Thank you Sensei!' Duran quickly bowed and hurried to find Rintarou.

He felt short of breath as he hurried across the courtyard toward Block-C, asking people he came across where to find him and was pointed to a group of guys hanging out on a bench underneath one of the trees before the block's entrance.

'That's him,' said a meek girl who pointed to the guy in the middle of the group.

He was the image of an athlete; tall and appealing with a manly face. There was a gentleness to his almond eyes that softened his features.

'Thank you,' Duran bowed and noticed her flushed cheeks.

He felt her eyes lingering on his back has he approached the soccer team captain.

He couldn't blame the girl. The man was an ideal fetch.

'Miyagi, Rintarou, I'm Kita, Duran.' He introduced himself.

'Yeah I know, the talented guitarist.' Rintarou acknowledged him.

'May I talk with you for a bit?' Duran asked politely.

'About?'

'Meiko Shouta,' he replied, taking longer breaths to calm his heart rate.

'Um, guys give me a moment,' Rintarou said to his friends as he stood.

'Let's go for a walk.'

They strolled slowly around the courtyard as they talked, oblivious of the appreciative or curious glances they both received from afar.

'Why would you be interested in Meiko-kun?'

'His homeroom teacher referred me to you for some insight on Meiko-san before the rumours.'

'So, you want to see if the rumours were true?'

'Not really. I just want to know what Meiko-san was like. He was on your team right?'

'Yeah. Our striker and one of the best I've come across. That kid has some fearsome raw talent.'

Rintarou sighed. 'I found it strange when those rumours started.'

'What was strange?'

'He was a quiet guy. Polite. A good team player. Brought us many victories. He seemed really sure of himself. I say that in a good way. He didn't need to prove himself to anyone. He never said a bad word about anyone either.'

'Why did everyone change their opinion of him?' Duran politely asked.

'Well, I mentioned he was a nice guy, but at the same time he kept a distance. I can't say guys on the team weren't jealous of him. This mysterious and talented junior comes along to save the day and steal girls' hearts. Some of the team saw him as threat to their positions and girlfriends. Ironically, I believe a lot of the girlfriends were to blame for the rumours.'

'Aah, I'm starting to see,' Duran said with realization.

'Yeah. Girls talk a lot and come to these weird conclusions. When they're jealous, some can get nasty.'

'Meiko-san is outed as gay and now a threat to steal their boyfriends.' Duran concluded and hissed at the absurdity of it.

'Bingo. People start connecting dots. The rumours keep circulating and getting nastier by the minute. They go viral on social media with more and more people jumping on-board to slam Meiko-kun. It got out of control. Meiko-kun didn't come back to school it made the rumours look like truth.' Rintarou released a weary sigh.

'Was Izuki, Isao at any of his games?'

'His childhood friend? Oh, yeah, he was something of our team mascot in the stands, waving a banner and yelling out to do our best with his quiet voice.' Rintarou chuckled.

His expression became serious.

'A lot of the guys realized what they caused after they had cleared their heads. I know a lot of them carry the shame and guilt. Especially when they saw a bunch of First Years' working hard to get him back to school. Even to go out of their way to make a music video message just for him. I think they came to see the actual damage caused by their own stupidity.'

'Do you see Meiko-san a good person?'

There was long pause before he responded.

'Yeah. It's a shame a talented player was stopped from playing the sport he loves because of all this.'

Duran felt certain he knew enough of Shouta.

'Kita-kun. When you see Meiko-kun, could you tell him

to come back, and we're sorry just like we showed on that video?'

'You think I'll be seeing him?'

'Yeah. I think he'll talk to you too since you're trying your hardest to get him back to school.' Rintarou smiled and gave him a pat on the back.

'I will, but I think it's better you tell him yourself too.'

Their conversation ended at the sound of the school bell. Duran bowed his thanks.

He reassured Rintarou that their conversation was confidential, before running of to enter his homeroom class just when Aimi-sensei was calling everyone to their seats.

His morning lessons passed uneventfully until Kato-sensei made an expected intrusion on Aimi-sensei's maths spiel before the lunch bell rang.

'Apologizes for intruding upon your lesson Aimi-sensei, but may I borrow Kita-kun,' Kato-sensei politely asked.

'Um okay. Kita please go with Kato-sensei.'

Duran packed up his bag and made a quick exit from class.

'Kita-kun, I received these for you,' Kato-sensei said as walked down the quiet hallway.

He handed Duran two USB flash drives.

'These the messages?' Duran asked excitedly.

'Yes, I checked both drives to be sure. I'm taking them to those boys now. I want you to come with me,' Kato-sensei said with a warm smile.

Duran followed his teacher to his car.

On the drive down Route 133, their conversations covered school subjects, book interests and other safe topic. Their journey eventually veered off towards a set of suburban streets crowded with apartment blocks.

They slowed to a block of architecturally designed apartments, which resembled Lego blocks buildings.

'Who lives here?' Duran asked taking in the building's weirdness.

'Meiko-kun,' Kato-sensei answered as he parked the car before a block entrance.

His teacher grabbed his satchel from the back seat.

Duran followed him into the building complex, up a flight of stairs to the second floor and down a balcony to the far end apartment. His heart raced when Kato-sensei pushed the intercom buzzer.

'Yeah?' Cracked a voice on the intercom.

'It's Kato-sensei.'

'Sensei what yah doing here? Didn't my father tell yah I'm not going back?' The voice responded in a dialect Duran wasn't familiar with.

'I have something you'd want to see,' Sensei replied and waited patiently for a response.

They waited patiently for the door to open. Behind the door was the shadow of a star athlete with messy hair flopping randomly over his bloodshot and dark rimmed eyes. His cheeks were sunken in and pasty. His T-shirt and track pants were too baggy on his body.

'Meiko-san?' Duran blurted with shock.

'Yah be?' Shouta frowned.

'I'm Kita Duran.' Duran bowed. 'Please may we come inside? I think you really need to see what we have brought for you.'

'Sensei what's this? Who's the kid with yah?' Shouta raised his voice.

'I'm a good friend of Izuki Isao,' Duran explained.

Shouta took a few steps toward him.

'Yah know Izuki? Have yah seen him? Is he okay?'

Duran shook his head.

'I've only spoken to him on the phone recently. Saying he's okay would be a lie.'

Shouta sighed and gestured for them to come inside.

'Sorry for intruding,' both Sensei and Duran said the formality.

The apartment was a bedroom, bathroom and kitchenette. Piles of clothes were strewn about the floor and unmade futon of the main room. Half-empty packets of instant ramen overflowed the bin in the kitchenette. A stale lived-in odour overpowered the air. Where was Shouta's parents?

'Meiko-san do you live alone?' Duran asked.

'My parents went back to Fukuoka. I'm here for now,' Shouta replied.

He cleared a spot for them to sit at his low dining table.

Duran made himself comfortable next to his teacher.

'Would yah like some tea?'

Both Duran and his teacher politely declined.

'What's it yah want me to see?' Shouta sat on the other side of the table.

'Something this boy organized for you,' Kato-sensei said and pulled out his laptop from his satchel.

Kato-sensei set up the USB stick and media player. He positioned the laptop before Shouta.

'Meiko-kun watch the whole thing. Don't say anything until it's finished,' he ordered.

He played the video file.

Shouta frowned as he watched the film. His expression eased with surprise when he saw his name and words on white cardboard held by many of his peers, in many classrooms and clubs. Tears welled in his eyes when he watched his homeroom classmates calling him back to school. The video ran for five minutes, the emotion in the room was overpowering to be felt for a lifetime.

'What is this? Why?' Shouta's voice trembled. Tears streamed down his cheeks.

'Meiko-san Everyone knows what they did to you was wrong and are remorseful. This was their way to apologize to you,' Duran answered.

'They want me back?'

'Yes.' Duran shuffled closer to him.

'Meiko-san we've never met, but I know Izuki-senpai, so I know he's a good guy. I asked people about what you were like before all of this. Not one person could tell me anything bad about you.'

'Then why did they believe those lies? Why did they kick us out?!' Shouta spat.

'It spun out of control. Before anyone realized it, the damage was done. I know a lot of people felt ashamed.'

Duran surprised Shouta when he bowed on all fours before him.

'Meiko-san. Please come back to school. I will kick any ass that says more bad things about you,' he said towards the molted carpet.

'This video was organized thanks to the Student Council, your homeroom class and a group of juniors who were courageous to stand up for you to the faces of others. This boy grovelling before you was the one person who believed in and fought for you the most,' Kato-sensei added.

Shouta pulled Duran into a hug. He didn't notice Duran holding on to his pain.

'Yah really did this for me?' His tears were soaking into Duran's shoulders.

'Yes, for you and Izuki-senpai.'

Kato-sensei stood and grabbed a box of tissues from the kitchenette counter. He handed a generous wad to Shouta who released Duran and started cleaning up his face.

'Okay, I'll talk to my parents about coming back,' he said with a smile.

'I thought you'd say that, so I also brought over your remedial work for mid-terms.' Kato-sensei slammed a folder full of sheets onto the table.

'And, geez, make sure you clean up this place and eat something healthy.'

'I can cook for you if you like until you feel well enough,' Duran offered.

'Yah cook Kita-kun?'

'I think I'm decent enough. I learnt from my father who's a chef.' Duran confirmed modestly.

'Really? Then cook for me too.' Kato-sensei joked.

'Nice try Sensei.'

'Nah, yah been too generous already. I don't wanna burden yah any more. I'll be able to eat right from now on,' Shouta politely declined.

'Says the guy who has stacks of empty instant ramen cluttering his bin.' Duran pouted. 'Actually, this isn't a request. I will come around and cook something more nutritious than ramen. For payback, you'll tutor me for history as I heard, from Sensei in the car, that's your strongest subject.'

'That's settled.' Kato-sensei sealed the deal with a clap. 'I expect you back to school next Monday with some of your remedial work completed. Kita-kun will cook for you, when?'

'I'll come every second day starting Monday,' Duran answered.

'Yes, he'll come to your house every second day to cook for you until you're our healthy sports star again.' Kato-sensei confirmed, not holding back his glee.

Shouta relaxed and returned their warm smiles. How could he say no?

Duran and Kato-sensei left one of the flash drives with Shouta. He was in good spirits when they said their goodbyes.

Kato-sensei let out a sigh of relief when they stepped into his car for their next stop.

'Wow Kita-kun. You did excellent work back there. I'm impressed, but are you okay to cook for Meiko-kun?'

'Of course, I wouldn't have offered if I wasn't. I do the cooking when my step-father isn't around. Himeko and my mother are absolutely hopeless in the kitchen.'

Kato-sensei chuckled as he started up the car.

'Well okay then. Next stop Izuki-kun's place.' Kato-sensei pulled the car out.

They drove down the road.

Duran and Kato-sensei arrived to Isao's home around

the time the last school lesson would have started.

Isao lived close to K-University, in a one large tatami mat room adjoined to others of a run-down communal block shared by university students.

Like Shouta, he lived alone. He worked at Matsu Ramen House to pay for his rent and other costs of living. It was permitted by their school to work certain hours, provided it didn't interfere with their studies. Since Isao had to share bathroom and cooking facilities with other tenants, he wasn't completely isolated.

They were let in by one of Kato-sensei's old university friends, which both surprised and made the teacher's day.

Duran had to drag his teacher away from the reunion and pull him back to the matter at hand.

'Focus Sensei!' He scolded his teacher, who responded with a cheesy grin.

Duran dropped his scolding with a sigh.

Isao met them when he returned from the communal bathroom.

He invited them inside his room and cleared space at his low table for Kato-sensei's laptop. He watched his movie and cried the same amount of tears as Shouta did.

'I never imagined you meant this when you said you'll show me that people wanted me back,' he said once his tears had eased.

'Senpai. I meant what I said. These people feel sorry for what they did to you. Please come back to school.' Duran kindly reassured him.

Isao agreed that he'll return on the Monday as well and received the same amount of remedial work from Kato-sensei.

It was the end of school by the time they finished up. Duran received permission to stay behind and help Isao with his catch-up homework.

Kato-sensei reassured Duran that he'd likely be around catching up with his buddy, so he could take him home.

'Sensei, you'd be drinking right?' Duran asked candidly.

'Well, um.' Kato-sensei fumbled.

'Then I won't rely on you for that lift. Go have fun being a friend, but don't drive drunk.' Duran smiled as he kicked the man out the door.

'Geez. Who's the responsible adult here?' Kato-sensei chuckled.

He gratefully left Isao and Duran to meet up with his buddy who was hovering around the hallways for him.

Duran sent a message to his parents and sister's phone to let them know where he was.

A thought of a goofy Kato-sensei shrieking out a karaoke ballad with full confidence entered his mind. He suspected his teacher was clingy and idiotic when drunk.

'That teacher is a weird one,' Duran mumbled.

He turned his attention back to Isao who was reading through the worksheets.

'Kita-kun. You really are one of a kind. No one else would have done or have been able to pull off what you did.' Isao smiled.

'Senpai, do you want to go for a walk?'

'Yeah. I think it'll be good to get some fresh air.' Isao stretched out his body.

Duran left the room to allow Isao to dress for going out. Whilst he was waiting in the hallway before Isao's door, he encountered a blast from the past he was hoping he'd never see again.

'Duran?' Said a low voice from the other end of the hallway.

A burly man appeared with his height and shadow towering over him. His brows were naturally set inward, so they carried a frown distorted by scheming eyes. His lips were twisted with a smirk.

'Kasamatsu-san?' Duran gulped nervously.

His mind flashed back to a memory of them talking on a set of playground swings. He was a middle-school student then. Yukio Kasamatsu was one of those guys who wasn't shy in showing what he thought of him back then.

'What brings you here?' Yukio asked.

'I-I'm visiting a friend.' Duran squirmed under that man's scrutiny.

'So, you're a high school student now. How's your English these days?'

'My English is fine, thank you,' Duran replied in English.

Yukio chuckled. 'You were always good with languages.'

Duran stiffened when Yukio drew close to him.

'You ran out on me that day and never returned my calls. I was hurt.' His voice dipped low with sadism.

Duran felt further discomfort beneath his stare.

'I thought I'd never see you again. Here you are. It must be fate,' he whispered into his ear.

The voice in Duran's mind kept screaming at him to move and run away. Go back inside Isao's room. Make excuses to leave. Anything to get away from the guy. His body wouldn't move. He was petrified.

'D-Do you l-live here,' he stuttered.

'Visiting a friend like yourself, but I come here often.'

His breath burned Duran's cheeks.

Duran felt Yukio's hands move around his waist. Why couldn't he move?

'Move feet, move!' Duran screamed in his head, but his body wouldn't budge.

'Now I know where I can find you. I won't let you go again.' Yukio's slimy breath ran down his neck.

'Kita-kun? Hey what you think you're doing to my friend!' Isao shouted as he entered the hallway and pulled Duran off Yukio.

'Hey, hey, Shorty. He and I go way back.' Yukio smirked.

'Kita-kun?'

'He is nothing I want to go back to. Kasamatsu-san, I don't know what delusions you have of me, but I'm telling you to leave me the hell alone!' Duran managed to shout

out.

He grabbed Isao's hand for support.

'Don't bother Kita-kun any more. I'll tell Kensuke-san you're harassing visitors!' Isao threatened and pulled Duran away from the scene as fast as they could.

They ran a block until they felt they were safe enough to slow down and catch their breath. They found themselves before a 24-hour eatery.

'You wanna go inside?' Isao offered.

Duran nodded his head and followed his senior to a seat near the window, furthest from the other dining guests and a place they could talk.

'Kasamatsu-san visits the house a lot because of his buddy. He's not a nice guy.' Isao shivered. 'Sort of resembles Mayuzumi.'

'No. Mayuzumi is a pussycat compared to that guy.' Duran timidly corrected him. 'With Mayuzumi I don't have fear.'

'Kasamatsu makes you afraid?' Isao gulped.

Duran nodded his head and started telling him about his second year at a British-international middle school, and experience with Yukio and his younger brother - Miwa.

♡ DURAN'S MIDDLE SCHOOL LOVE

Isao and Duran ordered a meal they could slowly nibble their way through whilst Duran recounted his past.

'I started my second year of middle school in a new school after Christmas...' Duran's voice became distant as his mind delved into the details.

⟜⟝

One and a half years ago—

Duran was set to make his new middle school life a typical experience.

His previous year had been traumatic and an unusual time, which saw to a separation from his childhood friends and the death of his first love.

But he felt it wasn't right to shut himself away from the world forever. His parents had suffered enough because of him. He owed it to them to face a new school life, do his best and be more of a genuine person. No more fake Duran to please factions. His heart would break if anyone else suffered because of him.

'A fresh life.' He sighed, as he observed himself in his bedroom full-length mirror.

The high neck-collar of his all-black school uniform felt stiff. Seeing himself in a uniform common to schools in the Edogawa region, it made him feel awkward and more foreign than he already looked.

'No. Don't think that way.' He slapped his own

face to snap him out of his typical loop of pessimistic thoughts.

Today was the chance to prove to his family that he had recovered from his ordeal and was strong enough to live life again.

It had stopped raining when he finally left his home and made his way to school, but still felt cold and miserable.

Dark thoughts seeded in his mind, as he felt apprehensive about his new class. Regardless, he was going to do anything possible to ensure a peaceful school life this time around.

Stepping into the grounds and finding his way to his new student orientation had been an uneventful experience.

His mind slipped into wishful thinking that he could nonchalantly enter his new class without stirring too much attention from his classmates. He followed his escorting teacher with prayers that the man could break the ice to his new class for him.

His heart raced when he entered his homeroom just as it had started and saw many heads turn his way.

'Excuse the interruption, Sakurai-sensei. I've brought your new student.'

Duran's escort had introduced him at the classroom's entrance.

'Ah yes, please come in and introduce yourself,' said a benevolent elderly man with tasteful highlights of black in his aged hair.

He gave a welcoming smile. The escorting teacher made his exit.

Duran stood before his new class, uncomfortable by their stares. He did have his promise to himself and his family, so he bowed and said, 'Good morning. I'm Kita, Duran, please take care of me.'

'Very good Kita-kun. Please make your way to the back desk, third row near the window,' Sakurai-sensei had dismissed him.

Duran had gratefully hurried to his new seat without making eye contact with others.

His teacher resumed his lesson.

A few of his classmates tested their bully tactics on him whilst the teacher had his back turned to the blackboard.

'Check this out,' a boy whispered at his back.

Duran felt a dull object hit the back of his head.

A short volley of paper balls and whispered snickers followed.

He rubbed at his head with a sigh and realization that this class wasn't going to be any better than his last one.

The bell for morning break rang, providing him an opportunity to face his attackers.

'That's your greeting for newcomers?' Duran said coolly.

He faced three surly boys with solid, mature builds already peaking early adulthood. They had bleached-blonde hair that was either spiky or a mop of dishevelled bangs. A mixture of blood was apparent in all of them. Their faces carried more European features than Japanese.

They were slouched in their seats with a bored expression.

'Have I enrolled in Yankee School? Bugger, this is annoying.'

Duran hissed, but he had been through worse situations and far worse forms of torture. And damn if he was going to be entertainment for three boys with zero tact and cliché attitudes. If his senior had taught him one thing was that tough appearances on the outside meant they were cowardly on the inside. Push the right buttons, and they'll be putty in your hands.

'Hah, you have the nerve to talk back to us. Cool, think I'm gonna have fun messing with you,' said the punk seated in the middle of the three.

He peered at Duran through cold, blue eyes. A smirk twisted his thin lips. They rose from their seats to approach Duran's desk and tower over him with intimidation.

Perhaps if he was in his old school, he would've been afraid by their show of butch bravado. Right now, he was ticked off and ready to retaliate.

'Kakeru-san. Thank you for teaching me to be strong.' His heart raced as he thought fondly of his senior.

'Fine.' He rose met their challenge for a fight.

'Reo, Tai, Tats, who's the new kid?' Another boy called out from the classroom entrance. He coolly made his way Duran.

Unlike the Three Putty Boys (Duran had termed his bullies), the guy making his way to him was a typical Japanese boy slightly taller than himself.

This Japanese boy stopped a few paces before him and stared him in the eye with a fierce gaze from his dark almond eyes. Duran met his stare with determination not to back down.

'Hah! I see you have some fight in you.' He acknowledged through a cocky smirk.

He sat at the seat of the desk next to him, relaxing with his feet up on Duran's desk.

Duran's heart raced, sensing a presence that was

similar to his beloved senior.

'At ease gentlemen.' He waved down the Putty Boys who returned to their seats.

'So, what do people call you?'

'Kita.' Duran frowned.

'What was that? I couldn't hear you.' The Japanese boy teased him.

'Oh, then how about Kissmyass,' he answered back with a louder voice.

The boy burst with laughter.

'You're late to class today Miwa. We're done with English already,' said one of the Putty Boys to the Japanese boy.

'I had a meeting for class presidents and bullshit,' Miwa explained with a bored sigh.

'You're a refreshing change aye?' Miwa said to Duran.

Duran cursed his stupid racing heartbeats and thoughts that retrieved his senior's gentle smile.

Miwa removed his feet from Duran's desk and sat up to give the foreign looking boy before him more attention.

'Seriously, what's your name?'

'He calls himself Kita, Duran,' a Putty Boy answered for him.

Miwa stood with eyes glaring daggers. He slapped the boy in the face.

Other chatter in the classroom fell quiet.

Duran saw some groups make their way out of the room. He groaned, feeling he had signed up to a school full of delinquents mistakenly, but it was too late to turn back now. His mother had made a financial commitment for the first two terms. If he had to change, he wouldn't be able to until at the end of spring.

'I didn't ask you to tell me his name did I?' Miwa hissed and turned his attention back to Duran.

'Is that your name? Kita, Duran.'

Duran nodded.

'You need to forgive these apes bad manners. They can't help it when they don't have much of a brain between their ears,' Miwa whispered to Duran.

Duran saw the guys tense and their jaws go stiff, but neither did anything to retaliate. He wondered what Miwa had done in the past to make the tough teens subservient to him.

'You just got here. Let me show you the school.' Miwa gave Duran a warm smile.

'You apes go hit a tree or something.' He laughed at the other boy's grumbles.

Duran wanted to reject the request, but he sensed it wasn't a good idea, so allowed Miwa to guide him out of the classroom and down the hallways.

He was expecting their direction to turn into a bathroom and his head requiring a towel-dry after being dunked. It didn't happen.

Outside the classroom, Miwa was living up to his example of a class president. His personality was amicable when the Putty Boys weren't around. Miwa was a polite, friendly and model student.

'Tell me about yourself Duran,' Miwa cordially asked as they strolled the classroom corridors.

The causal use of his given name had startled Duran that he was too stunned to answer.

'I can tell from your reaction, you're not used to people you've barely met calling you by your first name. We're in a British run school that encourages western customs. In western culture, everyone is called by their first name.' Miwa explained on the cultural norm.

It was the first time Duran heard a school using this custom and wondered if his class president was taking him for a ride until they encountered the escorting teacher a corridor.

'Oh good, Miwa's showing you around. I hope you enjoy your time here Duran,' he said before moving on.

'You weren't joking.' Duran was astonishment and felt weird, like his first kiss had been taken.

'Um, what's your family name if your given name is Miwa?' He blushed when the boy's given name came out of his mouth.

'Kasamatsu. Hey, if we strung our family names together it sounds kind of cool. Kasamatsu-Kita,' Miwa cheerfully said.

'Sounds like the name of a law firm.' Duran joked.

Miwa laughed and slapped his back, drawing out Duran's smile.

For the first time that day Duran felt the skies had opened and a ray of light to shone through to break away his dampened mood.

Their conversation was light and cheery as they continued their walk around the school, returning to their class before the lesson bell rang.

Duran was pleasantly surprised when the rest of his school-day had passed without incident.

As the day progressed, more of his classmates had opened up to him. Most of them girls who expressed their appreciation for his bravery against the punks even though it was Miwa who had saved him from their retaliations.

Miwa was his friend by the end of the day,

swapping email details with him. Duran was relieved he ended up being a nice guy. Although a screw came loose whenever the Putty Boys were around.

All in all, his first day was typical. He recapped on the bus ride home; mental images surfacing with his reflection on the bus's window. The day was good because of Miwa.

His mind lingered Miwa's image of piercing almond eyes on an appealing countenance with flawless skin and a serious smile. His black bangs and clean cut hair gently framed his oval face. He wore their uniform properly in a pristine condition that was downplayed by his coolness.

Duran's lips twitched with a lustful smile.

'Miwa.' He breathed on the window to make it frost.

His index finger drew the shape of a heart from the frost, stirring up his heart beats. They beat faster as he whispered Miwa's name a second time. He sighed, realizing his trouble and wiped away the heart outline.

'Here I go again.' He wiped Miwa's image clean from his mind.

If he wanted to blend in, he had to be like everyone else. He returned home, drilling this mindset into himself.

This new mindset was working for him the following days and weeks at school. He had formed a typical friendship with Miwa and another with a shy bookworm named Riko Shirogane.

Riko wore her black and white sailor's uniform conservatively; brown hair in braids with a delicate wisp of bangs brushing against her thin brows and soft round eyes of a mellow brown quality. She hid her dainty beauty behind thick rimmed glasses, which were balanced on her cute button nose and complimented her heart-shaped face.

'Kita-kun, it looks like you're enjoying school life now,' she said to him as they made their way down the school hallways for their next lesson.

'It did start off shaky, but it's all good now.' He smiled warmly at her.

She was the only one who referred to him in the correct manner, which he was grateful.

'Ugh, gross! Nerd freak alert.' A glamour girl badmouthed Riko as she purposely knocked into her shoulder as she strutted past them.

This girl was overly done up with make-up, hair in a fashionable ponytail with a soft sweep of bangs to frame a face that was pretty, but wouldn't be considered model material. Duran turned up his nose at the overpowering stench of sweet perfume coming off body. He frowned at her A-line skit that was riding too far up her thighs. He wondered why she wore a skirt at all.

She said more bad words about Riko to her group of clones that came up behind her.

The rude attitude from the bunch of try-hard idols ticked him off.

'At least she's not stinking of cheap air-freshener,' he answered back to the girls.

'Who are you? Her boyfriend?!' The girl jeered then blushed when she got a better look at his face.

Duran placed his arm around Riko's shoulders who twitched nervously within his hold.

'What of it?'

The girls gawked at him with gaping mouths and

puzzled expressions. It was clear they were unable to understand why a guy like him was with a girl they saw as distasteful.

'Whatever.' The glamour girl brushed off.

The girls moved on from them, whispering with disbelief.

'Haha! I love seeing those type of girls stumped.' He chuckled.

'Kita-kun you shouldn't encourage that behaviour,' Riko reprimanded him in a quiet scholarly manner.

'I know, you're right Shiro-chan. I can't help myself sometimes. I hope it doesn't cause you any trouble.' Duran grimaced realizing there might be a consequence.

'It's okay Kita-kun. You were standing-up for me. I'm thankful.' She reassured him and thanked him again with a courteous bow.

'Okay then. So, we have music now?' He asked to change the subject.

'Yes with Nakatani-sensei. He was once a professional concert pianist before becoming a teacher.'

Duran noticed a dreamy admiration to her voice and a fire in her eyes he hadn't seen from her before.

'Wow Shiro-chan, you seem particularly eager for the lesson,' he chuckled at the sight of her blushes.

It made him wonder what kind of teacher Nakatani was to steal the heart of his friend. He received his answer when they entered the music room and saw their teacher setting out worksheets on their desks. He was freaking hot! Nakatani-sensei was young for a teacher and a mix of some kind with bright-green eyes, an amiable face, well-formed body and brown hair kept in a respectable cut with a wisp of fringe over his brows. His clothes were less formal than the other teachers with his long sleeves rolled up and tie removed.

'Okay, I get it now,' Duran whispered to her who wasn't paying him any attention.

Her eyes darted between their teacher and the desk they were headed toward.

The music room was a small auditorium with the desks stepping downward toward a small stage that had an arrangement of instruments, music stands and chairs positioned behind a grand piano.

Duran and Riko took a seat in the second row of desks next to Miwa who had arrived before them.

'You took your sweet time,' Miwa said as he was getting out his music textbook from his bag.

'Says he who looks like he got here just before us. How did the meeting go?' Duran asked as he took his seat next to his friend.

Miwa had a meeting with his homeroom teacher to discuss some class business during their break.

'Looks like Reo's gonna get expelled,' he whispered carefully to him.

'Why?'

'He was caught stealing answer sheets by one of the teachers. It's not the first time,' he explained, not hiding his disappointment.

The topic changed directions to the lesson when they heard their other classmates take their seats near them.

Nakatani-sensei stood on the stage to address them.

'Welcome everyone. Today we're going to learn about a Polish pianist named Frédéric Chopin,' he said enthusiastically.

'Has anyone heard of him before?' He asked the class and received a lot of blank stares. He moved to the grand piano and started playing a piece.

Duran was spellbound by the romantic tale his teacher's fingers were drawing out from the piano's velvety notes. He realized he heard the song before at his old music school.

'That's a Preludes Op. 28!' He blurted and felt embarrassed.

'Very good,' his teacher called out and stopped playing.

Nakatani-sensei stood to see who had made the outburst and saw Duran sinking lower into his seat. All his classmates' eyes pointed his way.

'Aah, it was you?' Nakatani-sensei asked Duran.

Duran nodded.

'You play already don't you?'

Duran nodded again.

'I figured as much.' Nakatani-sensei smiled warmly.

He had the class open their textbooks, and went over theory on a whiteboard on the stage near a set of music stands.

'He performed his improvisation on a mechanical organ, which was ground breaking innovation at the time.

It eventually led to a recital before Tsar Alexander I. He was so impressed with the performance, he gifted Chopin with a diamond ring—' His lecture ran on.

Duran felt a sense of peace as his teacher told him more about the life of Chopin and the strange world he was from. He was sad when the bell rang to end the lesson.

'That was a good class Shiro-chan,' he said to Riko

with a wink.

Riko nodded her head in response and quickly packed up her bag. She froze when their teacher stopped them from leaving the room.

'Sorry, Kita-kun, is it? May I have a moment of our time,' Nakatani-sensei said.

Riko, Miwa and Duran shared glances.

'Sir, did he do something wrong,' Miwa said, his lips twitching to defend his friend.

'Um, sorry about earlier Sensei. I shouldn't have interrupted your lesson.' Duran apologized with a bow.

'No, no, I was curious if you could play,' Nakatani-sensei asked with a playful smile.

Duran sighed.

'I'm just a kid. I've only heard my music teacher play it,' he said with hope it would deter his teacher from the idea of him being able to play Chopin.

'Humour me.' Nakatani-sensei gestured to the grand piano on the stage.

Duran paused, thinking on a million excuses of why he couldn't play. When he looked into his teacher's imploring eyes, he ended up nodding his head and stepping on the stage with his friends and teacher behind him.

He gingerly took his position on the stool before the piano's 88 keys and stretched out his hands. He felt the eyes of his friends and teacher boring into his back as he started recreating the piece his teacher had played in class.

It was the same song, but the notes sounded lonelier under his touch. The music flowed and intertwined into everyone's senses, drawing them into a semi-cataleptic state. Time ticked by for a few silent minutes before they snapped out of their state.

'Wow Duran that was, wow!' Miwa exhaled his awe.

'Unbelievable. It was lonely, but beautiful at the same time,' Riko whispered through her reverie.

'I knew it was you. I saw your face and remembered a kid who brought the house down at last year's summer recitals at Suntory Hall,' Nakatani-sensei said with a beaming smile.

'Well that was last year. I don't play recitals any more.' Duran set the fact straight as he picked up his bag and shuffled off the stool.

'Why?' His teacher questioned.

'Because I don't. Sensei, I'm sorry again about before. I promise I won't interrupt your lesson again. I'm hungry. Please excuse me.' He ended the conversation with a bow and made his way up the stairs for the exit.

'Hey Duran wait up!' Miwa called out to him.

He and Riko bowed and hurried after Duran, leaving their puzzled teacher behind.

They caught up to Duran in the hallway.

'Why don't you play recitals any more?' Miwa asked Duran politely as they headed to the school cafeteria.

'Because I don't,' Duran replied.

'You're so good. I can't understand why,' Miwa said, pushing for more of an explanation.

Duran sighed and led them to a corner out of earshot from other people.

'I brought shame to my teacher at last year's performance,' he whispered.

'The general audience liked my rendition of Mozart's piano sonata, but the musical society committee thought my playing was unrefined and too emotional. One of the members said my playing was like a monkey wearing a cowboy hat banging on the keys.'

'Ouch! That's brutal,' Miwa winced.

'Tell me about it. I would've been crucified further if it was a proper competition. It's no secret that I'm not a Committee favourite. So, I decided to leave before I would cause further shame,' Duran said with remorse.

'That's ridiculous! You're really talented, I don't get it.' Riko piped up with passion that surprised the boys.

'When you get fired up, you get fired up.' Duran chuckled.

'I'm sorry Kita-kun it's just you're playing just now moved me. I don't know anyone here who could play as well as you except Sensei.' She blushed.

'It comes back to Sensei.' Duran teased her with a cheeky smile.

'What about Sensei?' Miwa asked, feeling he was missing out on something.

'Nothing.' Duran brushed off and led his friends back on to the path to the cafeteria, both he and Riko ignoring Miwa's insistent prying.

Eventually, another school-day had reached an end. He parted ways with his friends and took his usual route back to his home.

'Tadaima,' Duran said wearily as he walked through the front door of his apartment and removed his shoes.

A rich, beefy, aroma tickled his nose as he stepped into the modest sized lounge-room that was adjoined to a modern kitchenette.

'Okaeri,' Isagi-chichi greeted him warmly from the kitchenette.

He had all four burners balancing steaming pots and a colourful array of diced vegetables, rice noodles and bean curd portions spread out over the kitchen counter.

'Um, dad what's the occasion?' Duran dropped his bag and shuffled onto a stool before the counter to watch his dad in action.

'A new recipe I want to try,' Isagi-chichi said excitedly as he leaned over the counter to give him a peck on the cheek.

'Ugh, come on dad. I'm not a kid any more.' Duran cringed and wiped his cheek.

'Hah, I guess you're not. Can't a dad show a little affection to his son now and then?'

'It's embarrassing,' Duran said bluntly and pilfered a piece mushroom.

'Hey, wait for dinner!'

Duran flashed him a cheeky grin. His father sighed.

'So, how was school?'

'It was school,' Duran nonchalantly answered.

'And?'

'Nothing much happened. Had music today. The teacher forced me to play a Chopin song for him.'

'Really, in front of your class?' Isagi-chichi was worried. His mind relapsed to knowledge of his son's trauma the year before.

'Naw, just my two friends after the class ended,' Duran said to hopefully ease his father's tension.

'How did that go?' Isagi-chichi continued to ask with his attention to his cooking.

His mind was stewing on his worries. It would kill

him if his son faced another year of persecution. No amount of right and wrongs would be able to stop him from doing something unthinkable to protect his son.

'They seemed to like it.' Duran forced a lighter tone to reassure his father that he was fine.

'That's good then.' Isagi-chichi sighed. His grip eased on the spoon he was using to stir ingredients within the cooking pot.

'Speaking of music, did you have that talk with Masato-san?' Duran asked and waited for his father's response.

'Why would you want to know whether I talked with your former music teacher?' Isagi-chichi frowned, not liking where the conversation was going.

Duran sighed seeing the instant droop to his father's shoulders. The smile on his face had eased into an expression of bitterness.

'I'm sorry Dad.'

'That's okay. But son, what's between Masato-san and I are for adults to be concerned with.'

'I know, it's just, I thought it'd lead to a happy ending.' Duran had hoped that through all the previous year's troubles, something good could've remained.

He felt guilty he had broached the subject.

Isagi-chichi smiled and squeezed his cheeks.

'Coom owff it!' Duran protested between cheek squeezes.

He rechecked his jaw was still in place when his dad released him.

'Promise me you'll stay pure-of-heart forever,' Isagi-chichi said warmly.

Duran smiled and shuffled off the stool to see if

he could help. His father had him adding ingredients into the pots and cleaning up some mess. They were almost finished with their cooking creation when they heard a forceful rap on their door.

'You're expecting someone?' Duran questioned and felt concerned by his father's reaction.

'Keep cooking,' Isagi-chichi ordered him and went to check who was at the door.

Duran finished off the cooking in his father's place. A heated conversation caught his attention as he was turning off the burners.

He hurried to the door to see who was bothering them and saw a high school student shouting out curses like a madman at their door.

'What's going on dad?' He asked concern.

'Son, go back inside. I'll deal with this,' Isagi-chichi ordered him.

But Duran wasn't going to back down. All these intrusions to their life. Enough was enough.

'What's a high school student doing here? Who the hell are you raising your voice at my dad at our door!' Duran shouted at the guy.

'High school student? Wait one minute kid. I'm well over twenty.' The madman snapped at Duran.

Duran stepped forward to give him a good kick back from the door.

'You don't act like an adult. If you haven't got anything good to say, bugger off!' He yelled and slammed the door on the guy's face.

'Duran! What the hell you think you're doing?!' Isagi-chichi berated him.

'He was yelling at you Dad! Are you going to let someone like that curse you in our home? I've had it with people thinking they can give us shit and get away with it!'

His father surprised him when he burst with laughter. A smile relaxed his expression.

'You sometimes surprise me when that fight of yours comes out. Just like your mother,' he said fondly and ruffled Duran's hair.

There was knocking again. A lot quieter and void of anger this time. His father opened the door.

The madman was standing there with an expression of apology on his face. He bowed low before them.

'Please, accept my apology. I didn't realize you had a son home with you,' he said.

'What would've happened if I wasn't around?' Duran calmly asked.

'Could I please come in to explain myself?' He politely asked them.

His father gave Duran a signal to go further inside, which Duran obeyed this time.

He perched himself on a stool and watched his father lead the unexpected guest into the lounge-room. The guy looked even more apologetic when he saw he had interrupted their meal time.

His father went to the kitchenette to make some tea. Duran intensely scrutinized the stranger seated on their two-seat sofa from his perch

The man looked like a second year high school student based on his youthful image and style of clothing consisting of the latest fashion being an army style parka, Indie Rock T-shirt and jeans. His black fringe swept stylishly across his forehead and covered part of his right eye. The rest of his hair was cut in short layers, which aesthetically framed his heart-shaped face. His left ear lobe was garnished with a silver sleeper earring. Duran frowned at the man's black painted nails, wondering if he was a Gothic Metal-head.

He stared into the guy's chocolate coloured eyes, wondering why he'd try to lie about his age. His frown lifted with surprise at the mature coolness he sensed behind them.

'I see you're working out my danger level,' the guy said to break their silence. There was no malice behind his words.

'Why'd you—' Duran was cut short by his dad's return to the lounge-room with two cups of tea in his hand.

'Son, go to your room. I'll be fine,' Isagi-chichi said.

'No, someone's gotta watch your back.' Duran wasn't going to budge, determined to protect his father.

'Fine,' his father sighed and turned this attention to the man.

'Now, who are you and why were you raging before my door,' Isagi-chichi asked coolly.

The guy calmly introduced himself as Shintarou Akira. He explained that he was Masato-san's lover. Or so he was led to believe.

'I went to surprise Masato-san at his unit since I hadn't seen him for so long. I was going to take him out for our anniversary. When I got there, I saw him in bed with you. I ran out of the place and lost it. I came back to confront Masato-san. He confessed he was seeing another man. I keep demanding him to tell me a name, screaming at him. He broke down and told me who you were, so I stole your details from his contact list. It's been doing my head in for a few days now. I couldn't get it out of my mind. My anger drove me here. It didn't occur to me you met him through your son. When I saw your son, I...' Akira-san sobbed loudly.

Duran felt awkward by the revelation of a love triangle his father was knee-deep in.

He shuffled off the stool for the tissue box at the end of the counter and handed some to Akira-san.

'Th-Thank you,' Akira-san said as he grabbed them and blew out his woes.

'I'm sorry Akira-kun. I didn't know.' Isagi-chichi apologized.

'If it makes you feel better. We were both dumped by him. He broke up with me after I saw him at lunch with another man he was kissing passionately with. I confronted him, and he said it was a good time while it lasted.'

'Seriously?' Akira-san stopped his crying. He realized the truth from Isagi-chichi's eyes.

'Oh God! I'm so sorry. I thought you were the enemy. I thought. I'm sorry.'

Akira-san started bawling again, taking more tissues from Duran who was stood awkwardly before him with the box in an outstretched hand.

'Son, it'll be okay now. Why don't you go to your room?'

'Okay, but scream out if he gets psycho.'

Duran gave Akira-san the tissue box and a kill gesture before he ran off to his room. He kept his door ajar as he listened to his father and Akira-san's conversation, which lasted for a further twenty minutes. He re-entered the lounge-room when Akira-san was taking his leave.

'I'm very sorry for interrupting your dinner. Thank

you Isagi-san for being very kind to me, especially when I barged in crazily. You're a nice man.' Akira-san bowed and left their care.

'Well, that was interesting?' Duran sighed, relieved. He faced father and saw the man's crestfallen expression.

'Dad. There's a reason why Masato-san is a former for both of us. He doesn't deserve to be in our lives, right?' Duran reassured his father.

Isagi-chichi pulled him into a tight hug and cried onto his shoulders.

'I'm sorry. I didn't want you to see this. God knows you've been through enough drama.' He cried.

'It's okay Dad. It'll be alright, but I'm not sure about dinner,' Duran said lightly to break the mood.

Isagi-chichi chuckled and pulled away, wiping off his tears.

'Let's see what we can salvage,' he said, showing a bit of his usual cool self.

Duran helped him fix dinner and his father's sadness.

The rest of their night was uneventful, carrying that sentiment into the next few days.

Duran was happy to see that his father had found another reason to smile when Akira-san had returned the following days with further apologizes and peace offerings. He was relieved that the man ended up a nice guy, and seemed a good fit for his dad. Perhaps this time his father would have someone decent to love.

Love. This was another matter for Duran. A nerve-racking sentiment. One he wasn't sure he would be able to handle after his last brush with it. Regardless, he would have to face love anyway. On his birthday.

The day before his fifteenth birthday, he had his friend's over to secretly celebrate the day with him.

None of his friends and peers were aware that he was born on the same day as that St. Valentines celebration.

This year he did have fun making chocolates with Miwa and Riko at his place. They had made bags of bear shaped chocolate for their classmates and the teachers they respected as a good-will gesture.

On a windy cold Tuesday, he met up with Miwa outside their school footlockers and off-loaded some hoard to him for carrying.

Riko was also meant to meet up with them there, so she could start handing out the chocolates to their classmates and teachers since it would be weird for a guy to do it. But she was nowhere to be found.

'Wah, this bag is heavy do you think we went over-kill?' Miwa said as he slung a full shopping bag over his shoulder.

'I don't think so. It's for the whole class after all.' Duran frowned when he couldn't see Riko anywhere.

He pulled out his mobile phone that was vibrating in his back pocket, and saw a text from her that said she was running late and would meet them in class.

'She better be there. I'm not going to hand these out,' he declared as he pocketed his phone.

They arrived to their homeroom class that had most of their classmates buzzing excitedly around their desks about who had received or was going to receive chocolates. Riko wasn't among the group.

'Where is Shiro-chan? I can't believe that girl's

gonna pike out on us. It was her idea to begin with,' he complained and received an "I-don't-know" look from Miwa.

They both stowed away the goodies in their desks and went to look for her. They found her in the music room talking with someone concealed behind the whiteboard.

Duran was about to call out to her when Miwa slapped a hand over his mouth and drew him away.

They crept around the back corner that was away from her line of sight and the person she was talking to. Neither boys said a word as they watched their friend's love confession unfold.

Both her hands were holding out her bag of home-made chocolates to Nakatani-sensei, who was blushing like a fool at her gesture.

'Sensei, please accept these, showing my respect and admiration for you and,' Riko sighed away the rest of her words and bowed low with the chocolates shaking nervously in her hands.

'You made these?' He was surprised.

Riko nodded her head.

'Okay, I'll accept them Shirogane-chan. I do appreciate your feelings,' Nakatani-sensei responded warmly with a deep blush.

He removed them from her hands with a soft touch that surprised Duran.

Nakatani-sensei gently lifted her chin, so they were staring into each other's eyes.

Duran felt a moment of time pausing around them as they slipped into their own world.

'A month will change for me. I'll be able to give you a proper answer then. Will you wait for me?' Nakatani-sensei asked her and stroked her cheek lovingly.

Riko blushed and nodded.

'Arigatōgozaimashita,' she thanked him with a modest voice and slowly backed away to head to class.

Miwa and Duran crept out of the room before they could be spotted.

They hurried down the hallway, pumped with adrenaline.

'This is good, right, Miwa?' Duran said, hoping what he saw was a good thing for his friend.

'Good or dangerous. Duran, no one must ever know. It'll cause trouble for both of them if people knew,' Miwa whispered carefully with his eyes darting about to ensure no one was in eavesdropping range.

Miwa and Duran made a pact not to mention anything about what they had witnessed to anyone, even to Riko, to protect her.

Riko arrived to class when they did. She handed out the chocolates to their appreciative classmates and teachers thus completing their mission. Outwardly, she was her usual quiet, inexpressive self, but Duran caught her letting out a few dreamy sighs and smiles every so often.

'Hey Shiro-chan did something good happen?' He tested her during free-time of their English lesson, ignoring Miwa's warning looks.

'What do you mean Kita-kun?' She asked, struggling to hide her happiness.

'You seem on a high today. I like this side of you.' Duran smiled.

'Well it's Valentine's Day, the atmosphere has influenced my mood I guess,' she answered, evading the truth.

'I guess so,' Duran said to drop the conversation.

'Hey look who's the stud. Don't be jealous boys,' one of the apes gloated as he showed off his hoard to the other boys around him.

'Are you sure you didn't buy those for yourself Tats.' Miwa joked and laughed at the boy's embarrassed blushes and fumbled comebacks.

Duran sighed, hoping to receive chocolates from one person, but knew the chances of that ever happening were a million to none.

Throughout the day, they had fun keeping tabs on their classmates' confessions, and making bets on who would be answered on White Day.

The day ended quicker than usual with everyone coming down from the Valentine's buzz.

Riko was called into an after schoolbook club meeting, so Duran and Miwa made their way to their footlockers without her.

Duran frowned at the two large gift bags Miwa was carrying, filled to the brim with chocolates and gifts from many girls across their year. He felt a strong urge to throw them in a bonfire before Miwa had a chance to open them.

'You know, you have to give each one of them an answer,' he said coldly.

'I know, I know, but I can't say no to a gift that's been given with feelings.' Miwa sighed.

'Too many chocolates can make you sick.' Duran's frown deepened.

He didn't notice Miwa's eyes studying his expression as they approached their lockers.

'Don't tell me you're jealous that I got a lot and you didn't get any.' Miwa laughed.

'I wasn't looking for any,' Duran answered, not giving into Miwa's teasing.

'Really? So, there's no one that you want a confession from?' Miwa teased him further.

'I'm not telling you anything.' Duran opened his footlocker.

His frown turned into surprise when loads of fake cherry blossom petals, heart-shaped chocolates, and pink and red origami hearts scented with vanilla and strawberries, poured out of his footlocker.

'Woah! Check out Duran's locker. Some girl's gone all out.' A guy called out to his mates.

Duran was embarrassed.

He clumsily shoved the hearts, petals and origami back into this locker before more people could see.

'Back off guys. Nothing to see here.' Miwa pushed the onlookers away.

Duran quickly swapped his shoes and slammed the locker door shut.

He hurried out of the school grounds to get away from escalating attention. His mind and heart were racing to make his hands tremble with fear.

'Not again. Not again.' He mumbled as he blindly raced down streets to be as far as possible from school and danger.

Not aware that Miwa had been following him until he had overtaken him

'You're okay man? Was that too much for you?' Miwa asked him with genuine concern.

He had followed Duran at sprint out of the school gates and down a residential street leading to train station. It was the first time he had seen his friend look spooked.

Duran sighed. He took a diversion into a street playground and swing-set. They both occupied a swing next to each other as they talked.

'It was wonderful. Blew me away actually. Whoever set that up, they have strong feelings for me, and I feel sorry I can't return them.' Duran sighed.

'Why?' Miwa prodded.

Duran sighed again as he gave him an abridged version of his former school life, which saw to his ex-friends being traumatized like himself.

'I can't. Not again. I swear to make my heart off limits.'

'What's that supposed to mean?'

'It means just that.'

'Look. I understand your reservations, but you can't give up on love. You've got to keep living.' Miwa reasoned.

'I hear you Miwa. And I don't. I can't love again. I can't.' Duran argued back, feeling his nerves ease into anger.

'Bullshit! Sure you can. Or is it that you're so up in your head that you're above everyone else.'

'Why are you angry with me?'

'Because you're saying stupid things.' Miwa argued back.

'It's not stupid! I can't accept the feelings of a person I don't know because—' Duran stopped himself.

If he kept talking he would reveal that he had been thinking of Miwa in the same way he had regarded his ex-senior, which had caused a lot of trouble for everyone.

'Because of what?' Miwa goaded.

'Nothing.' He brushed Miwa's question aside and shuffled off the swing to resume their way home.

Miwa grabbed his arm to stop him. He yanked him around, so they could stare into each other eyes.

Duran gulped at Miwa's pain stricken face.

'What if I said I left those in your locker?' Miwa confessed.

'Yeah right, like you would do that.' Duran nervously laughed.

He stopped at seeing Miwa's serious expression.

'You're not shitting me? Why would you do that? Is this a joke!?' He demanded, hoping for the answer that he carried in his heart and prayed it wasn't a cruel prank.

'No! I would never be cruel to you like that.'

'Then why?' Duran whispered.

'I think you know why,' Miwa said and pulled Duran into a kiss.

Duran's heart thundered against his chest. He dropped his bag and wrapped his arms around Miwa's waist, not wanting to let him go as their kisses became deeper and more passionate. His entire body tingled with a lustful desire and an aching need to be held by him.

Gentle winds wrapped a protective shield of cold air around them as they burned into each other's embrace.

'W-Wait Miwa! What if someone sees us?' Duran forced himself back.

'Let them. I don't care. You love me too right?'

Duran swooned at Miwa's loving strokes to his cheek.

'My heart is going to burst.' Duran exhaled and received another one of Miwa's passionate kisses.

'Happy Birthday.' Miwa whispered between kisses.

The air became warmer with summer. Love

bloomed in Duran's circle.

Riko was quietly dating Nakatani-sensei who was no longer their music teacher. He had resigned from his post a month after her confession to work as an assistant music teacher in a high school within the Chiba prefecture. She spent time with him there. Any they could spare with permission and escort from her parents. Satisfying to their condition of being in a celibate relationship until she was of age for them to marry. It was fortunate that her family doted on her fiancé like he had always been part of the family.

Isagi-chichi was happy in love with Akira-san who enjoyed being a motherly influence to Duran. Not that Duran minded since he rarely saw his own mother.

Duran's own relationship with Miwa had deepened.

For the weeks following their transition from friends to lovers, it had been blissful.

'Too good to be true,' he mumbled to himself as he and his friends were headed to their homeroom class.

'What's too good to be true?' Riko asked.

'Nothing, just me mumbling nonsense.' Duran brushed aside her question.

'Are you staying over this weekend?' Miwa asked him with a suggestive grin.

'Yeah. Dad's spending a romantic getaway with Akira-san. Mom's still in Kyoto for work. I said I'll crash with you.'

'Cool. My uncle and aunt will be away, so it'll just be us.'

Duran knew he should have felt thrilled by the idea of him and Miwa having a weekend alone. He felt worried instead.

The last few nights he hadn't been able to sleep well with the memories of his recent past haunting his dreams. No one knew of the nights he woke up in a cold sweat and the brief throbbing pain he felt to his back from whiplash scars that had healed. Only just.

'What am I doing?' He panicked.

A boy loved with him for who he was. Couldn't he accept the happiness of his present and forget the past?

In his heart, he knew it wasn't that easy. The past had a way of catching up to people who chose to run from it.

Throughout the school-day, he existed in and out of his own thoughts. Trying to fight away his demons, which surfaced the more he embraced his reality with Miwa.

'What's going on in that head of yours?' Miwa whispered during their study time in the library.

He poked at Duran's head.

'Nothing.' Duran disregarded his question.

'You've been saying that a lot. Don't you love me any more?' Miwa frowned.

'What? Of course, I do. Don't say stupid things.' Duran reassured him.

'Then what's going on? You don't smile much these days. Sometimes you go into this trance.'

Duran wondered if he should tell him more about his previous year. Thinking about it made him feel tense.

'You're doing it now. Frankly, it's pissing me off.' Miwa growled.

'Oh man, I'm sorry. I have a lot of things on my mind right now.' Duran apologized and received a deeper frown from Miwa.

'I should be the only thing on your mind!' Miwa snapped.

He stormed out of the library.

'Shit.' Duran cursed under his breath.

He gathered his books and hurried after Miwa.

'Miwa!' He called out to him in the hallways, but Miwa kept on walking.

'Hey, please let me explain!' He called out to his lover again.

Miwa stopped and turned to face him.

'You know the term "let me explain" is commonly used when someone has lied to their lover, been caught cheating on them or breaking up with them.'

'I'm not cheating or breaking up with you.'

'Then you're lying to me,' Miwa stated.

'I'm not lying to you either,' Duran said, lowering his eyes.

'But you're keeping something from me. I can tell.'

Duran yelped when Miwa forced him into a corner away from prying eyes and pushed a kiss onto him. It wasn't the usual passionate, loving kind he was familiar with. This kiss was full of desperation and painful emotions. It was scary.

'Stop it!' Duran cried out, his mind racing with past fears.

Miwa slumped to Duran's chest and wrapped his arms around his waist.

'Can't you see what you've done to me? I think about you every night and day. How many times I want to hold you, kiss you. You tell me you have other things on your mind.'

'I'm sorry,' Duran whispered into his ear and stroked his hair.

'You have been on my mind. I've been stupid with worry that something might come along to hurt us. I don't want to see you hurt because I love you too much.' He reassured him.

'Yeah, you're an idiot. What could hurt two people in love?' Miwa said.

Duran didn't feel as sure as his lover. That sting of hurt from the past still lingered within him.

He could make up with Miwa and resume their happy relationship and friendship for the rest of the day.

The nagging foreboding kept surfacing in his mind the more he tried to push it away.

When he arrived home from school, he collapsed to his bed feeling drained.

He couldn't continue to wallow in the past, allowing it to affect his present.

The fear and feelings he felt from that time were becoming intense in parallel to his developing love for Miwa.

'Why can't you move on?' he yelled at himself.

He sighed and sat up from his bed to stare at his reflection in the full-length mirror nailed to the back of his door.

He removed his shirt. His eyes traced the lash scars he could see on his back.

Snippets of memory slashed into his mind, drawing out that intense cutting, stinging hot pain to his lower back, hips and knees. It hurt beyond imagining.

He collapsed to the floor short of breath.

'What am I going to do?' he panted and laid still to let the memory of the pain wash through him.

Move on. It was the only thing to do. He had

made that promise to himself for his family.

He sighed and closed his eyes.

The next days were calmer and lighter in mood as he gave Miwa extra attention than he had in the previous days.

'Keys, bag, phone.' He checked off before he locked up his home and headed out for a weekend at Miwa's.

The morning was fresh and bright like the feeling in his heart.

He had promised himself he wasn't going to spoil their weekend with all the negative thoughts and memories that had been plaguing him the past few weeks.

This was their moment to love each other openly, honestly and without restraint.

He carried his happy resolve all the way through the upper suburbs of suburbia to a large traditional house nestled in a corner of a street that was re-purposed with modern day apartments and houses.

Miwa was waiting for him on the wide front porch (engawa).

'You were quicker than I thought,' he said as he led him inside.

'Sorry for intruding,' Duran said as he followed Miwa to his room, which was simplistic and traditionally set with the typical tatami mats and a futon laid out in the middle of the floor.

Shoji doors were kept ajar to allow the summer breeze into the room.

Beyond the doors, Duran spied a tiny piece of paradise for a courtyard and feature garden.

'Wow this place is awesome.' Duran smiled as he

stepped out on to the courtyard engawa.

Miwa wrapped his arms around him and drew him into a kiss.

They made out on the porch under the sun's gentle warmth. The air was still around them as they slipped into their own world.

'Do you wanna have lunch?' Miwa pulled away, bringing them both back to reality.

Duran followed him into the kitchen.

They playfully made lunch together, which was a simple meal of noodles, rice, tempura fish and vegetables set out on a low dining table.

The sun's rays streamed through open windows and shoji ranma above the doorways, casting a gentle light over them as they shared their meal.

Having lunch in a house to themselves made Duran feel like they were a married couple. He was happy.

'I can't get enough of this,' he said dreamily.

He shuffled up close to Miwa, wrapped his arms around him and blew kisses on his neck.

'I'm still eating.' Miwa fumbled with his chopsticks.

'So am I,' Duran whispered as he licked and nibbled his way further down Miwa's neck.

His hands slipped underneath Miwa's T-shirt and played with his erect nipples.

Miwa dropped his appetite for food and drew Duran into a passionate kiss.

Abrupt knocking on the door paused their foreplay.

'Hey Miwa, open up! I lost my keys on the way here.' A deep voice bellowed from the other side of the front door.

'Who's that?' Duran asked and notice Miwa go

pale.

'My Aniki.' Miwa cringed.

The mood for love left them as they faced an unexpected intrusion.

Duran followed Miwa to the door.

'Man, you took your bloody time,' said a man who looked nothing like Miwa.

The proportion of his body was top-heavy, made obvious with his black t-shirt stretched tight across his burly chest and baggy jeans hanging low so the tops of his underwear were showing. His face was covered in a two-day growth and hair left scraggly.

A thought of ruffian entered Duran's mind the more he absorbed the man's appearance.

Miwa's older brother barged through the door and dumped his duffel bag onto Miwa's hands.

'Put that somewhere will yah,' he said as he made his way into the dining room.

'I smell something good. Man I'm starved.'

Miwa dropped the bag as if it was carrying a disease and stormed after his brother.

'What the hell are you doing here Yukio?!' He yelled.

His eyes narrowed at the sight of his brother scoffing down their lunch.

'Aunt saaid gof chukon 'em,' Yukio answered with a full mouth.

'That's not what I meant moron! Shouldn't you be in America?' Miwa cursed at him.

'I missed my Baby Bro too murch,' Yukio said as he swallowed down the rest of Miwa's fish.

He stretched his arms open for a hug.

'Not a chance Aniki.'

Yukio dropped his arms and turned his attention

to Duran.

'Who's the prince?' He eyed him suggestively.

Duran politely introduced himself and found himself pulled into Yukio's hug.

'I'll hug you since my Baby Bro is being stubborn.' Yukio teased Duran.

'You're cute. You sure you're just Miwa's friend, you're his type.' He fondled Duran's butt. 'With a nice perky ass.'

Duran blushed with embarrassment.

'Stop molesting my friend!' Miwa yelled as he yanked Duran off Yukio.

'Come'on Miwa. I was only teasing.'

'You can tell Aunty and Uncle I'm fine. Go find a girl to shag and get lost!' Miwa started pushing Yukio toward the door.

His brother surprised attacked him with a kiss.

Miwa slapped his brother's face.

'What the hell are you doing?!' He shouted, wiping vigorously at his mouth.

'Giving you a greeting kiss.' Yukio smirked, unperturbed by the slap.

'That's bullshit.'

'Shall I give Kawaii-kun one too?' Yukio pushed his tease further, clearly enjoying the boys' livid reactions.

'Don't you touch him!' Miwa threatened the man.

'Okay. I'll leave him, but I ain't going anywhere. I came back from the States to see you. You kids, as you were.'

Yukio headed into the lounge-room and made himself comfortable on the two-seat sofa before the family TV.

Duran and Miwa isolated themselves to his room.

'I can't believe that idiot is back in the country.' Miwa was trembling with anger.

'He's your brother right?'

'Half. Has a different mother. I wish we didn't have anything to do with each other.' Miwa clenched his fists and gritted his teeth when they heard Yukio calling out for more food.

Miwa took up Duran's suggestion of being somewhere else and quietly packed a bag.

They crept out of the house when Yukio was taking a shower and caught the bus back to Duran's place, which assumed a peaceful haven for them.

They were unaware of the many missed calls Yukio left on Miwa's phone as they resumed their peaceful time together in the safety of Duran's room.

The Saturday that Duran and Miwa shared as lovers was the last time Miwa would see his aunt and uncle alive.

Freakish storms belted across the highways the following Sunday, causing his uncle's car to skid into an oncoming truck. His aunt and uncle had died upon impact.

Having no other living relative in Japan, Yukio became his legal guardian since the man was of age.

Straight after the funeral, Yukio made it a habit of dropping off and picking up Miwa every day from school.

Every time Duran and Riko asked Miwa to hang out they were rejected with the same explanation.

'I can't. My Aniki's expecting me to be home.'

The only time they could be together had been at school. But even then Miwa wasn't with them, his mind and attention was always elsewhere.

'Miwa, is everything okay?' Duran asked during one of their science lessons. His heart knew the truth that something was far from right, having recognized the same expressions he had been giving the year prior.

Tears welled in his eyes when his lover flinched at his touch. It was like of that time too. Only he had been the one to brush away the hand of the boy he loved to spare him trouble.

'I'm fine. Don't ask silly questions.' Miwa had given a poor excuse and left things at that.

The days became lonely and frustrating for Duran as he watched Miwa slowly slip away under his brother's isolation. Recognizing the signs of abuse and feeling helpless to do anything. He cried when he tried to hug and kiss Miwa at the gym lockers and was pushed away.

'Don't touch me any more.' Miwa had said to him before he left the room.

The last straw of Duran's patience was when he saw a sly smile from Yukio behind the wheel of his car as Miwa stepped into the passenger seat looking lost and defeated.

He spent that night being consoled by Riko and Nakatani-sensei, who were at a loss on how to help him with a situation they couldn't comprehend.

Nakatani-sensei had suggested he could use the school counsellor to intervene and find out what was going on.

Duran felt involving others would cause more harm than good. His experience was evident of that. No, he had to find a way to solve the problem on his own.

One day, Miwa was absent from school. Duran panicked with thoughts for the worst.

He kept dialling Miwa's mobile number and sighed with relief when it went through. His relief turned to fear when the voice on the other line was Yukio's.

'Where's Miwa?' He demanded.

'Not here,' Yukio curtly answered before hanging up on him.

None of his calls could connect to Miwa after that brief conversation.

Miwa didn't show up for school the following days. Duran had expressed his concerns to his homeroom teacher.

Sakurai-sensei said his brother had made arrangements so Miwa could be home-schooled temporarily.

Duran had taken a trip to Miwa's house and had been chased out by Yukio. He became a nervous wreck as to how he was going to save his lover. Especially when his access to him was cut off.

Yukio was picking up his school work and dropping it back every day. Miwa had been maintaining his grades and didn't show any outward signs of distress when his teacher made his home visits.

Duran spent the rest of his summer drowning in his worry about Miwa. He stopped telling people about his concerns and retreated inside himself as he fought against the feelings of longing and frustrations for the boy he loved.

One afternoon when he was walking home from school-day, he was so lost in his thoughts that he didn't register Yukio blocking his path near a street playground until he bumped into him.

'Kasamatsu-san! What are you doing here? Where's Miwa?!' Duran yelled and yelped when Yukio grabbed his arm and dragged him toward the swing sets.

'Let go of me!' He cursed.

Yukio pushed him onto a swing and ordered him to sit there, so they could have a chat.

'Why are you doing this to Miwa?'

'You mean to you.' Yukio sneered with a frightening tone of voice.

'You annoyed me when you both ran away from me that weekend.'

'When my brother came home with pest marks on his body. I naturally had to cover them with repellent marks. You left a lot of nasty bites in hard to reach places.' His foul breath burned into Duran's ear.

'You bastard! Why'd you do this to your own brother?!'

'He's my brother. It's my given right.' He stated.

His lips twitched with an evil smirk.

'I remembered an ad I saw about dealing with the source of problems to deter further pestilence.'

Duran screamed when Yukio pulled him off the swing and pushed him face down to the ground.

He struggled with all his might to try to free himself from Yukio's attack, but he was too pinned down.

Fears and feelings of his past where keeping his petrified to move, making his struggles in vain.

He gagged from the loose dirt that went into his mouth.

'That's a boy. I want to see what my brother loves about you.'

Duran squeezed his eyes closed as he felt his pants being yanked and his butt being exposed.

'Please God. Someone, save me.' He prayed and pleaded in his mind.

He heard a scuffle and thud, and felt Yukio's weight removed from his back.

He spluttered out dirt and shuffled to all fours. He felt his pants being pulled up.

Miwa helped him to his feet and pulled him into a hug.

'Duran! My God, I'm so sorry. I'm so sorry,' Miwa cried and fussed over Duran.

Duran stared at Yukio who was unconscious on the ground. Next to him was the baseball bat that Miwa had used to knock him out.

'I found out what he was up to and followed him. I lost him back a few streets, but worked out where he'd be.'

'I missed you so much.' Duran whimpered and gasped at the sickly sight of his lover's withdrawn face and wiry body covered in baggy mismatched clothes. Nothing like the self-assured Miwa he knew.

'Not here. Let's go somewhere to talk,' Miwa whispered carefully.

They stopped off at a 24-hour café a few blocks from where they were.

Miwa told Duran about his brother's threat.

'When he saw us together at the funeral, he told me he wanted to hurt you. If he saw any more kiss marks on my body that wasn't his, he said he will kill you.'

'Miwa. That's insane,' Duran whispered with a shaky voice.

His worry for Miwa was paramount.

'He's crazy. You have to leave him. Find away!'

'I have Duran. I have a wonderful cousin on my

mother's side who's a lawyer in America. He knows about my brother's twisted complex. He'll be here in two days to take me back with him in secret. I have to play good with Yukio until then.'

'No Miwa! After today, he'll hurt you. You can't go back with him! Stay with me.' Duran pleaded.

Miwa shook his head.

'No. If I do, he'll kill you. You know he's capable of that.' Miwa's hands trembled.

His face steamed with tears. 'I can't see you again after we leave this place.'

'Miwa. How can I be sure you'll be safe?'

'I gave your email address to my cousin. He said he'll let you know when I'm in America.'

'That doesn't answer for today. How will I know he won't hurt you when you return home? I'm scared he might kill you,' Duran cried. 'Miwa don't go back.'

'You don't,' Miwa cried. 'B-But you have to have faith. We both do.'

'I have to go back for your safety. Please don't look for me again. I'll contact you when the coast is clear,' he said bravely and stood to leave.

'I love you Miwa. Please stay safe.' Those were the last physical words Duran said to Miwa.

He never saw him after he had walked out of the café.

A few weeks later he had received the text from his cousin telling him that Miwa was in America. Safe from his crazed brother.

Present Day…
Duran fell silent before Isao. He forked at his noodles absent-mindedly, wondering what his senior

thought of him now since learning of his past.

'Holy crap. I gathered that guy was twisted, but to think he'd do that to his own brother.' Isao sighed.

He shook his head with disbelief and bit-back his disgust.

'What happened after had Miwa left? Please tell me his brother didn't come after you again,' he asked, concerned.

'I moved to live with my mother in the city before the new school year,' he answered Isao's question with an uneven breath.

'You didn't see him again until now?'

Duran released another sigh.

Isao was shocked and horrified by Duran's stalking experience.

As soon as Miwa had left the country, Yukio had constantly spammed Duran's phone with death threats or crude sexual invitation.

Yukio attempted seduction numerous times when he had trailed Duran home from school.

Duran had been able to cleverly dodge his tail by taking different routes. The incidents repeated and became frequent that they were affecting his school and home life.

With the trauma from this previous year still lingering, he couldn't cope. Especially when he had no one else on his side to stop the man's bullying.

Yukio took advantage of Duran's past to hound his life like a plaque until Duran's parents had enough evidence for police support.

'My mom confided to her boss who referred us to a police officer we could report incidents. We moved out of the prefecture. I was pulled out of that school.'

Duran faced Isao with warm smile.

'It wasn't all bad news. Mom ended up marrying that police officer and I became an Onii-san. Although, I didn't realize that fact until after they were wed.'

'So, what are you going to do now? He's found you. Are you going to tell your step-dad?'

'I can only live day to day. I'm sure as hell not going to let that bastard ruin my life again. Nor allow anyone else to bully me and give me trauma ever again. I'll have to face him and my fears properly one day. Yeah, my step-father needs to know. It's gonna freak my mom and dad out though.'

'Oh man, I'm sorry Kita-kun. If you hadn't come to my house, he wouldn't have found you.'

'No. I can't shake the feeling that he knew I'd be there somehow. Senpai, I'm worried I might have brought you trouble.'

'Don't worry about me. I'm gonna move out of that place in the next few days anyway. My brother's come back from Australia and said he wants us to bunk together. He's nothing like Miwa's brother. He's cool.' Isao reassured Duran.

'I can't help feel my troubles are nothing compared to what you've suffered Kita-kun. I'm grateful you trusted me with your story. I promise to keep it between us. Don't worry. I don't think you're less than a good person as well.'

'Thanks, Senpai.'

Duran noticed the time was late and called Ryuu-chichi to see if he was in the area.

His step-father could pick them both up and dropped Isao home first.

He told Ryuu-chichi about his run in with Yukio shortly afterwards.

Neither said another word about it on the car-ride home. Duran could see Ryuu-chichi's face twitching with worry.

Duran pulled his mother into a big, squeezy, hug when he entered his home and saw her potting around in the kitchenette.

'I love you mom,' he whispered to her before pulling away and heading off to his room.

He slumped onto the stool before his keyboard and stared, absent-mindedly, at the keys for a long time.

He didn't hear Himeko and his mother enter his room. Nor notice them sit on his bed.

'Duran.' His mother's voice pulled him from his thoughts.

They wrapped him with a supportive hug.

'It's okay. I'm not going to cry about it any more.'

'That's not why we're hugging you. Son, you've gone through so much already. I hope you see what a strong person you are. When you deal with this Kas-bastard, I know you'll win against him this time and end this pain for good,' his mother said proudly.

'I have to face him don't I?'

'That and a lot of things you've been running from. One day.'

'Today, let's have pancakes. I feel like stuffing my face with a pork and ham flavoured one,' Himeko said lightly.

Duran chuckled.

'One day at a time,' he thought.

A smile lifted his expression when he realized that he could stop his seniors' bullying experience.

It was of that moment that he felt determined to ensure his past trauma could always be a strength for others against their own bullying situations. A sweet justice. One to celebrate with pancakes.

☠ THE GHOST OF 1-D

Shouta and Isao were back at school, doing well and looking healthy again. Duran was good with his word about cooking wholesome meals for Shouta to help his recovery for Mid-term examinations. He cooked at Shouta's place every second day.

When word leaked about his delicious home-cooked meals that was boosting Shouta's high scores, Shouta's place eventuated as the preferred place for studying or mucking up with a meal.

Shouta entertained Himeko, their friends, Isao and his classmates on the days Duran cooked.

A few times Rintarou had dropped over to study with them, mentoring them on some curly parts.

Mid-term examinations eventually came to a conclusion with Duran and his friends passing decent grades.

Duran was still waving around his results slip proudly to others and bragging to Himeko.

He annoyingly waved his straight A's at her face as they made their way across the courtyard for the gymnasium, knowing this would stir a reaction from her. He was in a devilish mood.

Their homeroom classes shared a Physical Education lesson towards the end of a Wednesday. So, both were geared up in their sports uniform of navy sweat pants and white T-shirt, ready to burn calories and break a sweat.

'Hey. Check my flush A's. Take that Himeko!' Duran teased his competitive sister.

'It's not poker Nii-san,' Himeko pouted. 'You got lucky with your answers.'

'Hah! Luck has nothing to do with being a genius baby.'

'You mean being a smart-arse. I still say the results were rigged.'

'Then what does yours say eh?'

Himeko zipped her lips and stormed a head of him.

Duran laughed. He had heard about her mixture of B's and C's from Mei and Kou, and her outrage and whining about being robbed from the 'A ' that she deserved.

Kou had laughed when he recounted the puffy flared up expression on her face, comparing it to the Incredible Hulk's.

He followed Himeko's trail into the gym and saw her complaining to Mei near the gym ropes.

'Man. Is Hime-chan still pissed with her B's and C's?' Fumio asked as he came up behind Duran.

'What you guys talking about,' Aki asked as he came up behind them.

'Himeko.' Duran answered.

'Aah. She still peeved about her B's and C's,' he said nonchalantly.

Aki and Fumio laughed as they told him about a sports relay the three of them were in back at their middle school.

She was fully pumped and boasting with bravado at how they were going to win and the other teams were sad-sorry losers.

When they lost, she was like Nick Kyrgios on a tennis court, swearing aloud foul curses and throwing batons everywhere that almost struck a teacher.

'Thing is, we came second and won by default,' Aki chuckled.

'Hey. What's funny?' Saski came up behind them.

'Himeko.'

'Haha! Still moping about her B's and C's.' Saski grinned.

'Alright, alright, everyone front and center!' Watanabe-sensei called for everyone's attention.

The students giggled at his sports get-up. He was wearing a sweat shirt with a loud message of *wake me when you go-go*, bright blue neoprene pants, black nylon shorts and a matching blue sweat band across his forehead.

'Pfft. Sensei what's with the #badboy eighties look.' Kou let out a mocking laugh.

'*Tsk*. This is the proper attire for teaching physical-ed.' Watanabe-sensei replied seriously.

'I can see why your day job's a science teacher.'

'If Moriyama-sensei didn't come down with the flu I would've been happily mixing my concoctions in my lab. Since I'm here, NO TALKING!' Watanabe-sensei blew his coach's whistle so loud it screeched throughout the gymnasium.

He organized the students into five lines and pushed them into sprints, jumps and rope climbs until their breaths were burning against their chests.

'Water, I need water.' Himeko collapsed to the floor, spread-eagle and panting.

'Com'on Suzuki-kun! No pain, no gain!' Watanabe-sensei blew his whistle over her head.

She jumped up and cursed at her teacher who was chasing her up and down the gym with terms that was supposed to motivate her.

'Damn you *baka* teacher!' Himeko cried out as she found herself pushed to the limit with non-stop laps.

All her classmates erupted with laughter at the

sight of her flailing limbs and the contorted expression on her face.

She eventually called it quits and collapsed next to Duran who tried to hide his laughter whilst rubbing feeling back into her back.

'Well done Suzuki-kun. Take five,' Watanabe-sensei said proudly. He went off to find another victim for his motivation.

'Why does he have to be our club adviser? Why God? I ask why?!' Himeko cried out.

'He got you running.' Duran snorted.

'That man's gonna kill us.' Aki collapsed next to him and guzzled down a full sports bottle of water.

'Hey, you'll get a tummy ache drinking like that.' Mei warned Aki as she sat next to him.

'My whole body's aching. What does it matter?' he said wiping at his mouth.

'Why aren't you sweating like the rest of us?' Aki eyed Mei suspiciously.

'Unlike you, I can easily handle these tests,' Mei said with her usual serious manner as she re-adjusted her glasses on her nose.

'Or maybe you're good at skipping out.' Aki grumbled.

Mei ignored him.

All the students sighed with relief when the end-of-lesson bell rang. They scrambled into the change rooms to redress in their uniforms.

Duran made his way to his English lesson back in his homeroom class.

Harada-sensei was apparently the English expert, which amounted to the vocabulary of a first year middle school student. As Duran was quite versed in the language, the class was his time to zone-out.

He was about to nod off during free-time when he caught on to a hush conversation Chiasa and her friend were having about strange things that went bump at night at an old abandoned classroom of the Clubroom Block behind the gymnasium.

'I tell you Chia-chan, the old 1-D class is haunted.'

'Suki-chan that's stupid.' Chiasa brushed off.

'It's not stupid! You remember that guy who, like, drowned last year at the summer festival? That was his class before they moved all the rooms to Block-B and C. Like, my boyfriend swears he heard howling and heavy footsteps from that room late one night.' Her friend emphasized dramatically.

'He was passing near the lower-ground floor stairs and, like, heard the noise. He got to the floor and 1-D's door. The noise stopped. There was no one there. No lights. The door was locked. He went back up the stairs, it started up again. It freaked him out, he ran outta the place.'

'I don't believe you. That guy died nowhere near the school.'

'Doesn't matter. His spirit must be, like, attached to that room, like they say in those ghost shows and stuff. Hey, maybe a girl he crushed on was there. Like, he didn't tell her before he died. He still has unfinished business. Oh! The boiler room is near it too. Like, he could get in from the pipes and taps,' her friend said excitedly.

'Nah.' Chiasa try to brush off again, but found her friend's explanation so farfetched it could likely be true. 'You really think his ghost is there?'

'I believe it. I mean, it's like The Ring. That movie was based on a true story you know.'

'Wow, explains why no one wants it for a

clubroom.'

Duran frowned, wondering what door his clubroom keys opened. He wouldn't be surprised if the Student Council thought it was hilarious to allocate a haunted old classroom for the music club.

'Hey Tsubaki!' Duran called out to him after the lesson was over and everyone was filing out of the room.

'I'll catch up with you in a sec.' Saski told Osamu who was almost out the door.

Both Saski and Duran failed to notice Osamu's chuckles directed at them before he left the room.

'Kita-kun.'

'About the clubroom for the music club. Which one was allocated?'

'The only vacant one in the Clubroom Block. The old 1-D class on the lower-ground floor,' Saski said with a serious face.

Duran knew him well enough to tell when he was suppressing a laugh.

'Ha! You think this is funny don't you.' He wasn't laughing and felt annoyed by Saski's smug attitude.

'Oh come on Kita-kun. Surely you don't believe the ghost rumours are true.' Saski smirked.

'How'd you know it's not true? Nebuya-chan said her boyfriend heard strange noises that couldn't be explained. I don't like strange noises that can't be explained.' Duran shivered.

'Come on! There's no such thing as ghosts Kita. Anyway, putting the ghost rumours aside. That room is perfect for the music club. You can make all the noise you want and no one will complain.'

'If you're so sure, you won't mind coming with me and the guys when we go to open the room after school.'

Saski peered at him.

'Fine. I'll bring Hayashi with me.' He sighed.

'Yeah, yeah, good idea. We can use him as distraction because he's got that "I'm a bad-ass mother" vibe going on that ghosts like to play with. He can keep it busy while we find out how to vanquish it. Maybe we'd need a Power of Three spell and three booby-babes to say it,' Duran thought aloud.

Saski rolled his eyes and clicked his tongue, annoyed by his classmate's stupidity.

'What the hell are you going on about? He needs to come for reporting purposes.' He reasoned.

'Yeah, okay, good idea. I'll meet you guys outside the Clubroom Block after school,' Duran answered, not really listening to Saski's voice. His mind had latched onto the type of magic he'd need to dispel ghosts.

'Wonder where I can get some wards and charms,' he mumbled in thought.

'Oh and bring some of Watty-sensei's distilled water with you, just in case,' he said to Saski as an afterthought.

He left the room with his mind circling around his ghost-buster plan.

'Kita's an idiot,' Saski said out loud and laughed at the ridiculous conversation they just had.

Ghosts became the theme of the day. Duran and his friends chatted about the music clubroom at their usual hangout spot on the rooftop during their lunch break.

'I'm telling you Nii-san, those ghost stories are silly rumours. There is no substance to them,' Himeko said to try to reassure the twisted truths her brother had in his mind about their allocated clubroom being haunted.

'You sure about that? Nebuya's boyfriend isn't the only one who's said something like that. There's been nine events since that guy's death.' Aki rebutted her argument with a shiver.

'Ridiculous! The whole situation is absurd.' Mei scoffed.

'Nine events?!' Duran said to Aki, ignoring his sister and Mei's voice of reason.

'Yeah, listen to this,' Aki said excitedly.

Aki recounted an urban myth of when three girls were coming down the stairs from an after school meeting and heard a lot of scratching and thumping noises in the pipes on the lower ground floor. They told the teacher who accompanied them to the floor. There they saw a pair of eyes hanging off a pipe that ran along the ceiling trim. The eyes were floating in space. The teacher tried to keep her cool, but ended up running away in fear with the rest of the girls.

'No way!' Duran gasped.

'That's stupid. For starters, if there was a ghost in that building don't you think the whole building would be haunted?' Mei reasoned again.

'Maybe it's stuck in that spot.' Fumio added to the conversation offhandedly. He was more interested in relieving Duran's uneaten fish stick from his hand.

'You eating that?' He asked his friend and licked his lips when Duran handed him the fish stick.

'That makes no sense Fumi-chan.' Himeko sighed. She couldn't understand why her brother and Aki were buying the ghost crap.

'I get it. It's something to do with water.' Duran

perked up when a dormant thought in his TV and film show archives went ding.

'Maybe it can't move from that spot because of too much water keeping it there. Something like a water wall.'

'Huh? Anyway, how did it get there in the first place?' Mei questioned.

Duran pondered hard for an answer and replied, 'The water brought him there. Yeah, like a conduit.'

'So, water brought it there and trapped it? Kita-kun that doesn't gel.' Mei argued.

Duran frowned and saw Fumio's eyes hovering around the rest of his fish sticks in his lunch box. He offered them to his friend who scoffed them down greedily and had a very satisfied look on his face afterwards.

'Honestly Kita-kun. I don't know why you're getting worked up with fiction. Tsubaki-kun is right when he says that the room is ideal for our club.'

'Of course I'm right,' Saski said as he took a seat next to Mei with Kou and Osamu next to him.

'What brings you here Tsubaki-kun?'

'I figured you might be talking about ghosts, and that Kita-kun would be suckered in by the nonsense.' He chuckled.

'You disbelievers! I won't be the one laughing when something unexplained gets the drop on you.' Duran shivered.

'Duracchi. You're talking about the Ghost of 1-D aren't you,' Chiasa said as she came up behind him and wrapped her arms around his waist.

'Ugh! Chia-chan. I told you a million times don't do that. I'm freaked out enough as it is.' Duran berated her and shook off her arms.

'You're so funny Duracchi.' Chiasa cooed and rested her head on his shoulder.

Duran sighed and gave his friends a pleading look.

'Suki-chan thinks it's true, don't you Suki?'

Nebuya Suki (who was an uncanny resemblance to Chiasa) approached their group with their other pop-idol clone friend.

'I only know what I've heard. All those people believe in what they heard and saw. I can't see why they aren't true,' Suki confirmed.

'But, you don't know for yourself.' Duran fished.

'They think it's true, so I think it's true,' Suki said quite convincingly.

'Bah! There's gotta be a proper explanation for those weird occurrences.' Kou piped up.

'Agree with Hayashi-kun. It could be leaking pipes, sound of someone flushing a toilet, even rats running around in the roof.' Saski added to Kou's reasoning.

'Rats! I hate rats.' Duran eyes bulged.

'That doesn't explain the weird thumping, floating eyes and howling.' Aki retorted.

'You saying my boyfriend's a liar Tsubaki-kun?' Suki's eyes narrowed at Saski.

'I'm not saying he lied, Nebuya-chan. I'm saying there is a perfectly reasonable and scientific explanation for what he experienced.' Saski rationalized.

'Hate to admit it but Tsubaki-kun talk's sense.' Mei agreed.

The group's argument about whether the ghost was real or not became heated.

There was a split with Team Tsubaki who believed in reasons explained with science and Team Nebuya who believed there were spiritual phenomenon out there. Sitting on the fence was Fumio and Osamu enjoying Duran's food.

'Hey!' Dai'chi shouted when he approached the group. 'What the hell are you guys making a lot of noise about?!'

'Dai-chan, we're talking about ghosts.' Duran filled him in.

'Really? Okay,' Dai'chi said.

He sat next to Fumio and joined the fence-sitting team, helping Fumio and Osamu finish off Duran's tasty bento.

'This show's better than Switch Girl.' he chuckled.

'Ugh! Nii-san you're a Flush-A's Idiot. There's no ghost at 1-D!' Himeko yelled out at the top of her voice. She was backed by Mei and Kou.

'What the hell has my results got to do with ghosts?! I won't be an idiot when I hear your blood curling screams from the other end of that floor!' Duran argued back who was backed up by Aki, Chiasa and Suki.

'Hah! Flush-A's Idiot. Couldn't agree with you more Suzuki-chan.' Saski chuckled.

'Vous sœur stupide!' Duran shouted out his retaliation.

'Woah! Kita-kun's now speaking in tongues. This show's getting good,' Osamu commented.

'Hey Yamaguchi any tempura left?' He looked into Duran's lunch box and was disappointed when it was empty.

'Vous êtes tous des idiots!' Duran screamed. His face was flaring bright red.

'Hey everyone calm down. We're getting the Flush-A Idiot too excited,' Kou said coolly.

Duran stood and threw down a gauntlet before

them all.

'Right. All of you at the Clubroom Block after school! We'll see whose right. Let's pray to Okamisama I was wrong, but don't say I didn't warn you when you're left shaking in your boots!' Duran had the final say.

He grabbed his empty lunch box and stormed off the rooftop with Chiasa and her friends trailing his heels.

'Well at least the Power of Three left with him.' Saski joked.

Duran's friends and few others from the rooftop debate were waiting for him outside the entrance of the Clubroom Block. Along with Watanabe-sensei and Yoshinori-sensei who was his home economics teacher.

When she found out what he was doing after school, she decided for herself she would be there. Duran was in no position to deter her when she had been gripping her wooden longsword (shinai) tightly.

He saw his sister waiting on the steps between Mei and Kou. She had a miffed expression on her face, obviously still annoyed at him.

'Fine, let her seethe for a while.' He thought, vexed by her senseless grudge.

'Ready to meet a creepy ghost.' Aki joked as he came down the steps to greet him.

'To be honest, I hope my sister and Tsubaki-kun are right. I'd rather look a fool than be ghost mincemeat.' Duran glanced at his sister again and sighed.

'She's still pissed at me isn't she?'

'Heehee, yeah. She kept complaining what an idiot for a brother she had during science. It didn't help that Hayashi-kun kept geeing her up with his dry sarcasm.' Aki laughed.

Watanabe-sensei made his way to them and pulled out a set of keys from his lab coat pocket.

'Here you go,' he said smugly as he handed Duran the keys.

'Eew! What's with the keychain?' Duran screwed up his nose at the mangy rabbit's foot dangling next to a shiny newish set.

'It's for luck since you have the fabled haunted clubroom. I believe the only thing that will haunt you there is bad music.'

It was only nature for a science teacher to debunk supernatural activities at their school.

'You say that with such conviction Watanabe-sensei,' Yoshinori-sensei said as she made her way to them.

The glare in her dark round eyes made Duran shiver.

Yoshinori-sensei was a stern presence, carrying a pale face that would have otherwise been considered pretty. She wore a hakama in the school navy blue complimented with a cotton white blouse. Her presentation was plain, but perfectly set so not even a crease showed on the hems nor a strand of her raven hair was out of place from her ponytail.

This image strengthened her impression of authority, along with the shinai she carried and used without hesitation to whack out bad behaviours from her students.

Duran wasn't sure what was scarier, the ghost or being in the middle of a showdown between two teachers who didn't see eye to eye.

'Hey sorry I'm late.' Dai'chi panted from his mad

sprint from the Student Council's office.

'That Saito-kun had me signing my life away on release forms.'

'Then you have these.' Duran tossed him the set.

Dai'chi dangled the set before his screwed up nose. 'Nah, you keep them safe for me.'

He threw the setback to Duran who threw it back to him, they ended up playing hot-potato with the keys.

'Oh for Pete's sake!' Yoshinori-sensei intervened and grabbed the set between a toss.

'You boys will get these back when the clubroom has been cleansed.'

'Of course, I imagine a lot of waste particles have gathered that needs cleaning away,' said Watanabe-sensei offhandedly.

'I meant cleansed of unworldly energy,' Yoshinori-sensei corrected him.

'Pfft! It's unlikely we'd need that sort of effort.'

'You still deny there are forces that can't be explained,' Yoshinori-sensei argued.

Duran and his friends slowly backed away as their teachers' argument became heated, and Yoshinori's grip to her shinai tighter so her knuckles were turning white.

'Everything can be explained through science.' Watanabe-sensei affirmed.

'Science bah! If science was the end all and be all our culture wouldn't be steeped in Yokai,' Yoshinori-sensei rebutted.

'Yokai are stories parents tell their children to shut them up.' Watanabe-sensei refuted.

Duran stood uneasy at the sight of his two teachers growling at each other like kids.

'Hey! Watanabe-sensei, Yoshinori-sensei. Please, can we get back to the matter at hand?' Saski interrupted them for a time out.

Their teachers were still grumbling at each other with their science verses the occult arguments as they filed into the Clubroom Block and down the hallway to the stairs of the lower ground floor.

Duran felt his argument on the rooftop paled in comparison to the one his teachers were having.

All chatter stopped when they came before a sepulchral sight of the stairs.

Flickering fluorescent lights stopped at the third step from the bottom, accentuating the pitch blackness of the way beyond.

An eerie chill blew towards them.

'Um, I just remembered that assignment I need to finish.' Aki's voice shook nervously as he turned to run away.

'Oh no you don't Aki-man. You're not getting out of this.' Dai'chi held his arm, stopping him from running away.

'You go first Hayashi-kun,' Duran said and pushed him to the front of the group.

Kou looked back and saw all of them cowering behind him in a huddle.

'You're all pansies.' He scoffed with full bravado and took a hesitant step to the lower ground floor.

'Hayashi-kun don't!' Chiasa gasped and buried her head in Saski's chest.

'Kou-kun do it, so I can get Chia-chan off my chest.' Saski mouthed.

Kou rolled his eyes and resumed his way down the stairs.

He stopped at the third step when he heard a

blood curling howl coming toward him from the darkness.

His eyes widen with a mixture of fear and disbelief as a pair of glowing green eyes raced for him.

He sprinted up the stairs as fast as legs could carry him and ran squealing with a high-pitched voice down the hallway with everyone else hot on his heels.

Everyone came out of the Clubroom Block panting with adrenaline.

'What did I tell you?! That floor is haunted,' Yoshinori-sensei confirmed with a bit of smugness.

She fished around the pockets of her hakama and pulled out small vials containing salt. She threw a vial at Kou, Duran, Saski, Aki, Fumio and Dai'chi.

'What's that going to do? Make it extra tasty for dinner?' Watanabe-sensei said sarcastically.

'What are these for?' Saski asked.

'Throw the salt at the ghost to dispel it,' Yoshinori-sensei answered knowingly.

'Bah! What utter nonsense.' Watanabe-sensei scoffed. He ignored the daggers from Yoshinori's eyes.

'Huh? I'm not going back there.' Kou declared, putting his foot down.

'What was all that talk about ghosts not being real?' Aki teased him.

'Ghosts aren't real but that, that was, was...' Kou struggled to explain and gave up.

'Oh for crying out loud! Give these to me!' Mei said bravely and took all the vials.

'I'll go in there if you boys aren't man enough to face one little supposed ghost threat.'

'Gaah! Since you put it that way. Okada, give me them!' Duran volunteered and took the vials from her hands.

'No! Don't do it Duracchi! Stay with us.' Chiasa wailed.

Duran found his arms locked into the hold of Chiasa and Suki's embrace.

'I gotta go now,' he said and shook himself free.

They followed Duran back inside, ignoring the whispered gossip and giggles directed at them from other students making their way up and down the main stairway.

Duran took a deep breath and cautiously made his way down the lower ground floor stairs with the salt vials gripped tightly in his hands.

He stopped at the same step Kou did and waited for the apparition to appear.

On cue, he saw the floating eyes racing toward him. He flipped one of the vial's lids and braced himself for impact.

'Duracchi!' He heard Chiasa whimper.

He steeled his will with a few deep breaths. He had come so far for a music club, one little ghost wasn't going to end it for him now.

He threw the salt at the eyes with all his might and heard screaming and cursing from the darkness.

The eyes fell to the ground and started revolving about in circles.

Chiasa and her friends went screaming back up the stairs and disappeared.

'What the hell Kita?!' A voice cried out, cursing his name.

Lights flickered on in the darkness to reveal Osamu and a mechanical set of toy eyes blinking on and off in a hallway.

He was furiously wiping out salt from his eyes and

glasses.

'Mikumo-kun?' Duran said, momentarily confused.

He glanced behind the *megane* boy and saw nothing untoward.

Realization dawned on him.

'It was you wasn't it!' He approached him angrily. 'You were playing the ghost!'

'Hey, now calm down Kita-kun. Aren't you glad there's no ghost?'

'Come here and let me hit you!' Kou shouted out behind them.

He grabbed Osamu by the cuff of his shirt, ready to take a swing.

'CALM DOWN!' Yoshinori-sensei shouted, tapping her shinai in her freehand.

'You, spill.'

Osamu gulped and started telling them about his prank.

It all started around the time of their Entrance Ceremony at the beginning of the year. He was running late to the event and had decided to take a shortcut behind the Clubroom Block.

There he noticed a litter of kittens moving in and out of a small hole near the vents of the boiler room.

The hole was cleverly concealed behind a long section of wild grass. He wouldn't have noticed it if it weren't for the cats.

Not long into his new class, he learned of the urban myths about the ghost on the lower ground floor and wondered if it was the cats causing the noise. He chose to find out for himself and followed their trail to the old 1-D classroom.

'It was such an opportune moment. I couldn't help myself.' He nervously laughed.

'The look on everyone's faces when they ran to high heavens was priceless.'

'Hold him down Hayashi-kun, Kita-kun while I whack some discipline into him,' Yoshinori-sensei ordered with her shinai ready to strike his butt.

'Settle down Yoshinori-sensei! You dare strike my student!' Watanabe-sensei intervened.

'So, it was cats making all those howling and thumping noise.' Duran recapped.

'Yeah. No ghosts or anything supernatural. Just a bunch of strays running around the pipes and calling the boiler room their home.'

'This was your twisted sense of fun? Do you know how many people you freaked out?!' Himeko berated with fire in her eyes.

'Okay, okay. I can see you're all really pissed about it, but I did it for the cats. If the school found out they were there, they'd be taken to a shelter.' Osamu tried to reason.

'Right everybody. Now we know there aren't any ghosts at this school. We can all get on with the task at hand and setting up this music club.' Watanabe-sensei concluded.

'Fine, but I'm not done with you.' Yoshinori-sensei glared at Osamu, pointing her shinai at his face.

She threw the clubroom keys to Duran, turned and stormed up the stairs.

'Now. Keep still while I take a swing.' Kou eyes narrowed.

'Let him go Hayashi-kun. Mikumo explained his reasons. He'll get his from Yoshinori-sensei,' Duran said to calm Kou down and eased him away from a nervous Osamu.

'Well I feel like an idiot.' Aki breathed out a sigh of

relief.

'That's because you are an idiot.' Dai'chi joked.

'Shut up Santo Shonky. You were scared like the rest of us.' Aki shot back.

'Shall we open up the club?' Watanabe-sensei said jovially.

Duran could tell his teacher felt fantastic about being right.

'Fine.' He agreed, not feeling as happy about the situation as his teacher.

He opened the door and fumbled around the side wall for the lights. He flicked a switch and watched the room flicker to life. It was a dusty, dirty room with piles of desk junk and other school paraphernalia overrunning the free space.

'Crap.' He hissed.

'Yep. Lots of it.' Watanabe-sensei chuckled behind him.

He tensed when a pile of chairs wobbled before him then relaxed when a tiny black kitten emerged from the shadows.

He crouched low and placed out his hand in a friendly gesture.

The black kitten crept cautiously toward him and allowed its head to be pat. It meowed with a strained voice and fumbled on the spot under Duran's touch.

'Oh my god. It's too cute.' Himeko cooed.

'To think you were the scary ghost of our school.' Duran chuckled to the kitty.

He faced Osamu with a smile.

'I understand your prank now Mikumo-kun. It's all good.' He reassured him.

'Kita-kun may have forgiven you. I'm still gonna bust your ass later Miki-chan,' Kou said, crunching his knuckles and glaring at his childhood friend.

'Drop it Kou-kun. It's like Kita-kun said. It's all good.' Saski sighed.

'That aside. What are we going to do about this mess and the cats? Kou-kun and I have to put something into our reports.'

They saw more cats come out of hiding the more they talked about them.

'We clean up and dispose of the junk. About the cats, nothing,' Duran answered.

'I don't know about that Kita-kun. They pose an occupational health and safety hazard with this many running around.' Watanabe-sensei advised. 'I could solve the problem by keeping them in my laboratory to...'

'NO! Sensei don't you dare or I'll report you to animal cruelty!' Himeko pointed an accusing finger at him.

'What if we ensured they didn't Sensei? I mean, we're the only room on the floor. If we could keep them contained, couldn't they keep their residency? They've been here all this time and no one's been hurt.' Dai'chi reasoned.

'Yeah. I mean you can't kick them out. They're already members of our club.' Himeko added and giggled when a cute kitten of brown and black fur patches licked at her outstretched hand.

'Hime-chan. Careful. They could be carrying diseases. You better wash your hands when we leave,' Mei said with a cautious look in her eyes.

'Settle down Mei. They're too cute for that,' Himeko said and released her contact with the kitten.

Duran's attention was pulled toward a black male cat distinguished with a white strip of fur on its head like a mohawk.

It had its back arched as it padded its way toward the kittens and mewed loudly to recall them back to the shadows. He frowned wondering where he had seen the cat before.

'This might be nothing, but I get the feeling I've seen this cat before,' Kou said, voicing Duran's thoughts.

Duran and Kou shared a knowing look as they both remembered.

'The ramen house!' They said in unison.

The cat hissed one more time before it fled into hiding with the others.

Watanabe-sensei recommended they leave the place and lock up, so they can figure out their next steps.

They made their way back to the main hallway feeling relieved and embarrassed by the whole ghost situation. Other students gawked at them with disbelief, surprise and awe as they emerged from the lower ground floor talking causally and looking composed.

'You're alive!' An unsuspecting girl cried out.

'Of course I'm alive, why wouldn't I be,' Aki answered back and laughed at the feverish gossip that was shooting up the main stairway.

Duran chuckled as they made their way out of the Clubroom Block, appearing to others as surviving heroes from a movie.

✪ HOTAKA MUSIC CLUB

A new Hotaka High School urban myth was created the day Duran, his friends and teachers walked out of the lower ground floor of the Clubroom Block unscathed. Chiasa and her friends recounted the event up to the moment they saw Duran throw salt at the ghost to all their friends and classmates. The rumours of Duran vanquishing a ghost had spread like a wild fire within a day.

Despite Duran telling people the truth about stray animals being the reason for the raucous (minus Osamu's involvement), his peers decided it was way cooler to believe the urban myth. Once again, Duran was the deviant hero the school's First Years.

'You think, for a school that prides itself on logical subjects, its students wouldn't be suckers for myths and fables.' Duran grumbled to Himeko as they made their way to their morning homeroom classes.

'Suppose the flip side for being grilled on subjects about real world facts and science, your brain begins to crave the ridiculous.' Himeko reasoned.

Duran was glad that they were on good terms again, not that they ever stayed angry with each other for long anyway. In this recent case, he forwent his pride and admitted to being a gullible idiot more than once.

'Well, whatever. I'm glad we have a clubroom now,' he said.

His mind began to work through ideas on dealing with the junk since the school didn't have other space in their storage units to accommodate.

Saski and Kou had gone back to the Student

Council to see what budget they had for a clean-up and counted peanuts for surplus funds. Principal Kimura was adamant that the school's budget didn't cover for those sundry inconveniences.

'Isn't this why we have a club budget?' Principal Kimura had smugly told Saski and further added that since the Music Club had inherited the room, the responsibility was theirs.

This drove a further wedge between Dai'chi and President Saito's already unfriendly relationship, especially when Dai'chi poetically told the Student Council President to shove the school's lack of funds up their proverbial backsides.

Thankfully, no one had made mentioned on the cats still running about the room and floor.

Saski saw it as some compensation.

'Aah, geez, what we gonna do with the junk.' Duran sighed.

'I think we maybe in luck. Dad said he knows of a friend who's starting up a community youth center. They could probably take some desks and stuff that the school is happy to write off.' Himeko smugly offered to save the day.

Duran flashed here a goofy grin and wrapped her arms with a bear hug.

'You've been holding out!'

'Dad said he didn't want to tell you until he was sure. We'd still need the school's permission for removal.'

'I don't think they'll deny it. Until then, I guess we'll make do and stack everything to one side.'

They parted ways at their homeroom classes, which kicked off the school morning with a seating change. Duran groaned when he found himself sitting next to Chiasa at the window side of the middle row.

He felt a bout of butterflies in his stomach when he saw that his desk was in front of Saski's. He heard Fumio grumbling about being stuck to the front where he couldn't doze off without their teacher seeing him.

His mind was too preoccupied on the Music Club to care much for his seating arrangements. He wanted to try out his new toy and enjoy the company of some cute kittens.

The bell ringing was music to his ears when lunch came around. He sprinted out of the classroom block for the clubroom with his keys jangling in his pocket. Fumio wasn't far behind him.

'You're both grinning like idiots,' Aki said when he saw Fumio and Duran skipping down the clubroom's lower ground floor stairs.

'I'm not the only one,' Duran replied when he saw all his other club members talking excitedly and not hiding their eagerness to enter the room and make their own. They were greeted by their clubroom cats when he opened the door. They ran about their feet and bellowed out with chirpy mews.

'Okay. No pushing. Here you go,' Himeko said as she pulled out a packet of cat kibbles from her bag and fed them in empty ice cream contains she had pilfered from one of the science labs.

'Hime-chan! Don't feed them. They'll never want to leave,' Mei scolded her.

'Don't mind the cat hater.' Himeko soothed the kittens who greedily chowed down on the food.

Mei sighed and stepped further inside.

Aki and Fumio opened up all the blinds. They coughed back clouds of one-year-old dust in the process.

Gentle rays of summer daylight streamed through the high windows caked with dust rings, revealing dark spots that had been hidden for a very long time. The gloomy atmosphere of the room was gradually eradicated as they cleaned up and created as much space as possible.

They managed to push most of the junk to one end to create a few square feet of space when Saski, Osamu and Kou rocked on up to do their inspections.

Osamu joined Himeko and Aki's play with the cats whilst Duran and Dai'chi talked business with Saski.

'I'm really annoyed the school doesn't want to clean their own junk, but that's how things are I guess,' Saski apologized.

Neither Duran nor Dai'chi were mad at him about it.

'That's okay Tsubaki-kun. You did try. I think my step-father has the solution anyway.'

Duran told Saski about the Community Center donation. Saski agreed to handle the asset paperwork and offered his aid should they need help with the removals.

'Oh and this is for the club. When I offhandedly mentioned the school starting up a music club, he said his associate was looking to donate an instrument to a worthy cause,' Saski said as he pulled out a business card from his pocket and offered it to Duran with both hands.

Duran accepted the card and frowned as he read it. The card belonged to an account executive for a pharmaceuticals giant.

'I don't get it. We're being donated drugs?' Dai'chi

said as he read it over Duran's shoulder.

Saski sighed and rolled his eyes. 'Turn the card over.'

Duran's frown turned into glee when he read the make and model of an outdated upright piano. It was accompanied by a pick up address.

'Is this for real?'

'Yeah. It belonged to his late son. My father's associate wasn't willing to part with it unless the cause was worthy. When he heard about a music club starting up in the school his son had attended, he wanted to donate the piano.'

'Thank you Tsubaki-kun. I can't express how grateful I am by the gesture,' Duran said with a humble voice and low bow.

'Er, well, I think you'll be doing him a service actually. You'll need to pick up the piano yourself, but it'll be a start for the club.' Saski said, unable to hide his blushes.

'Leave that to me,' Duran said.

Saski and his friends joined in with the cleaning, making the old 1-D classroom resemble some of its former glory by lock-up time.

Duran stayed on a high with his thoughts floating between the music club and Saski who was proving more of a guardian angel in his life. He stopped questioning the guy's motive, enjoying their deepening bond.

Sounds of shuffling paper behind his back reassured him of Saski's presence.

He delved deeper into fantasies of them being together, realizing how much he was falling madly, deeply, in love again.

'That's a problem,' he muttered to himself.

Being in love was one thing, action to make his love a reality wasn't something he was ready for. Especially when he felt strong enough to face his fears for the time in his life. Miwa could return to him anytime now.

His current relationship with Saski was enough for him. He disregarded further thoughts on the matter.

He finished his school-day with the clearest mind he had had in a long time, reflecting on the day's highlights as he made his way to his footlocker with Himeko and Mei.

Out of the blue, he received a text from his old boss as he was swapping his shoes for the journey home.

'Shiro-san's asking if I can come back to work. He'll pay me this time,' he said to the girls.

'You think that's a good idea?' Himeko frowned.

He had finished up his punishment at Matsu Ramen House a while ago, but he and his friends continued to visit the place as patrons. He was happy to see its business was booming since their time there.

'Business must be booming if they need the help,' Duran answered.

He thought about funds needed for the club. The job was an opportunity to boost its budget. He came to a conclusion that one day a week shouldn't affect his studies. So, he returned the message saying he'll be there shortly to talk it over.

Duran and Himeko arrived to Matsu Ramen House that was booming with patrons crowding the compact restaurant.

Some tables were active with hearty conversations from salary-man and women from neighbouring offices, mother clubs with their kids in strollers and elderly couples at quieter tables, enjoying a steaming bowl and the sight of youngsters. It was certainly a lot busier than usual for that time of day. Isao was so flat-chat with orders, he walked right past them.

Further inside, most the stools on along the bench was occupied with students from his school.

He noticed all the seniors of the Student Council at a table before the window. They were engrossed in a meeting over half-eaten bowls of ramen soup.

'Hey. Kita-kun.' Teppei waved Duran over to him.

'Aah the pork fried special,' Duran said when he approached their table and noticed the familiar recipe in Teppei's bowl.

'My favourite here.' Teppei smiled. 'How's the new club going?'

'It's getting there,' Duran replied.

'How's it feel being a hero in the process? I heard you vanquished ghosts with table salt.'

The other Student Council Members stifled their chuckles.

'Kiyoshi-san. The ghost situation is a misunderstanding,' Duran stated levelly.

'No need to be modest Kita-kun. Students calmly move about that building now that they know there's no supernatural threat any more.' President Saito smirked.

Duran sighed. Believing in the myth or playing along for a gag was their choice. He wasn't in the mood to entertain them on either.

'Nii-san. Didn't you come to see Shiro-san?' Himeko gently reminded him as she interrupted on their conversation.

'Of course. Sorry for intruding on your meal,' Duran said with a courteous bow and followed

Himeko into the small backroom behind the open kitchen.

'Shiro-san! What happened?!' He gasped when he saw the state of the small preparation room that was separated from public view by a noren partition.

The place was usually an impression of order and cleanliness, with jarred and canned goods organized neatly on wall shelves that maximized the tight space.

A good flow of orders could be churned out on the island bench and hot plate cooking area.

Today, the stainless-steel island bench was cluttered with random bowls and containers of ingredients, causing more of a mess than efficiency. Small food crates, boxes and containers were half-opened on shelves or stacked unevenly near the island bench's hot plates and burners.

The small built-in pantry, next to the back door, had stock out of its order. In short, the prepping room was a sight of culinary chaos.

'Where's Jiro-san today?' Duran asked when he didn't see the man's brother.

He dumped his bag near the pantry and rolled up his sleeves to help.

'At an omiai with our investor's daughter. Sasaski-kun is sitting his employer's exam. Izuki-kun is handling the tables all on his own.' Shiro-san groaned, stirring ingredients in a wok and pot steaming on the burners.

'So you need me to work today?' Duran offered.

'Please. I'll pay you by the hour,' said Shiro-san almost pleading.

'What about you Suzuki-chan?' He stared at her with imploring eyes.

'Oh me? Um, I'm not good in the kitchen, but I

could help Izuki-san with orders.' She suggested.

'Great! I'll pay you both 700 yen an hour each. Now get to it!' Shiro-san, thanked, offered and commanded in one breath.

Himeko informed their parents then donned wait staff apron and made herself useful to Isao who was extremely grateful for the relief.

Duran assisted in the prepping room so Shiro-san could return to cooking in the open kitchenette. When Shiro-san was working to his usual efficiency, Duran waited on the tables.

Himeko surprised everyone when she could capture the orders correctly and wait the tables as if she was a regular staff member. Her excuse was that she had eaten there so much whilst her brother was on shifts, his routine was etched into her brain.

It was close to 8:00 pm when Jiro-san walked through the door, sighing and looking as drained as the staff. Business had slowed by then.

'Suzuki-chan! You're waiting tables,' he said surprised.

'Shiro-san asked for help,' she politely replied as she attended to a table.

Jiro-san made his way to the backroom and saw Duran preparing the ingredients for his brothers cooking orders.

Isao was in the pantry restocking the shelves. The place was running to its usual efficiency.

'Wow. Looks like you didn't need me at all.' Jiro-san joked and copped a whack on the ear from his older brother when he had stepped into the open kitchen area.

This display of brother love stirred chuckles from the regular business patrons who enjoyed this added benefit to their meals.

'Don't be stupid. If Kita-kun and Suzuki-chan didn't show, we would've been screwed.' Shiro-san grumbled. 'Out of the blue, a sales team from the Kawazaki Corporation down the road showed up, it was mom's day out and the old timers from the Shogi Association was having their meeting.'

'Another unexpected killer day?'

'Yeah. We pulled through because of my two lucky charms here.' Shiro-san flashed Duran and Himeko a proud grin.

'Well I'll take over Kita-kun. You and Suzuki-chan can take off.' Jiro-san offered as he ruffled Duran's hair.

'Phew, thank you.' Duran bowed.

'How was the omiai?' He asked with cheeky grin.

He sized up Jiro-san's navy suit, which was nicely fitted to his body's muscly contours and complimented his conservative maroon tie. The man's good-looks and solid fashion sense were sure to impress a woman.

'Huh? Well, she's got the looks of a princess; a nice girl from a good family background. How'd you think it went?' Jiro-san sighed miserably as he removed his tie and jacket.

'Yikes. It was like that was it?' Duran felt bad he had asked the question.

'Yeah. I was clumsy like a middle school kid and looked like an idiot through the whole date.'

'I'm sure she could see you were nervous.' Duran consoled. 'Do you like her?'

Jiro-san thought hard before he answered, 'Yeah. She's a good sort.'

'Then I'm sure it'll work out.' Duran reassured him

with a pat to his shoulder.

'What about you Kita-kun? You got a chick you fancy?' Jiro-san questioned him.

Duran's face when beetroot red. He wasn't sure how to answer.

'Haha. I see it's like that.' Jiro-san laughed and slapped his back.

'Hey grab your sister. I'll get your pay.' Shiro-san interrupted their conversation.

Duran gave Himeko the okay to call quits.

'I'll just finish up with this order,' she said, being mid-way through serving dishes.

He re-entered the backroom to grab their things and started telling Jiro-san about the music club.

'Really? So, you have any other instruments?'

'No. Hotaka High School doesn't do music classes, so I'll have to spend the budget on some pieces,' Duran replied.

'I know where you can buy a drum set for next to nothing in price. Probably more nothing than price too.' Jiro-san offered.

'Seriously? That'll be great!'

'Yeah. My band mate purchased a new set and wants to get rid of his old. I'll hook you up. Also, do you and the club want to see us do a gig?'

'Are you for real? Yes, please! It'll be an excellent experience for us. If it's a place we can get in, we'll go.'

'It's a public gig during the day, so don't worry about that.'

Jiro-san told him he'll contact him about the drum set. Himeko entered looking enervated.

Shiro-san gave Himeko and Duran their pay, which they accepted with a grateful bow.

They both agreed to work a regular shift of Thursday's a week to fill their staff shortage for that day.

'Kita-kun, for the piano pick up. I know a roadie who could help with that. Send me some details, I'll organize it.' Jiro-san offered.

Again, Duran was very grateful and accepted his offer.

Himeko and Duran walked the safe route home and arrived at the same time as Ryuu-chichi. They told him about the part-time job, which Ryuu-chichi wasn't too thrilled about for Himeko's sake.

When Duran said he'll work with her on her grades, his step-father reluctantly agreed on the condition Himeko would leave work if her grades didn't show improvement.

'What's wrong with my grades?!' Himeko bellowed as she followed Duran to their rooms.

'So, you're okay with your B's and C's?' Duran chuckled.

Himeko was quiet when she entered her room.

Duran was still chuckling when he entered his room to call it a night.

Next day, he woke earlier than usual for a Saturday morning, too wired to sleep beyond the crack of dawn. It was just as well, since he had made prior arrangements with Jiro-san and Saski to meet at the ramen house for the piano pick-up. He was tickled pink with happiness at having to spend time with Saski outside of school hours, under the guise of club business.

He pushed off his bed covers and scratched at his arms as he expelled the rest of his sleep with a hearty yawn. Daylight was still finding its way into his room as he readied his clothes and bag for the day.

He stumbled toward the bathroom and attempted to open a locked door. He heard the shower running and Himeko humming a chirpy tune.

Ever since she found out his weird habit of showering his body in the morning and washing his face at night, she followed pattern. The competition for morning bathroom time was a frustrating disruption to his long-standing routine.

'Don't hog the hot water!' He yelled out as he banged the door.

'Get lost!' Her voice carried across to him from the other side.

He gave the door another bang and padded down the hallway to the living areas.

'Morning.' His mother greeted him as he stepped into the adjoined dining and kitchenette area.

She was dressed in a business suit, running around the kitchenette, dining and lounge room doing many things at once, so she could leave home without looking back for the day.

'You have work mom?' He asked as he shuffled into one of the dining chairs.

'Yes. Big case in the city. I'll be late tonight,' she said whilst checking through her laptop bag on the table.

Duran studied his mother as she went about her checks.

She carried a youthful appearance with a number of grey hairs and wrinkles you could count on one hand. They shared the same green eyes. Her eye colour was the only obvious feature, which associated her to the Kita-Dubois bloodline. The rest of her was Japanese. She kept her long, raven hair up in a tight bun with wisps of fringe falling to her eyes. The natural rouge of her cheeks, flawless pale skin, soft full lips and gentle shaped eyes formed a classic beauty. Behind her feminine features and petite build was an intelligent mind and sharp tongue that was capable of slaying giants.

'I bought more eggs for *tamagoyaki*. Make sure you eat well before leaving for the day. *Sois sage*,' she told him with a mother's peck to his forehead.

'Ain't I ever?' He said with a wry expression.

She hurried out of the room.

He heard the front door close at the same time the shower was turned off, and raced for the bathroom.

'Outta my way,' he said to Himeko as she stepped into the hallway.

'Hey! Stupid Nii-san,' she cursed then laughed when the shower went on, and she heard his swearing.

'Goddamn Himeko!' Duran swore at his cold shower, and could only tolerate five minutes underneath semi-arctic temperatures.

Duran made sure they both had a decent breakfast before leaving their home for the day. Himeko had a date with Mei for quality girl time. That meant paying visit to the boutique and beauty stores in the city that his friend liked to drag his sister to. He never pictured that bossy-boots into fashion, but then again she did dress stylish when they weren't in uniform.

They parted ways when they stepped outside.

Duran inhaled the fresh morning. His skin tingled under the crisp cool air and gentle sun as he strolled along the waking urban streets to the ramen house.

Saski arrived out the front of the restaurant the same time he did.

He felt an urge to turn tail and go into hiding when he saw how good looking his love interest was in his light jacket, blue polo shirt and jeans. He looked drab in his blue gingham short sleeve shirt and jeans in comparison. His eyes widen when he saw they both wore the same type of runners, although Saski fitted a size a lot bigger than his.

'Kita-kun, um, morning,' Saski greeted him.

The man had his hands in his pockets, eyes lowered toward the pavement he was toeing.

Duran felt an unusual awkwardness between them.

'Morning Tsubaki-kun.' He returned the greeting with a light blush.

His heart went for a pounding when he noticed a similar flush to Saski's cheeks. Damn cute!

Saski started talking about his father's associate.

'Tadatoshi-san is a very proper man. Please be mindful of this. I wouldn't mention his son unless he does even then best to keep the talk short on the matter. His son died two years ago. It's still a touchy subject.'

'Um, so he knows your dad well?'

Saski looked uncomfortable with the question.

'I suppose. He's known my father since he was as a resident doctor at Sakurai General.'

Duran didn't ask any more questions and started looking around for Jiro-san.

At that moment a pick-up truck pulled up to the curb before them. Jiro-san called out to them from the front passenger side.

'Hey you two. Hop in the back.'

Duran and Saski shuffled into the back passenger seats.

'This my good mate Taco,' Jiro-san introduced his

driver from the rear vision mirror.

'Howdy,' Taco greeted them with a generous smile.

Duran felt genuine warmth behind his eyes and features. He gawked at the size of Taco's guns poking through his long sleeved shirt and figured he worked-out as much as Jiro-san.

'Hello. Thank you very much Taco-san for your help,' Duran said politely.

'Hah! You weren't kidding when you said we'd pick up two polite kids,' Taco said cheerfully as he kicked the truck into drive.

'Dudes. Just call me Taco. You make me feel a hundred years old with the honorific.'

'Oh.' Duran blushed

'At ease mate.' Taco chuckled and flashed him a reassuring smile.

Duran relaxed into a smile of his own. He glanced at Saski from the corner of his eye and could see he was tense.

'Hey, it's okay,' he whispered his reassurance.

Saski lips twitched with a weak smile in response.

'So, where to?' Taco asked and received the address from Jiro-san.

Duran's heart raced at the same speed of the truck when Saski and his hand made skin contact for a moment.

He felt a pang from where his rib had been cracked and gripped the bottom part of his seat belt. He turned his attention to the rushing world outside his window to distract his pain and flurry of feelings.

Saski frowned when he noticed Duran's tension. He tapped his arm to draw his attention to him.

'You still feel pain in your ribs,' he asked in a hush voice.

'Rarely. It's nothing major.' Duran reassured him and forced himself to relax.

'Hey you guys are pretty quiet back there,' Jiro-san said as he glanced at them through the rear vision mirror.

'Just enjoying the ride,' Duran responded cordially.

They turned into a street that had a lot of large traditional houses spanned across spacious lots. Tall elms and Sakura trees dotted the nature strips providing a serene atmosphere.

The truck slowed before a set of security gates and stone wall that kept guard over a tranquil bonsai garden of various varieties. The garden formed a picturesque view around a traditional two-story-house, which sported the typical triangular shaped rooftops and cornices that were common of the Showa Era. A generous sized engawa porch ran around the edges of the ground floor with a similar type of balcony of the upper level.

Duran's mind flashed back to the weekend he had spent at Miwa's and recalled the bitter-sweet feelings. He sighed them away and fixed his mind back to the present.

'Dude must be from a well-do family,' Taco said as he parked the truck.

Everyone shuffled out and stood before the security gate.

Saski announced their arrival at the gate's intercom. They then waited for a response.

'Please come to the front door.' Cracked a mature voice from the intercom a few seconds later.

The gates swung open.

'You guys go up first. We need to get out equipment,' Jiro-san said to Duran and Saski.

Saski led the way down a path that snaked its way to the front porch and entrance door.

A distinguished gentleman in blue cashmere, grey slacks and loafers stood tall before them.

His hair was kept in a respectable cut. There was a slight cow-lick to the left side of his hair so his sparse fringe flicked over and up off his narrow forehead. His grey eyes and thin lips beamed with a welcoming smile.

'Tsubaki-kun. It's been a while since we last saw each other,' he greeted Saski fondly with a peck to each cheek.

Duran knew it was only a customary greeting. He felt slightly nauseous watching the interaction.

'Tadatoshi-san. Yes, it has been a while. Thank you for seeing us today and for your generous donation.' Saski said formally with a low bow.

'My, my, you don't have to be formal with me. I've known since you were a child. But, excuse me for being rude. Are you Tsubaki-kun's friend who has started up the music club?' Tadatoshi-san said to Duran.

Duran followed Saski's lead and formally introduced himself.

'Hmm, I have a niggling feeling I've heard of your name before. Well, you are a treat for the eyes and polite too. I'm not surprise Tsubaki-kun would take you under his wing.' Tadatoshi-san chuckled.

Duran and Saski stood with nonplus expressions on their faces, unable to respond.

Jiro-san and Taco entered the scene to save them from the moment.

Tadatoshi-san lead everyone around the porch to a spacious back room, which had a studio upright piano positioned in the room's center.

Duran smiled with appreciation when he saw the piano *was* a Wagner. Its mahogany finish was aged but still in good condition with a few preloved scratches and chips to the fallboard. The face of the pedals had typical worn marks from many shoes pressed upon them. The red material of the stool showed a few tell-tale indents of where Tadatoshi-san's son sat. He sensed an energy of love and care from the instrument.

He glanced about the room and noticed very little furniture and decorations. The only images Duran saw on walls were photographs of a boy around the same age as himself. All of them captured a pleasant face with warm brown eyes and a friendly smile.

He peered closer at the photographs. His mind went back to a time at Suntry Hall. He had been waiting at the backstage corridor for his turn to play, trembling with nerves and muttering to himself to not screw-up. An older boy had entered the corridor and saw him pacing. He had given Duran some advice.

'When you're nervous think of the prettiest flower in the whole of creation. A flower that makes your heart at peace. Hold it in your mind as you take a few deep breaths. All your nerves will fade away,' he had advised Duran with a kind smile and gentle pat to his shoulder.

Duran could play his Mozart because of the advice and smile of that boy.

'Tadatoshi, Kobori,' he whispered to the photo when he remembered the boy's name.

'My son,' said Tadatoshi-san next to him.

'He was a happy child and loved playing the piano from the bottom of his heart.'

'I met him once when I was a middle-school student. He was kind to me,' Duran said politely.

'Aah, now I remember, you're Kita-kun. You played at the summer recitals a few years back.'

Duran faced Tadatoshi-san and noticed a pained expression behind his eyes.

'Please forgive me Tadatoshi-san. I didn't mean to bring back a memory,' he apologized.

'It's perfectly okay Kita-kun. I'm quite honoured to talk with you. My son couldn't stop raving about your performance at that time. He kept saying "how could a kid of that age understand Mozart so well". I'm sure, if he was alive, he would have loved to have known you.'

Duran acknowledged his words with a courteous nod.

Jiro-san and Taco were positioning themselves to lift the piano onto a dolly trolley when Tadatoshi-san politely intervened and asked if they could wait five minutes.

'Please Kita-kun, before it is wheeled away, would you mind playing a song for me?'

Duran nodded his head and stepped up to the piano. He gingerly pulled up the fallboard to reveal a set of keys that still had some sheen to them. He noticed the keys of the third and fourth octaves had slight worn patches from being pressed by fingers numerous times.

'This piano was definitely a friend,' he whispered to himself.

He sat before it and turned to Tadatoshi-san.

'What would you like me to play?'

'I'd love to hear that Mozart piece again,' said Tadatoshi-san.

Duran inhaled deeply and began to play *Piano Sonata No.16 C major.*

He pictured that moment with Kobori-san and how at peace he felt with those few words. His mind started flowing with flowers and the colours of spring enriched by the ditty trills and upbeat notes of the song. The music sprinted from his fingers to embrace the world around him with a moment of joy.

A smile teased his lips when his hands came to rest at the end of his playing. The room assumed a peaceful silence.

He looked to Tadatoshi-san again and felt concerned when he noticed tears glisten in the man's eyes.

'Tadatoshi-san?'

'Oh my. A far different experience from Suntry Hall,' Tadatoshi-san exhaled. 'You must have found a piece of happiness in your life since then.'

He surprised Duran with a courteous bow.

'Thank you Kita-kun. I've treasured this piano for far too long. Now, I feel okay to let it go, knowing it is in good hands,' he said with a warm smile.

Tadatoshi-san gave Jiro-san and Taco the signal to go ahead with the removal.

He approached Saski who had been quietly observing them from a corner.

'You have a one-of-kind person here. Treasure him the way you had wanted to with Kobori-kun, even more so,' he whispered inconspicuously into Saski's ear with a knowing smile.

Saski's cheeks flushed a deep red. He acknowledged his words with a bow.

They followed the piano's plight along the porch, down a temporary ramp that Taco had set up for the removal and all the way to the truck.

Duran and Saski bowed their thanks again to Tadatoshi-san as Jiro-san and Taco secured the piano safely in the truck's hold.

'When we are open for a public display, would you like to visit our club room?' Duran politely invited Tadatoshi-san.

'I would love that Kita-kun and to hear you play again.' Tadatoshi-san agreed.

Duran and Saski stepped into the back seats and waved their goodbyes as Taco drove them away from the house and down the streets toward their school.

'Man, Kita-kun! Do you always play like that?' Jiro-san said excitedly.

'Um, guess so.'

'Kid you play better than the pros. You should play with us sometimes.' He offered then lapsed into conversation with Taco about trivial topics.

'You do play like a professional,' Saski commented. 'Although your style is a bit arrogant.'

Duran shot him a funny look and saw Saski holding back a laugh. He slapped his shoulders and poked out his tongue childishly at him. They both broke out laughing.

'Hey Jiro-san, could we stop off at the convenience store I need to buy something,' Duran called out.

They pulled up before a Family Mart near the school. They guys waited in the truck for Duran as he ducked into the store to purchase some cat kibbles.

When he returned, they were back on the road again and arrived inside the school parking grounds a few minutes later.

The Kobori (Duran had penned the piano) was set in a spot toward the middle of the clubroom's free space, where sunlight from the high windows kissed the keys.

It was not too close to the air vents and moist areas to disrupt the tuning.

Jiro-san and Taco had left their care to attend a gig both had somewhere else.

Saski had stayed with Duran to attend to the cats and see that the piano fitted well into its new home.

Duran sat before the Kobori and tested a few of the keys.

He noticed the lower-G and a few others in the fifth octaves had been knocked out of tune from the move, which was something he was expecting.

'Looks like I'd need to tune you back into shape,' he said to the piano as he tenderly stroked its keyslip.

'Stroking the piano like that is really creepy,' Saski said with a screwed up face.

'Haha! Well, this piano is a fine piece. I can't help but admire it,' Duran said with a goofy grin.

Saski sighed and gestured for Duran to make room on the stool, so he could sit next to him.

'I know I organized this for you, but now that it's here, I feel weird about it,' he said.

'Why's that Tsubaki-kun?'

'This piano was Kobori-senpai's. It's the remaining part of him.' Saski sighed away the rest of his explanation and started fingering a key lovingly.

Duran frowned, wondering if there had been more to the relationship between Saski and Kobori-san.

'I have a feeling you two were close.' Duran cringed as he said the words.

'We were. Sort of, but not in the way I wanted us to be I guess,' Saski said soberly.

'But, that doesn't matter any more.' He brushed off

the matter and faced Duran.

'Kita-kun. Teach me something.'

Duran glared at the keys, not sure if he wanted to touch them again.

He stared into Saski's eyes and noticed a longing behind them. A twisted feeling in his heart made his hands tense and stomach nauseous. He felt a strong defiance to his request. He didn't want Saski touching the piano any more.

'Sorry Tsubaki-kun. Not now. The keys are out of tune.'

He slammed the fallboard back down to hide the keyboard, and shuffled off the stool to play with the cats.

'Hey Socrates,' he called out to the small kitten with black and brown fur patches.

It was sitting near the large blackboard on the back wall. The kitten padded toward him to be petted. It mewed animatedly under his playful strokes and rubs.

'Kita-kun. What was between Kobori-senpai and I died when he did. There wasn't anything there to begin with.' Saski explained as he approached him.

'I don't know why you're telling me this. I didn't know you back then, so why should that matter to me,' Duran said coolly, but the pain he felt in his heart was becoming overwhelming.

He didn't like the idea of Saski being in love with Kobori-san or anyone else for that matter. He couldn't look at him without letting his feelings show.

'But, my past with Senpai bothers you. I can tell. Your body shows quirks that betrays your feelings. Like the way your shoulders tense when you frown. How you lower your head when you're afraid or ashamed. The goofy smile on your face when you're happy. You walk away when you're angry. There are so many things I see of you, I don't want anyone else to see.' Saski came at him and met his eyes.

Duran felt his chest was going to collapse.

'You like me Kita-kun,' Saski said not dropping his eye contact.

Duran's heart was racing a million miles per hour. He wanted to say something, but he was speechless.

Saski leaned in and kissed him. Duran returned the kiss with all the passion that was welled up inside him. He wrapped his arms around Saski's waist. Their kisses became intense as they delved further into each other's embrace.

'I like you too,' Saski whispered into Duran's ear as he licked and nibbled at his lobe playfully.

His hands slipped underneath Duran's shirt and stroked his bare skin.

Duran moaned with pleasure from the tingling, flushed sensation he felt from Saski's tender strokes, playful pinches and teasing of his nipples.

'Promise me no one else sees this side of you ever.' Saski demanded at the sight of Duran's aroused expression.

He pulled Duran into another passionate kiss. His hand started working its way toward Duran's throbbing member.

Duran struggled to keep his mind from going blank. In the process, memories of his time with Miwa and all his past loves surfaced. Followed with the suffering they faced because he was their lover. He feared a cursed fate befalling to Saski. He would rather deny his love to protect him from future harm and trouble.

'No!' He gasped and struggled out of Saski's

embrace. He stood and pulled himself together.

'I-I'm really sorry Tsubaki-kun, but we can't be like this,' he said, flustered, and rushed out of the room to get some air.

Saski collapsed to the floor and stared up to the ceiling with a troubled sigh. He couldn't understand what had gone wrong.

He started pouring out his questions to Socrates who had jumped onto his chest and laid down to rest on him.

The following days, Saski didn't say anything to Duran about their time in the clubroom. Duran had continued their relationship as if they had never kissed. It was weighing on both their minds a lot. Fortunately, the club set-up was keeping them busy.

Jiro-san came good with the drum set and dropped it off to the clubroom a few days after Kobori's arrival. Duran had to fork out ¥15k for the set from the club's budget.

It was worth it when he saw it was a Tama Imperial Star-five-piece that he knew was worth a hell of lot more than what he paid for. He felt content that Jiro-san had scored a bargain for the music club.

Around the same time, Ryuu-chichi's friend picked up the unused desks and chairs for his community youth center after receiving permission from Principal Kimura who was surprisingly happy to donate.

Duran suspected it gave the school good community brownie points with the desk donations being written off as a charity gesture.

Isagi-chichi and Akira-san had also helped with the disposal of the rest of the junk. Akira-san had donated his old two-seat sofa, a couple of pedestal fans and a bar fridge he no longer needed since he and his father moved to a smaller apartment near the city.

Dai'chi had given their club a name that everyone was excited about.

The Hotaka Music Club sacrificed their weekend to clean-up, sound-proof and set up the room for jam sessions and their six cats.

Finally, after a week and a half since its door's had opened, the club was ready.

Another school day commenced at the height of the sweltering summer heat with June around the corner.

Dai'chi had to prepare for his university submission and entrance exams for the upcoming weeks leaving the president's duties to Duran who was the club's vice president.

At lunch time, Duran was pouring over event schedules and budget with Aki (Treasury) and Mei (Secretary) at the desks they had retained and positioned toward the cooler side of the room near the sofa, fridge and cat feeding area. Whilst the others were getting to know the instruments.

Himeko had brought in her spare guitar. Dai'chi had lent the club his old Yamaha electronic keyboard all-rounder, so they could be a proper band. The only instrument missing was a base, which Duran was researching models and prices with Aki.

Himeko, Fumio and Dai'chi started jamming away in the background, but stopped mid-way when arguments, about timings and the type of the music they should play, was getting the better of them.

'Ugh! I can't stand it.' Aki cried out and dumped piles of paperwork to intervene.

'You guys are bloody useless if you can't agree on

one song!' He stated.

'So, what song you think we should do?' Himeko shot back.

'What song do we all know as a band?' Aki threw back and got the cogs of everyone's brains working together.

Without further arguments, they all started playing the song that Duran had written for Isao and Shouta's messages.

Duran stopped reading through the paperwork he had been engrossed in and made his way to the band. Mei followed suit.

'What you think Kita-kun?' Dai'chi tested him.

'Amazing, but I think we can work it differently,' Duran said as his spinning cogs pictured additional sounds and arrangements to give the song a new kick.

He threw out ideas for his friends to accept or reject, seeking when things didn't work and keeping them collaborating.

There were a few occasions where he had to pull Aki and Himeko's egos in line with clever keywords. Before the end-of-lunch bell, they had established roles and a rhythm as a band.

'I think we need an actual band name,' he suggested to his friends as they made their way across the courtyard to the classroom blocks.

'We can't be the Hotaka Music Club?' Mei innocently asked.

'Er, I guess, but it'll be good to have a name that signifies us as the original members and friends.'

'Okay how about the Freeloaders.' Aki joked and received a whack on the head from Himeko.

'Aki, be serious!' She cursed at him.

Duran frowned as he rummaged through the junk

in his brain for a name.

'Hey, what about Original6?' he asked his friends and saw them mulling it over.

'I like it,' Dai'chi decided.

'Me too. Sounds cool like Day6.' Aki agreed.

'Okay with me either way.' Fumio added.

His sister and Mei both nodded their acceptance of their band name.

'That's sorted. We are Hotaka Music Club's Original6.' Duran confirmed with a huge smile on his face.

'Maybe we should make up some T-shirts.' Aki joked.

'All in good time Aki-man.' Dai'chi patted his back.

They parted ways for their next class.

Saski and Duran's relationship was civil after their kiss. They continued their usual friendship without so much as stealing glances. At least not making the other aware.

During classes, and in-between lessons, their conversations were limited to one or two polite words before moving on to other things.

As much as it broke Duran's heart for them to be this way, he was convinced it was the right thing to do for the boy he loved.

He was prepared for Saski to eventually get over him and silently reflected on their non-relationship whilst going over his school work in the clubroom during lunch.

The data on worksheets weren't making much sense to him after a while. He decided to take five.

'Damn Fumio. I can't believe we did it and with a lot of support.'

Duran dumped himself to the sofa next to his friend who was appreciating their hard work with Nekito resting contently on his lap.

He was grateful for the cool relief the fans provided against the sticky summer heat.

Duran raised his hand to pat the white-mohawk cat and received a hiss that clearly told him to *piss-off*.

'Nekito still pissed at you.' Fumio chuckled.

'Well Hayashi-kun and I did chase it half a block for its fur.' Duran sighed.

Fumio had named the cat Nekito because it was the first one that came to his mind. The cat had bonded to him straight away.

At that moment, Socrates hopped up on Duran's lap and pawed at his legs to make himself comfortable before settling down to rest.

'Speaking of, haven't seen Tsubaki and Hayashi here since the piano was dropped off. Mikumo comes a lot for the cats.'

'They're Student Council guys. Guess they busy with that sort of stuff,' Duran said causally.

Although he knew why Saski hadn't set foot back in the club. He wasn't comfortable to share his fact with anyone else.

'Yeah, but Tsubaki-kun always found a way into our talk. Now, he's like a ghost,' Fumio said, calmly pressing the matter.

Duran frowned, picking up on his friend's fishing. Sharp as always the guy was.

'Well, we have the school trip coming up and all. Life's busy.'

Chiasa, Suki and their friend Meiki entered the clubroom at that moment.

'Wow, this clubroom is awesome!' Suki said with awe as she glanced around the room.

'Duracchi. Can we join your club?' Chiasa chimed in as she pushed in between himself and Fumio, disrupting the cats' quality moment.

Socrates jumped off Duran's lap to go into hiding.

Chiasa dodged an angry swipe from Nekito before he jumped off Fumio's lap and escaped through a hole in the dark corner of the room.

'Ooh that cat's nasty.' She shivered and snuggled up to Duran.

Duran sighed and let her have her way this time.

'Why do you want to join?'

'The music club's so cool,' she answered and rested

her head on his shoulder.

Fumio gave up his seat for the other girls who eagerly joined Chiasa's side and her fawning over Duran.

'Do you play an instrument?' he asked, but doubted she did.

'No, but I like music and stuff. Hey, like, we can be your groupies.' She perked up.

'Groupies, hmm. What you think Fumio?'

'Huh? Whatever,' Fumio replied not really paying attention to the question. He was too busy getting into his bento at one of the desks.

Duran didn't think the music club should only be for musicians. It could also be for others who could contribute in different ways. Even if they were just there for appreciation.

'Okay, you're in.' He decided.

'Us too?' Suki piped in.

'Sure, all of you.'

The three girls squealed with delight and started buzzing animatedly amongst themselves about what they could do for the club.

Duran moved to the Kobori, hoping to distract his thoughts from his troubles.

'You and I have issues with a certain someone don't we?' He whispered carefully to the piano.

He lifted the fallboard and started to play a random song.

Himeko, Mei and Aki entered the room at that point. They gawked at the three groupies hanging out on their club sofa.

'Um, Nii-san. What's the pop-squad doing here?' Himeko whispered inconspicuously to him.

'They're the club groupies,' he answered.

'What?' Mei gasped with eyes bulging.

'Yeah. Okada take note of their names on the members register will yah.'

'Are you out of your mind?' She hissed at him.

'Nope. They could come in useful,' he said carefully in a low voice whilst he kept playing.

'I hope you know what you're doing Kita-kun,' Mei said and moved to the new bass, which was propped up on a stand next to an amplifier positioned behind him.

Aki and Dai'chi had scored a deal for it at their local music store. They could purchase the guitar and amplifier as a package.

Duran changed his random playing to a song he had heard on YouTube the other day. It was a foreign song by an Australian band penned *5 Seconds of Summer*, which he felt was current to the feelings and concerns that he was going through with Saski.

'Hey Duran, what's this song? I think I've heard this one somewhere.' Aki called out as he positioned his acoustic guitar against his front.

Fumio abandoned his bento and joined them on drums.

'Amnesia.' Duran answered and started dissecting the song for his friends to learn.

The club groupies' chatter fell silent as they watched Duran and his friends learn a new song.

It took a bit of curve-balling to have everyone understand their part and be in-sync. After fifteen minutes of jamming, they could play the basics of the first verse and chorus.

Dai'chi stormed into the clubroom at that moment looking as if he had gone through the mill with the intense study session he had had with some of his classmates in the library. He didn't say anything as he dropped his bag and joined in on his Yamaha.

Duran recommended a few tones and notes to him, and gave him cues of when to chime in. When the end-of-lunch bell rang, they had jammed through the whole song with basic roles and parts mapped out.

'Okay, we're gonna keep practising this one,' he said to them as they packed away the equipment.

'I'll email you the YouTube link so you can learn it better.'

No one complained against it as they filed out of the room for their next class. The rest of the day passed uneventfully and pleasantly.

The next morning, Duran saw his sister was brooding about something when they left their house for school.

She let out pensive sighs here and there on their way to their homeroom classes.

'Sis, what's up?' He gave her a soulful look as they neared his classroom.

'Nothing Nii-san,' she sighed and carried her mood to her own class.

'Nice talking with you.' He sarcastically shrugged off and headed inside his room.

'Morning D-man,' Fumio called out to him from his desk. He was surrounded by Saski, Osamu and few of their other classmates.

'Morning all,' Duran greeted warmly and pulled up a seat into the group next to Osamu.

'I fed the cats for the day so don't need to do,' Osamu said with chipper smile.

'Thanks Mikumo-kun,' Duran said with a friendly pat to his back.

His phone started ringing in his back pocket. He pulled it out and saw the call was from an overseas number he didn't recognize.

'Who's that?' Osamu asked, snooping over his shoulder.

'Give me a moment.' Duran excused himself and took the call into the hallway.

'Hello?'

'Hey, it's been a long time.' A voice from the past greeted him.

Duran felt his mind pulled back in time.

'Miwa.' His voice drifted through the receiver. 'H-how are you?'

'Good. I'm sorry I haven't called you sooner. I didn't know if your number had changed. I took a punt.' Miwa apologized.

Duran knew he'd be able to get through since he had refused to change his number from back then. He was always wondering when he'd call.

'So, what's been happening in your life?' Duran felt his heart doing somersaults. He toed the marred linoleum before him.

'A lot. My cousin introduced me to a good therapist. He's been really good to me,' Miwa said calmly.

'I was a mess when I got there, but I'm better now. I felt I could call you now to let you know. Also, I've got a guy in my life who's been my support throughout.'

Duran felt tears well in his eyes. He was happy to hear Miwa was doing well, but the fact he had been able to move forward from him was breaking his heart.

'So, you're in a relationship.' He tried to sound

stolid.

'Yeah. He suggested I call you to let you know.'

It was that type of call.

Duran walked to a corner that was away from people and the sound of the school bell drawing everyone to their classes. He wanted to tell Miwa how much he had had to endure after he left a hole in his life and this call was unfair.

'That's good you're okay. Y-You sound like you're in a good place.' His voice trembled.

'But, I left you behind to deal with shit and that wasn't good. For that I'm sorry.' Miwa apologized.

'So, you called me to say you were sorry.'

'That too. Ah, man, we both have different lives now Duran. I need to know you're happy.'

All the tears Duran was holding back flooded his face.

'I'm not going to hear from you again am I?' He asked with a tear stricken voice.

'Please don't say that.'

'Miwa, be honest with me.' Duran pleaded.

'No, probably not.' Miwa's voice trembled through the cracking line. 'I need to hear that you're doing okay. Please Duran, tell me you're doing okay.'

Duran's mind ran through a million excuses and reasons that could keep Miwa on the line, keep him connected to his life. He had been waiting for his return for so long.

'Since you left, I moved places. My mom remarried. I have a sister I adore and w-we're re-really close friends. S-so you don't have to worry about me. I'm doing fine.' He bravely reassured him.

'That's good.' Miwa exhaled. 'Hey, I have to go. Take care Duran. Be at peace also.'

'Bye Miwa. You too.'

Duran held on after the call had ended, listening to the long-drawn-out beep and staring at an empty hallway.

His broken heart and his overwhelming pool of tears pulled him down to the cold, hard floor.

Deep down, he knew their relationship had ended with their last meeting at the café, but there was never that closure. The call was the final full stop.

He pulled himself up and ran out of the classroom block.

His running took him to the refuge of the music clubroom. Inside, he let out all his grief and tears. After a while of crying, he could recompose himself and return to his class toward the end of the first lesson.

'Please excuse me for coming in late.' He bowed with his apology to his teacher when he had entered.

'I wasn't feeling well all of a sudden, but I'm fine now.'

Aimi-sensei accepted his excuse and allowed him to take his seat.

He ignored the concerned and questioning looks from his friends, and consolidated his focus to his lesson and the plans he had for the day.

Duran had set aside his call with Miwa and assumed a happy face as he moved from lesson to lesson.

Some of his friends had expressed their concerns with gentle questions, but he brushed them off with flippant excuses and laid their questions to rest.

He felt a lot more refreshed as the day went on. Being in school and surrounded by friends really helped. There was another reason he didn't want to wallow in self-pity.

Today was a special day he didn't want to screw up.

'Another school day done and dusted.' He said as he headed to the music clubroom with his sister and friends.

He glanced at his sister and saw her dampen spirits.

'Hey sis, what is going on in that junkyard you call for a brain.' He teased her as he shook her shoulders.

'Shut up Nii-san! You're so stupid you didn't notice what day it is today.' She snapped at him.

'Um, it's a Wednesday right. Hang on, you didn't miss an assignment deadline did you?!' He gasped and copped a whack to his stomach.

'Okay. I take that as a no.' He groaned and shook off the pain.

'Since you're in the know. What day is it sis?'

'It's my birthday you moron!' She shouted at him and stormed off to the clubroom ahead of everyone else.

Duran's lips twitched with a smile and hurried after her.

Himeko kept complaining and whining about how she had heartless friends for forgetting it was her birthday and her sixteenth too.

Taking her complaints all the way to the lower ground floor. All her whining stopped when she opened the door to the clubroom.

'HAPPY BIRTHDAY!' her classmates and some of Duran's shouted out with poppers and streamers going off.

Duran and all her friends burst out with laughter.

'We got you!' Aki called out.

'Wah?' Himeko tried to speak, but she was left for words.

The whole clubroom was decorated with happy birthday banners, balloons and decorations for a party.

Watanabe-sensei started up some party music on a portable stereo Fumio had secretly brought in that morning and hid in the club's backroom.

Himeko was patted on the back and wrapped in happy birthday well wishes and hugs from her class and friends.

Even the cats came out of hiding to celebrate, skittering about feet and holding out for friendly pats.

Tomoe, a ginger tabby, padded toward her and affectionately rubbed itself against her ankle.

'Oh Tomoe,' Himeko cried with happiness. She picked the cat up and snuggled it.

She was led to the sofa where Duran and her friends wheeled out a triple layer chocolate cake (Duran had made himself in secret) on a trolley.

Everyone sang the happy birthday song with all their cheer and clapped as she blew out the candles. The cake was enjoyed, gifts were presented, the merriment continued beyond after school hours.

The celebrations ended in the early evening.

Duran, Kou, Osamu, Saski and her friends were left behind to clean up the mess.

'Nii-san, Fumi-chan said you ran out before homeroom began and came back late to class with red eyes,' Himeko said to her brother as he was cleaning up streamers off the floor next to her.

Duran paused his cleaning and sat on the ground beside her.

His eyes darted around the room to be sure no one

else was in earshot.

'Miwa called,' he said revealing some of his heartbreak on his face.

'Oh,' she said with understanding.

'I'm sorry Nii-san. I can see it didn't end well.'

'I always knew, deep down, our relationship was over. I needed the closure.' He heaved a weary breath.

'Anyway, this is your day, enjoy it. But, I want you to take back all your complaints you gave us before the party started.' He wagged a finger at her and stood with his hands on hips, looking down on her.

'Fine, I'll take it back,' she said and poked her tongue at him.

He pulled her into a hug with one of his goofy grins on his face.

'Luv ya, Sis. I'm glad you were born and you're here. Thanks for taking me in as your brother,' he whispered.

'Aw come off it Nii-san. Don't get all mushy on me. Stupid Nii-san.'

'Stacks on!' Aki cried out and jumped on the two of them, knocking them to the ground.

They were joined by Dai'chi and Fumio.

'Get off me you morons!' Himeko yelped. She was grinning from ear-to-ear.

'Hey! You're not kids! Stop mucking around! We have to get this place back together.' Mei called out as she made her way over to them and found herself pulled into the group hug.

'Ugh, okay, I get it, get off me!' She cried out and was released from their hug.

The group resumed their clean up in high spirits and finally came to rest when the room was back to boring.

'Hey Kita-kun, about that call, I hope it wasn't anything serious.' Osamu was mindful of his words. He sat on the ground next to Duran.

'Nah. I wasted time arguing with a telemarketer about how I didn't need a lifetime supply of Viagra.' Duran joked.

'Pfft. Okay, I get it Kita. If you ever need to talk, I'm here,' Osamu said with a friendly pat to Duran's back and stood to start up a conversation with Mei.

'Mikumo-kun, thanks,' Duran replied solemnly and saw Saski watching them from the sofa with Socrates on his lap.

He went to join him.

'You're okay now?' Saski asked him with a straight-face.

'Yeah. Why wouldn't I be? But, thanks for asking,' Duran said politely and patted Socrates's head.

The cat was purring contently from the affection it was receiving.

'It's obvious that call had left you upset. Your eyes were red when you came back to class.'

'Got something stuck in it. Nothing more. I'm fine,' Duran said impassively.

Saski told him point-blank, 'I haven't given up on you. I've thought long and hard about that day I kissed you. I'm still sure about my feelings.'

'Right.' Duran sighed, giving his attention to Socrates.

His mind went back to the phone call he had with Miwa. There had been closure, but the wound was still raw for him. He had too much baggage to off load. Too many fears he had to face before he could contemplate a relationship with anyone.

Saski met his eyes.

'I'm willing to wait for you Kita-kun. When you're ready to let go of whatever is holding you back, I'll be there. Just keep talking to me like you always do. It gets weird if you don't,' he said and flashed a smile.

Duran acknowledged his words with a courteous nod.

He shuffled off the lounge and moved to the Kobori. He started playing the song the band had been practising.

His friends made their way to their instruments and joined in. Kou, Osamu and Saski became audience to the song, Original6, had come to master.

Duran had the uncomfortable task of excusing Himeko's last-minute absence to Shiro-san when he arrived to start his shift for work.

He had given his boss a white lie by saying she was sick. In some sense it was a truth. She had a last-minute stress attack when she realized she had forgotten to do an assignment she needed to hand in the next morning.

Her stressing caused a fictional bout of the flu to hit her. He made her promise him that she'd have the work completed by the time he came home from his job.

He joined Isao in a busy run of serving patrons and keeping the dining area clean.

It was close to late evening when Kou, Osamu and Saski showed up looking brain-dead.

'Hey, Kita-kun.' Kou waved Duran over to their table.

'Sup. What are you after?' Duran flashed a smile and saw Saski sizing him up with suggestive eyes.

He dropped his attention to his notepad as he took their orders. Then hurried to the kitchenette as fast as he could, leaving them alone to talk among themselves.

'It's good to see you two talking again,' Kou commented to Saski.

'Since when weren't we,' Saski coolly answered.

'I heard that Chia-chan and her friends joined his club.' Osamu jumped in to change the subject.

'*Pfft.* Sexy K-Pop girl group. Check.' Kou joked.

Chiasa and her two side-kicks entered the ramen

house as if they had been conjured from the boys' talk about them.

'Oh shit! Psycho bazooga alert!' Kou muttered to his friends.

'Saskicchi!' Chiasa squealed excitedly and hurried to Saski before he could get away.

The girls hijacked their table.

Duran was coming out of the backroom when he saw Chiasa talking with Saski. He retreated to hide.

'I'll do your tables,' he said to Isao with a high pitched voice, as the man was getting ready to start his shift.

He picked up Isao's orders that were for the tables away from the line of fire and started to deliver them. He didn't see Jiro-san laughing at him.

Isao looked confused by the sudden change of his layout, but shrugged it off and started taking over Duran's tables.

'Chia-chan, why you here?!' Saski's voice croaked with surprise.

Chiasa beamed a cutesy smile his way and pulled up a free chair next to him.

'Do I need to join tables so you can eat together?' Isao asked innocently when he approached the girls.

'Yes,' Chiasa answered at the same time the three boys let out a definite no.

Isao chuckled and actioned in favour of the girls.

Kou, Saski and Osamu found themselves locked into place with the Hotaka Music Club groupies.

Chiasa snuggled up close to Saski's side and giggled when his body tensed.

The girls placed their orders then continued their fawning for the boys next to them.

'You keep breaking my heart,' Chiasa whispered

into Saski's ear as she stroked his hand.

Saski retracted his hand from her touch. In the process he knocked his glass of water to the floor. Some of it splashed on to his pants.

'Goddamn it,' he cursed.

'Oh Saskicchi it's just like our dates in the old days,' Chiasa grinned as she wiped up his pants with a napkin and an obvious attempt at seduction.

'That's before I knew you were a psycho-hose beast,' Saski mumbled.

His words went over Chiasa's head.

Isao rushed over to pick up the glass and mop up the spill. Muting his laughter at the sight of three stiff looking guys surrounded by glamour girls.

'Can I get some ice in a cup,' Saski asked Isao with an awkward voice.

'Make that two,' Osamu said with a weirder voice when he felt Meiki's hands becoming familiar with the sheen of his pants.

'*And maybe a cold shower for three.*' Isao laughed in his head and disappeared from their view.

'Um, so, yeah, you joined the music club.' Osamu attempted conversation to distract his uneasiness.

'Yeah. Duracchi wants us to be part of the club,' Chiasa said dreamily.

'I'm sure he does, not,' Kou commented sarcastically, which also went over Chiasa's head.

'Saskicchi. Been meaning to ask. Since we've been in high school why haven't you had lunch with me?' Chiasa asked Saski (who was trying his best to move away from her).

'Huh?! Why'd I do that?'

'We used to have lunch back in middle school.' She pouted and toyed with the buttons on his shirt.

'Um, no we didn't, and we only fake-dated for a week. We fake-broke up, so you could make your senior jealous. Didn't you get the memo?!' He knocked her hand away.

'Oh you, cracking funny jokes again.' She brushed off and snuggled further by his side.

'By the way. Where's that Kita-kun?' Osamu looked around and saw Duran waiting tables outside.

'Piker,' he muttered and gulped when Meiki snuggled closer to him.

'Oh, just remembered I had a thing,' he said.

He picked up his bag and shuffled past her chair. His voice let out an awkward yelp when he felt her hand brush past his front.

'Excuse me.' He hurried off and found Kou and Saski follow his lead.

The three boys bolted for the door without looking back.

Duran laughed when he saw them scurry past him with the shivers. He could avoid the club groupies throughout his whole shift thanks to Isao.

Although, they did try to call his attention to them a few times when he was inside serving other tables.

Isao didn't seem to mind the flirtatious attention the girls showered him as he waited on them.

'Man, those girls are man-eaters aren't they?' Isao said to Duran when they left the ramen house for other fun.

'That they are.' Duran sighed. 'They're good people.'

'Haha! They're not your cup of tea right.' Isao laughed as he sat down behind the counter for a well-earned respite.

Duran joined him.

'They come on too strong for Japanese girls. If they toned it down by 500 percent, they'd attract the boys they're after. Unless they're after someone like me.'

'Well I think they're cute. Unlike you guys, I don't mind a girl who's sassy since I'm a wimp. I do fancy the quieter one with the big adorable eyes. She seems nice,' Isao said with a dreamy smile.

'You'll be talking about Mabuchi, Meiki. If Senpai is that interested. I could put in a good word for you. I think she's single.' Duran offered and saw Isao giving it some serious consideration.

More patrons entered the restaurant interrupting their conversation. They resumed their shift.

Sasaski-san arrived not long afterwards to relieve them both for the night.

Jiro-san approached Duran when he was grabbing his gear from the lockers next to the small pantry. He held a wad of tickets in front of him.

'Hey mate. These are for your club,' he said proudly as he handed entry tickets for Day-2 of the Summer Sounds Music Festival at the Mariner Stadium near the coast.

The tickets were for the second weekend of July.

'Wow Jiro-san this is that gig?' Duran asked excitedly.

'Yeah. We're only a warm-up band for the evening acts but it'll be good experience for you guys. Some big names on that day too,' Jiro-san said with a ruffle to Duran's head.

'Cool! How much are these?'

'Nah. I got them for free by the organizers. Sort of a lottery hand-out. Just make sure you show up.'

'Jiro-san that's way too generous. I have to pay you

something,' Duran politely protested.

'Turn up. That'll be your payment,' Jiro-san said.

Duran gratefully accepted the gift with a generous bow of thanks.

'Hey. Maybe take that girl you like as well.' His boss added with a wide grin on his face

'Girl I like?' Duran wondered if Jiro-san had seen him react to Chiasa's entrance and misunderstood.

He blushed at the absurd thought.

'Yeah that one that came in with her friends. She looks like a pop idol with a nice rack. You should take her. There's enough tickets for a plus one.' Jiro-san added with knowing wink and pat on his shoulder.

Duran sighed. He didn't know where to begin to explain the misunderstanding and decided not to bother.

He thanked his bosses again for his well-earned pay and the tickets, and stepped out of the ramen house into a warm summer evening and a street still alive with the bustle of people going about their business.

He was giddy with excitement about the tickets that he couldn't wait to tell his friends.

He started sending a mass text to them with the tickets gripped tightly in his hands. Too enthralled with his texting that he didn't see Kou, Saski and Osamu approach him until Osamu waved a hand before his face to draw his attention.

'I saw you guys run off into the high heavens.' Duran chuckled and copped sarcastic look from Kou.

He quickly pocketed his phone and the tickets in his top jacket pocket.

'We're on our way home,' Kou said not giving into Duran's tease.

'What are you hiding?' Osamu asked with a sly smile on his face and wrapped his arm around Duran's shoulder so his hand was close to his pocket.

'Club business,' Duran answered and cursed when he saw one of the tickets in Osamu's hands.

'Hey! Give that back!' He shouted and found himself in a game of "catch-me-if-you-can" with Osamu who was waving the ticket about for him to try and catch it.

'Let's see. Oh, ticket to the Summer Sounds Music Festival. Wow, these aren't cheap. You're taking your girlfriend aye,' Osamu asked both impressed and attempting to return Duran's tease.

Duran managed to grab it from him after a few attempts and stow it away in his pocket.

'None of your business. Anyway, you know I don't have a girlfriend.'

'I dunno about that. You and Chia-chan are awfully friendly these days. Now she's your club groupie, you have plenty of opportunities to get up close and personal.' Kou joked.

'*Tsk*. I thought you said you were going home. Get going.' Duran frowned and braved a glance at Saski who was observing him with an aloof expression, but his eyes danced with excitement.

'Nah. Teasing my honey-buns is much more fun.' Osamu chuckled.

'But I'm sad my sweet honey isn't inviting me. I'd love to come too.'

Duran sighed and quickly calculated that he had enough to hand all three of them a ticket.

'Fine, here,' he said as he fished out tickets and handed out one to each of them.

He gave Saski a coy smile when Saski accepted his

with both hands.

'For real?' Osamu asked excitedly. 'This is seriously for me?'

'Yeah. I got them from Jiro-san as the music club's first excursion. Now you have one, you have to go otherwise you'll be offending Jiro-san.' Duran had explained and felt a seed of happiness at Kou and Osamu's excitement.

'That means you too Tsubaki-kun,' he said to Saski nonchalantly.

Saski was doing a good job at not showing his excitement.

'I guess I have to come to keep them in line. Honestly, those two are like kids at a theme park when it comes to these sorts of events,' he said soberly and pocketed the ticket without looking at it.

Duran felt his heart banging against his chest as if it wanted to break through and join with Saski's.

Saski did say he would wait for him, but he had so many issues to work through. Holding him back from relationships didn't seem fair. Surely he was like every other hot blooded teen.

'Look, I have to go. Nice talking to you.' Duran moved past them to make his way home.

'Kita-kun thank you!' Osamu called out with a genuine thanks. 'I'll come by the club tomorrow to feed the cats.'

Duran nodded his head and resumed his way down the street.

♪

When Duran's class started to hear how good the Original6 band was becoming with their practice sessions, a few would drop into the music club during lunch to hang out. Most of his peers played with the cats as they listen to them practice.

It didn't bother Duran, but he could see it made Himeko and Mei slightly uncomfortable.

'Nii-san. Is it okay for any tom, dick or harry to hang out here?' Himeko whispered into his ear during a lunch-time practice session.

'Yeah, I'm okay with it and Dai'chi doesn't see a problem either. We both agree it's good experience for you guys to play with an audience around you that way you'll be able to handle public performances.'

Himeko sighed and nodded her head in agreement to her brother's logic.

'So, we're really gonna go public?' Aki asked having overheard their conversation.

'Yeah, and while we're on that. I notice we don't have any stage presence yet, which is to be expected since we're still coming into our own style,' Duran said.

'What yah mean?' Fumio asked with a frown.

'Hey Fumio, don't pout. You know what I mean. We're good at the instruments and connection with each other, but we're in our own world at the moment. That world is still a developing place too. If we want to draw in crowds, we'd eventually need to come into our own and be something like 1-D.'

'Huh? Aren't those guys breaking up?' Mei threw out.

'Sabbatical, apparently.'

'Sounds like a break-up to me.'

'Okay so maybe 1-D wasn't a good choice. Grandrodeo then. You see those guys rock-out. They have a unique stage presence and band connection, the same goes for Old Codex. They get out there and do their thing with this swag and self-assurance but neither of them isolate their audience. Rather they draw them into their world. We need this too whilst keeping true to our own music.' Duran said animatedly and called the band to the blackboard.

Everyone sat on the ground before Duran and his lecture.

He started going over what he knew about famous bands spanning across history.

'You have the British band, The Beatles, who lead rock generations around the world. They weren't good looking like the pop bands we have today, but they carried a charisma and self-confidence that got into girls hearts and sent fans screaming with delirium any time they were near. They opened up a standard for other artists and genres to follow like Death Penalty and then when they became Boowy—'

Duran drew a timeline that highlighted the unique stage presence and style of each artist.

The whole clubroom became enthralled in his lecture. A lot of sad sighs could be heard around the room when the end-of-lunch-bell rang to call them back to their classrooms for their next lessons.

All the students stretched out with relief when the afternoon break bell finally rang to take their minds away from being a sponge for knowledge or out of a bored stupor.

Watanabe-sensei overhead some of the students (who had visited the music club during lunch) eagerly talk about Duran's musicology lesson when he was passing through the hallways to the staffroom for his break.

He was instantly curious being the club adviser, and had mentioned it to Kato-sensei, Aimi and

Harada in the staff smokers' room.

'It seems Kita-kun is teaching music history.' He chuckled between puffs.

'Well, he is an academic genius. It does seem his brain is a walking encyclopedia on the subjects he likes. A contradiction to his step-sister,' Harada-sensei said offhandedly with cigarette smoke lazing around his stoic expression.

'I'm interested to see what kind of teacher he is to his peers,' Kato-sensei said enthusiastically.

'Hey, Aimi-kun, you're his homeroom teacher. What's he like in class?'

Aimi-sensei thought carefully before answering the question.

'He's well liked, quiet, polite and easy going.'

'Not to mention good looking even with western features. No wonder the girls can't get enough of him.' Kato-sensei laughed.

'Hmm, well. As cute as it sounds, I guess I need to listen into one of his lectures as the club's adviser. I wouldn't want him to be in trouble for giving other kids bad ideas.' Watanabe-sensei sighed.

'Off topic. You've met his mother at the parent-teacher night Aimi-kun. What's she like?' Kato-sensei asked and chuckled at Aimi's deep blushes.

'Kato-sensei. I can't help feel this question alludes to a highly inappropriate discussion.'

'Hah! You don't have to be a gentleman around me. Come on, face it, she's pretty fit.' Kato-sensei smirked.

'And she's married to a police officer whose daughter happens to be in Harada-sensei's class.' Aimi-sensei chided him.

'Yeah, well. Unlike you stuffy old men, I still

appreciate the fine beauty of women,' Kato-sensei answered for himself before taking the last drag of his smoke.

The end-of-break bell twanged, calling the teachers back to their classes.

Watanabe-sensei and Kato-sensei's minds were piqued with interest on how Duran was running the music club.

'Hey, Watanabe-san. Let me know when you're paying a visit to the club. I'd like to join you,' Kato-sensei called out and received an eye-roll from Watanabe.

'Fine.'

The teachers resumed their way to their classes.

♪

It was the first time Duran and Himeko were having their friends sleep over the night before a music festival. They were all going to go there as a group and rock out as long as they could for a Saturday.

'Nii-san I'm too excited to focus on homework,' she said with a giddy step in her stride as they walked home from school.

'Hah - since when do you focus on homework,' he joked.

'Shut up Flush-As Idiot. I have you know, I take my school work seriously.'

'Neglecting deadlines for assignments, until the last minute, is really taking your work seriously,' said Duran with a sarcastic grin on his face.

'Unlike some, I wasn't born with a genius switch,' she came back at him and felt embarrassed by the stupidity of her words.

'Haha. You said it.'

Himeko's mobile ringing saved her from putting her foot further into her mouth.

She started a conversation with Fumio who was on the other line asking when he should arrive to their place.

At that moment, Duran got a call from Dai'chi asking the same thing.

Their phones rang non-stop as they walked through the door of their home, dumped their school gear to their rooms and donned their everyday clothes.

'Who's that now?!' Himeko cried out as she heard her brother's phone go off just after he had hung up on a call with Aki.

Duran's heart fluttered when he saw it was from Saski.

He took his call to his room and slammed the door on his sister's face.

'So rude,' Himeko pouted.

Her expression relaxed into a smile when she saw an incoming call from Mei on her phone. She answered it and carried the conversation to her own room.

They both emerged to the living areas an hour later and went about making the place fit for entertaining.

Himeko tidied up whilst Duran made canapés they could savour throughout the night.

Duran's phone rang as he was cleaning up the kitchenette. He answered a call from Osamu who was trying to tee-up a time to meet them at the festival.

'Geez, we need secretaries.' Himeko joked as she

watched her brother finish off his cleaning with his phone propped to his ear.

Duran had just ended his call when his phone went off again. He saw the number belonged to Akira-san.

'Akira-san, how is everything—' he took the call to the sofa.

Himeko heard the intercom bell ring and went to answer the door.

'Fumi, Aki, come in.' She invited them in.

'Sorry for intruding,' they both said as they entered the apartment and removed their shoes.

They followed her to the lounge room.

Duran had ended his call as he saw them come in and greeted them warmly.

The intercom bell rang again. He answered the door this time and welcomed Dai-chi and Mei into the house.

He led them to the lounge room where the others were. All their friends lapsed into friendly conversations whilst he placed plates of canapés on the dining table.

Fumio caught a whiff of the savoury treats and hit the plates straight away.

'Fumi-chan, don't scoff them down like a pig!' Mei scolded him.

He flashed a cheeky smile and continued with his devouring.

Duran laughed and went to get more.

The lounge room was crowded with hearty laughter and heighten conversation when Sakura entered the house with her arms weighed down with shopping bags.

'I'm home,' she said wearily.

Her eyes bulged when she saw her lounge room overrun with teens.

'Oh, you're all here already.'

'Welcome home mom.' Duran greeted her warmly.

'Wow, there's a lot of them,' Sakura said as she counted the number of heads in their small lounge room.

'Is that alright?' Duran asked nervously as he took the bags from her.

'I guess, but I'm concerned there are a lot of boys around Himeko. Especially, since your step-father and I will be staying in the city tonight.'

'Mom, no one here thinks of Himeko as a girl okay. These guys are her childhood friends. Not one of them will ever dream of hurting her or Okada. I'm here too to keep an eye on things.' Duran reassured her as he started unpacking the groceries into the cupboards.

Dai'chi and Aki rushed in to help quicken the pack away task.

Duran noticed they were too polite and well-mannered around his mother. His eyes narrowed with realization of their intentions.

'Okay guys, we're done now!' He said as he pushed them back to the lounge room.

'I see your friends are nice. I guess that's a bit more reassuring,' Sakura said with a clueless smile and disappeared to her room.

'Your mom's a freaking hot fine woman,' Aki whispered to Duran.

'Shut-up. Don't talk about my mom that way.' Duran snapped at him.

'You should feel proud you came out of good sort.' Dai'chi smirked.

'Right, say one more word about my mother in that way and I'll deck you!' Duran growled.

'Fine, fine. I'm sorry I think your mother is desirable.' Dai'chi apologized.

'Me too, I'm sorry I had inappropriate thoughts about her.' Aki followed suit.

Both burst out with laughter when they saw Duran's face tense and go red with anger.

'Mate we're playing with you.' Dai'chi laughed and slapped Duran's back.

Duran relaxed and started talking about other things.

They were still laughing and talking in the lounge room when Sakura said her motherly goodbyes to Duran and Himeko. She left them the care of the apartment with stern warnings.

The boys moved their banter to Duran's room whilst Himeko and Mei transformed the lounge room into a makeshift bedroom.

Aki and Dai'chi got stuck into exploring the nooks and cranny of Duran's stuff.

'Hey this book is printed entirely in English,' Aki called out as he held up a Lord of the Rings novel.

'It's thick enough to knock the block off someone.'

'That's just for show, right Kita-kun? No way you understand all that.' Dai'chi scoffed.

Duran took the book off Aki and started reading out a random page effortlessly.

'Shit! Your English is better than Harada-sensei's,' Aki said with awe.

'That's why you fall asleep in his class. Here I thought he was boring you to death.'

'What are you talking about Aki? He is boring.' Duran joked.

'Duran, where is this?' Fumio called out as he was flipping through a school album.

'Oh, that's the last school I came from. I wasn't there for long cause I had to move.'

Fumio's brows rose when he saw a school emblem in one of them.

'You went to Emi-Daiki.'

'Not a crash hot place for academics.'

'Hang ten. These guys with you, I've seen them before,' Dai'chi said over Fumio's shoulder as they were looking at a shot of Duran standing next to four idol-boys with stylish hair where fringes swept across foreheads or had geometric layers cut around their faces. They were dressed in the black blazers and grey slacks of the Emi-Daiki Senior High uniform.

They both started brainstorming on who they could be.

At that moment Himeko and Mei walked into the room.

'Hey Nii-san. Looks like your privacy's being invaded.' Himeko noticed.

'We're all friends. I guess that's okay.'

'That's it! They're that pop idol band Elicit!' Dai'chi piped up with his eureka moment.

Fumio snapped his fingers drawing to the same conclusion.

Himeko noticed her brother's shoulders flinch at the mention of their name.

'Hey! That's enough guys. Stop snooping through my brother's stuff!' She berated the boys and took the album off their hands, shoving it back in the cupboard.

'Dude. You know Elicit?' Dai'chi asked Duran.

'Not really.'

'Who met Elicit?' Mei perked up.

'Duran,' Fumio answered.

'Really?! What are they like? Are they cool, kind...?' Mei fired off a million questions at once to Duran.

'Um, I guess you could say professional,' Duran replied.

'Nii-san, if you haven't figured. Mei is a big fan of that group.' Himeko warned him.

'Okada, really? Wow, did not see that coming.' He muttered his surprise.

Dai'chi sat before Duran's keyboard. 'Can I?'

'Sure, go ahead.' Duran sat on the end of his bed and watched his senior play a few random notes.

'Do you think you could play this?' He said as he rummaged through a box on his shelf and pulled out sheet music.

'I guess. Hey is this something you wrote?' Dai'chi said when he saw the notes written out.

He started playing the song on the sheet. Duran joined in with his guitar and started singing out the words.

Fumio tapped out the beat on a box.

Himeko rushed out of his room and came back with guitars and a bass for Mei, Aki and herself to use.

They honed their vocal and instrumental harmonies as they learned the new song and recapped over the other three songs they had been practising.

They spent the rest of their night playing music in Duran's room.

By morning, they were more of a band with the confidence of four songs under their belts. They made sure the house was in order the next morning before leaving for the festival.

Calling the music festival just a community gig was

a modest explanation from Jiro-san.

Duran and his friends arrived to a massive stadium overrun with music fans from all walks of life.

They entered a line before the entrance gates and found themselves pressed into a packed queue, which was worse than the ones awaiting to board the sardine train carriages of the weekday morning rush, then on to other connecting lines for the sports fields and convention centres along Tokyo Bay coast.

The late afternoon was steamy from an early morning down pour.

Storm clouds loomed overhead with a threat of more rain to come.

Duran was glad he, his sister and guy friends chose comfortable outfits of a shirt or light jersey, t-shirt, trainers and jeans.

Of course, Mei stood out as their fashion queen with her light cardigan, frilly navy blouse, ballet flats and floral skort.

'Make sure you don't wander off when we enter,' Mei said to them as she readjusted her satchel bag to her shoulder.

She was carrying a heap of stuff to keep them going for the day. Even a tent, which he had no idea how she could fit inside that small bag.

'Yes mom.' Aki joked and received a hefty whack to his shoulders from her.

'Don't be a smart-arse. We could easily loose each other among the crowds here.' Mei scolded at him.

'Are you sure you don't want me to carry the bag,' Duran asked her to be polite and found himself dumped with the heavy satchel.

'You boys should take note of Kita-kun's good manners.' Mei lectured them.

'Hah! Good manners or kissing ass.' Aki snorted and copped another light whack from her.

'The others are waiting for us inside.' Duran summarized the text he had received from Saski to change the subject.

He told them where they were waiting, which was near the first food stall before the stadium's main entrance.

'I'm starving,' Fumio grumbled and rubbed his noisy stomach.

'Do you think of anything else but music and what goes in your stomach,' Himeko said to him.

'I'll get back to you on that one. Man, I hope there's a pancake stall. Could go with a pork flavour.' His mouth salivated as his mind drifted into a happy place filled with red bean buns, pork flavoured pancakes and all his other favourite foods among heinous rock and roll.

Music from the stage beyond sailed into Duran's ear. He felt the ground vibrate under his feet by the sound of a roaring crowd. His body was pumped with the stadium's energy.

'I can't wait to get in there,' he said to Dai'chi who looked as eager.

They inched their way closer toward the entrance gates and saw the line, behind them, had extended out onto the barricaded road.

'Man - here I thought our part in the queue was long enough,' Himeko noted.

After a slow crawl to the gates they finally made their way through and could move about freely.

Duran's heart skipped a beat when he saw Saski with the others, looking fine in his grey shirt, t-shirt, jeans and boots.

Osamu and Kou looked ordinary in comparison wearing similar outfits as himself. They were next to a pancake stall before the stadium entrance.

He took in the entire circumference of the outer area, which was populated with rich food stalls, loud advertisements, vibrant, colourful banners staked to the grounds and patrons eager to purchase their wares. The place was crazy busy.

He understood what Mei was on about with getting lost. He could easily to be swept away with the crowds if he wasn't paying attention.

'Hey!' Osamu waved out to them.

The made their way to the three guys.

Fumio disappeared into the pancake stall's queue. Saski was called out by a couple of older guys ahead of them. Duran watched his warm meet and greet with the guys.

'Hey, Mikumo-kun, are they from our school,' he asked.

'Them? Yeah, they're our seniors. The tall, dark and handsome guy with those sparkly brown eyes and devilish lips is Konekomaru, Taiga. He's the kendo club president. The angry looking short-stop next to him is Suguro, Ryuji.' Osamu described to him.

Duran eyes narrowed and his stomach churned with unease at the happy grin on Saski's face.

He had never seen him show an expression of adoration before. He clenched his fists and suppressed the urge to butt in and yank him away from the guys.

Saski's seniors said their goodbyes. He rejoined their group.

At the same time, Fumio resurfaced with two containers stuffed with pancakes. He growled at

Himeko when she attempted to take a piece out of one of them.

'Don't be a spoilt brat!' Himeko yelled at her childhood friend and received a glare from him in response.

Fumio cleaned out both containers without sharing, which clearly pissed her off.

'Here,' Mei said to Himeko as she handed her a packet of Pocky sticks.

Himeko poked her tongue at Fumio and got stuck into them.

They entered a full-scale baseball field that had been transformed into a music arena, and headed toward to the outer edges a short distance from the massive main stage erected at the arena's center.

Beef-cake security guards patrolled the stage perimeters, which was enclosed by metal barriers to keep the mosh-pit crowd from stampeding onto the stage.

Performances could be seen on a humongous digital TV screen fixed underneath the scoreboards of the back walls.

White marquees and first aid tents stuck out as sore thumbs near the entrances and backstage barricades. Some people had pitched tents on the outskirts.

Duran glanced up at the upper bleachers crowded with people moving in and out of seats, having a good time and dancing in their own world.

'This is amazing,' Kou murmured.

He was agog by the vibe and energy surrounding them.

'I've never been to something like this before.'

'Me neither,' Duran responded with the same

awestruck.

'So many people.'

They were taken in by the electric vibe flowing down from the bleachers and the pulsating music stirring the arena and mosh-pit masses into a dance frenzy.

Mei led them to a practical section of grass at the stage's far-right outskirts, which was handy to facilities. The boys started pitching the tent.

Duran felt his phone vibrate through his back pocket. He pulled it out and saw a text from Jiro-san. He called his boss and received directions to meet him at the barricades of the backstage area.

'Hey Himeko come with,' he said to her before she had the chance to sit down on the picnic blanket Mei had spread out for them.

They made their way across the field (through patches of people) to the barricades where Jiro-san and Taco were waiting for them.

'Hey Boss. You look ready to rock.' Himeko grinned as she sized up Jiro-san's swag of loose jeans, T-shirt, gold bling and teased hair held together with a black bandanna.

'You must be this dude's baby sister.' Taco gestured to Duran as he greeted her warmly. He was dressed in a similar outfit minus the bandanna.

She nodded her head politely.

'Good to see you made it across to us in one piece.' Jiro-san smiled.

'Yeah, you could get lost in this place. It's crazy,' Duran said excitedly.

'We're on after the next band.'

'Cool bananas. We'll be watching you over there,' Himeko said pointing to the stadium entrance, near a colourful wallboard advertising an anniversary flavour of Georgia, on the opposite side from them.

'We're really excited to see you play Jiro-san. Do your best. We'll be going wild for you.' Duran encouraged his boss.

'Haha, do that. Enjoy the experience. I'll talk to you later,' Jiro-san said when he saw he was being called backstage by an assistant.

Duran and Himeko headed back to their group and saw the guys ducking in and out of the tent or annoying the hell out of Mei who was trying to keep stock of the snacks she had packed for them.

Saski had saved a seat for him on the blanket. Duran felt his skin tingle as he sat down next to him.

The energy of the grounds went to a standstill when the stage changed bands. It soon kicked off again with dance tracks that sent the masses into a roaring fit.

Duran noticed a few groups of girls' direct skanky, filthy looks toward his sister and Mei as they passed them. He wondered if it looked weird for two girls to be surround by seven guys. It made him more conscious for their safety.

'This is insane!' Osamu cried out when a screaming hoard of people flocked to the arena's center and started dancing wildly to the music with their hands punching the air.

The ground underneath them grumbled with threats to split open and swallow everyone whole.

Aki pulled a complaining Mei to her feet and started moving her into a dance. Himeko and Dai'chi joined them.

Duran sat with Saski, Kou and Osamu, watching their friends moving their bodies to the beat.

'Thank you for the invite. This is awesome,' Saski whispered into his ear.

Duran gulped down a nervous knot he felt in his throat and nodded his head.

He felt his phone vibrate in his pocket and saw a text from Akira-san asking to see him near the backstage marquees on the other side.

He looked at the way before him and cringed when he realized he'd have to squeeze through people sandwiched together in a heightened, music infused state.

'Hey Akira-san.' He decided to phone him instead.

'Kita-kun please tell me you still keep in contact with Akashi-kun. My label only has his group performing today. They're meant to be the act after the next one, but I can't get through to him anywhere. He's a no show. His manager is freaking.' Akira-san was frantic on the other line.

'Sorry Akira-san. I haven't spoken to Akashi-kun for a long time.' Duran apologized.

'Can you come over please?' Akira-san pleaded and hung up before Duran could answer.

'Hey, I have to meet Akira-san on the other side. Let my sis know I'll be back in a moment,' he shouted out to Kou who was having a hard time hearing him through the deaf defying music.

Kou eventually worked out what he was saying and nodded his head.

'Come on Miki-chan,' he shouted and dragged Osamu into the dance with the others.

'Tsubaki-kun come with me,' Duran said into his ear and grabbed his hand.

The early evening sun disappeared behind storm clouds.

Trickles of rain landed on their skin as they pushed their way through the crowds and gyrating bodies mingled in sweat and salt. Duran felt his own heat and sweat meld with Saski's hand as he tightened his grip.

They continued pushing through a path until they eventually came upon the backstage marquees and saw Akira-san stressing before the security barricades ahead of them.

'Kita-kun!' Akira-san called out and met him at a barricade.

'Akira-san. What do you need of me? I'll help if I can.' Duran offered.

At that moment a stylish boy dressed in dark skinny jeans, a navy double breasted jacket (unbuttoned to reveal a cotton t-shirt) and steel capped boots coolly walked up to Akira.

Saski was taken in by the guy's symmetrical, Japanese-western features that almost rivalled Duran's. His grey eyes carried an aloofness, pale clear skin accentuated the natural red of his plump lips. His light-brown bangs swept across his perfectly shaped brows.

'He's definitely a pop idol.' Saski concluded.

'Where the hell have you been?! I had to drag Kita-kun here to see if he could get through to you. You had Fukuda-san nervous!' Akira scolded the pop idol with a hard slap to his shoulders.

'I was stuck in traffic. I sent you a million messages.' The pop idol explained unperturbed by Akira's anger and coolly shook off the pain.

His eyes lit up when he saw Duran.

'Kita, Duran! You came to see us.' He grinned with smug attitude.

'Not on your life Akashi-kun. I had no idea your

group was on today.' Duran glared at him.

'I see.' Akashi-kun's brows rose when he saw Saski next to Duran.

His eyes narrowed.

'Make sure you stay and watch us. I'll blow your mind,' he whispered seductively to Duran.

'I'll call you afterwards,' said Akira-san to Duran.

Akira-san and Akashi-kun disappeared into a marquee.

'Who was that?' Saski frowned.

'No one special,' Duran answered with deep frown. He grabbed Saski's hand to lead them back to their group.

Torrential rain poured on them as they forced their way through crowds.

They found themselves caught in a muddy wave of people headed for the mosh-pit.

'Hang-on!' Duran called out to Saski as they twisted their way free from the partying mob and emerged to the less crowded outskirts near the arena exit and their group of friends.

Saski gripped Duran's hand tighter and steered the course toward the exit.

He dragged him into the stadium corridors and a secluded corner away from people and prying eyes.

'Tsubaki-kun. What are we doing here?'

Saski wrapped his arms around him and pulled him into a deep and passionate kiss.

'I'm sorry. I know I said I'll wait for you. Seeing that Akashi-kun guy look at you in that way. It fired me up.' He apologized and lowered his head to Duran's damp neck.

Duran clung to his mud-stained and steamy body with a burning desire to lose himself in his embrace.

'Go out with me. I'll handle whatever comes with you.' Saski kissed into Duran's ear.

Duran met his eyes.

'What am I gonna do? I find you too irresistible to refuse.' He delved into Saski's passionate kiss.

The kiss would've led to other steamy affairs if they hadn't heard people come up the corridor near them.

They reluctantly pulled away from each other and resumed their path back to their friends.

'Nii-san! Tsubaki-kun! You took your time.' Himeko called out.

Her eyes carried questions that neither of the boys would have answered.

Duran saw all his friends were also drenched. He was surprised to see Mei dancing and laughing with Kou, Osamu, Aki and Dai'chi in the rain.

'She's getting into it,' he said to Himeko who burst out with laughter.

'Yeah. Once the guys got her dancing, she wouldn't stop.'

Jiro-san's band kicked into action as Fumio came up next him. He was happily chowing down on *watame* candy. His hands carried plastic bags full of a boy's confectionery wants and wishes. He finished off his snack and dumped the treats inside the tent next to Mei's bag.

Duran and his friends danced like idiots in the rain to the cool music played out by Jiro-san's band.

★♫ END COMMENTS ♪★

Thank you for reading this revised edition of I'm Kita Duran. I hope it was as an enjoyable read as the first time around. A lot more was added to give better context to this book and the series storyline. Cheers.

☆Veronica Purcell ☆

twitter: @veronicapurcell

www.ingramcontent.com/pod-product-compliance
Lightning Source LLC
Chambersburg PA
CBHW061427150726
47987CB00001B/126